THE DEVIL
PLAYS SIX STRINGS

VINCE E. PINKERTON

6/6/23

This book is dedicated to three amazing women:
To my wife, Brooke Pinkerton,
without whom you would not be reading this.
Thanks for fixing my spelling, correcting my comma splices and
being my biggest supporter.

To my mom, Dorothy Pinkerton,
for teaching me to love reading at an early age.

And to Sue Buchanan,
my cheerleader and go-to for questions about writing.

THE DEVIL PLAYS SIX STRINGS

"We can see God in the works
He does every day in our lives,
but if you're not looking,
you might just miss Him.
Now the Devil, he will walk right up
and shake your hand."

Joseph Mann
1934

ELIJAH

PART 1

CHAPTER 1

1930

The sun bore down on Seraphina Parker from a cloudless sky above, and the dry, dusty dirt beneath her feet reflected its heat back at her from below. She had never been so hot and uncomfortable, and being very pregnant only added to her misery.

She stopped chopping at the dirt with the hoe she was using and looked to the sky, hoping for some relief from a passing cloud, but there was none. She went back to work, trying to cut weeds from a row of late-season corn.

Seraphina had signed on to work at the farm along with her husband two weeks before, never expecting that the pregnancy would become a problem. She reminded herself that black women had been having babies and working in the fields for as long as anyone could remember, and it would go on long after she was gone.

The last two days, the baby had been kicking something fierce. Sometimes causing her to hurt in her ribs, and last night there had been some blood in her underthings. As if the baby knew she had been thinking about it, she received a hard kick that radiated down through her lower back. She stopped working again and stretched to try and ease the pain.

"You just hold your horses in there baby, you don't want to be born in this heat," she whispered to the restless life inside her.

The baby calmed as Seraphina smiled and lovingly ran a hand over her enormous midsection. She looked out over the field of weedy corn then looked up to the heavens and whispered a prayer.

"Lord, I know you tell us to do all things without grumblin' or questionin', but if you don't mind, I shore would like to have this baby soon. It's tired of waitin' and so am I. Amen."

Seraphina turned back to her work, secure in the belief that her prayer had been heard and would soon be answered.

Elijah Parker stopped working and pulled an already-saturated handkerchief from his back pocket. He used it to wave away the gnats before running it across his face, only managing to move the moisture around instead of soaking any of it up. Then he pressed the cloth against the back of his neck to try and dam the river of sweat that currently traveled down his back and into his trousers.

He looked over at Seraphina, or Sera as he called her, who was working two rows over. From where he stood, he could see the stains that had formed under her arms and around the collar of her work dress. He could also see them surrounding the bulge of her very pregnant belly. The moisture on her arms and face made her skin glow and only intensified her beauty. Elijah had fallen in love with Seraphina the first time he had laid eyes on her five years before.

A hot field of late corn was no place for a woman as far along as Sera, but she wouldn't hear of taking it easy while everyone else worked. One thing Elijah had learned about his wife over the last five years was that she was stubborn. It was one of the things he most admired about her and the one trait of hers that drove him the most crazy.

Seraphina looked up at him and their eyes met. For a moment she smiled, then it changed to a grimace.

Seraphina fell to her knees.

Elijah threw his hoe to the ground and raced toward her.

Ella, a young dark-skinned girl from some island Elijah had never heard of, was a row closer and beat Elijah to Sera's side. She helped her get off her knees and into a sitting position as Elijah dropped down beside them. He used his handkerchief and tried as best he could to wipe the sweat from Seraphina's forehead. She took a deep breath and laid her head against his chest.

"Micah!" Ella called over her shoulder to her husband, who was working across the field. "Fetch Seraphina some water!"

Micah, a tall skinny man with mahogany-colored skin had not noticed what was happening. At the sound of Ella's voice, he ran from the field toward the nearby farm house.

"Breathe easy sister," Ella said in her comforting island accent. "You don't want to have no baby out here in the dust."

"I told you that you shouldn't work today, now just look at ya," Elijah scolded her.

Seraphina took the handkerchief from him then waved him off and used it to wipe under her chin and dry her chest.

"For God's sake Elijah, you are smothering her." Ella shooed him away. "Move back and give her some air."

Elijah looked from Seraphina's face to Ella's, then scooted back, but just a little.

Seraphina gave Ella a quick knowing wink before handing Elijah's handkerchief back to him. She reached into the pocket of her apron and pulled out her old worn Bible. Breathing heavy, she looked up at Elijah. "You would have me sitting by the fire every time I sneeze if you had your way."

Seraphina smiled at him. "I'm just havin' a baby." She switched to a more comforting tone. "Folks been doin' that for a long time now. Besides, the Good Book says that if a man should not work, then neither shall he eat. I *believe* what the Good Book tells me, and I *live* by what the Good Book tells me, and if it tells me to work so I can eat, that is just what I'm gonna do."

Micah arrived with a bucket of water and a dipper. Ella filled the dipper and raised it up to Seraphina's mouth, helping her take a deep drink. Some of the cool water dripped down her chest and caused her to shiver. After a few more sips, she nodded and smiled at Ella.

"Thank you, Ella."

Seraphina started to get up but had trouble getting her feet under her. She wasn't very graceful in her condition, so Elijah took her by the arm and helped her. Once on her feet, she dusted the dirt off her dress, then noticed that the three others were watching her every move.

She put her hands on her hips. "That's all I needed, now y'all quit fawnin' over me and get back to work." She spoke to them like a mother talking to three naughty children.

Micah started back to his section of the field, but before Ella left, she leaned in and gave Seraphina a quick kiss on the cheek. Seraphina in turn whispered a *thank you* in her friend's ear.

When Ella was out of earshot, Elijah took Seraphina by the shoulders and looked worriedly into her dark brown eyes. "I really wish you'd go back to the camp and rest."

"It's okay baby, I'm fine." Seraphina kissed Elijah's cheek and smiled. "Now, go on back to work, we've got a lot to do before this baby comes."

Elijah nodded and uneasily returned to his place a couple of rows away, all the time keeping his eyes on her. Seraphina placed the Bible back into her pocket. She used her sleeve to wipe the sweat from her forehead, then took a deep breath, looked up to heaven, and returned to work.

* * *

A small fire burned in the workers' campsite, and even though the night was hot, some of them still chose to sit around it, talking and drinking coffee.

Elijah and Seraphina sat outside the fire's reach in hopes of catching a cool breeze. A light wind rustled the leaves of the tree they were sitting under as Elijah smoked and strummed an old guitar. Seraphina looked up from her Bible that she had been reading with the help of some light from a candle.

"Umm, that's nice," she purred, feeling the breeze blow across her face.

"Are you taking about the breeze or my playin'?" Elijah asked.

She shut the book, then closed her eyes and listened.

"That's pretty, baby. You know I love listenin' to you play."

He continued humming along with the guitar as she turned her attention back to her Bible.

"I've been reading this book for a while now, tryin' to figure out what to name this little one, but for the life of me, I just can't find nothin' that feels right. This baby gonna be here in another few weeks, and I don't know what to call it."

"You worry too much." Elijah stopped playing and set the guitar to the side. "I bet you take one look at that baby and a name will just jump out your mouth."

Seraphina smiled and reached up to caress his cheek. "I hope it's a boy and that he looks just like you."

Elijah wrinkled up his face. "Why you want such a ugly baby?"

Seraphina smiled and returned to looking at her Bible.

"I'm gonna go over there and see if there's any of that coffee left. You want some?" he asked.

She shook her head as he flicked his cigarette away and leaned in to kiss her on the forehead. Instead of getting up and going to the fire, he continued to stare down at her as she read.

Her eyes lifted from the book. "What are you looking at? I thought you wanted some more coffee."

"I'm just lookin' at the prettiest girl in the world. If that baby is a girl and looks just like her momma, I'm gonna have to get me a shotgun to keep the fellas away."

Seraphina rolled her eyes, then leaned forward and pushed Elijah toward the fire. "Stop your foolishness and go get some coffee."

He stood and gave a small bow in her direction. Laughing, she waved him on, then watched as he walked away. She couldn't help but smile and shake her head, wondering how she got so lucky as to marry a man as kind and gentle as Elijah Parker.

Ella and Micah were sitting and talking next to the fire when Elijah stepped into the circle of firelight.

"How's Sera feelin'?" Micah asked. "She about scared the living soul out of me this afternoon."

"Me, too," Elijah said. "She's tired, but I think she'll be okay after she gets some rest."

Elijah pointed at the kettle on the fire. "Any of that coffee left?"

Ella got a towel, picked up the coffeepot and swished it around, checking to see if it had anything in it.

"There's a little bit left but it's gonna be mighty strong."

Elijah smiled. "Just the way I like it."

She found a metal cup up on the ground next to the fire and rinsed it out with a dipper of water from a bucket heating on the coals. She emptied the contents of the kettle into the cup, managing to fill it about halfway with thick black liquid, then handed it to Elijah. Steam rose up out of it as he lifted it to his mouth and blew on it.

"What y'all gonna do when the baby comes?" Ella asked him.

Elijah tried to take a sip from the cup and winced as the hot coffee touched his lips.

"I've been thinkin' a lot about that, and I think I'm gonna send Sera back home to her momma till the harvest is over. Field work ain't no place to try and raise a baby."

"You think she'll go?" Micah asked. "Sera is the toughest, most stubborn woman I ever met."

Ella playfully slapped him on the arm.

"Exceptin', of course, for you, honey."

She gave him a dirty look, and they laughed.

Elijah thought it over for a minute, then smiled and nodded. "It may take some convincing, but I think I can get her to see it's for the best."

He blew again on the coffee, then sipped it and grimaced.

"*Ooh-wee*! You wasn't lyin' when you said it'd be strong. That'd take hide off a mule!" Elijah dumped the rest of the coffee into the fire, then pulled his makin's from his pocket and started to roll a cigarette.

A scream from the darkness stopped him before he could pour the tobacco from the pouch into the paper.

He dropped everything and ran toward the tree where he had left Seraphina. Micah and Ella followed close behind.

They found Seraphina lying on her side with her legs pulled up against her stomach. She screamed again as Elijah fell to the ground beside her and drew her into his arms. Ella knelt at her feet and slowly eased Seraphina over onto her back. The movement caused a shudder of pain to run the length of her body and she screamed again, turning her face against Elijah's chest.

Micah picked up the candle Seraphina had been using to read. He struck a match, relit it, and came closer, holding it down near Ella to help her see. In the candlelight, Ella saw that her hands were covered in blood. A few of the other workers gathered around them, looking on with concern. At the sight of the blood on Ella's hands, one woman started to cry and another to pray.

"This baby's coming now," Ella said. "Micah, y'all go and find me a sheet or a towel and fetch that bucket of warm water from the fire." She turned to Elijah. "You hold her tight and keep that sweat out of her eyes."

Micah and a few others rushed off to follow Ella's directions as Elijah gently wiped Seraphina's forehead with his handkerchief.

"It's okay baby," he whispered in an attempt to keep her calm. Deep down inside, he was truly scared for the first time in his life.

Seraphina took in a deep hitching breath, then her back arched with a contraction. She screamed and shuddered. Her chest rose and fell fast as she tried to breathe through the pain. By the time the contraction passed, she was exhausted. She closed her eyes and let her body lean against Elijah. He looked over at Ella and their eyes met. Elijah didn't like the look of concern he saw there.

"My Lord, Elijah," Ella said, "there's a lot of blood. I think something's wrong."

Seraphina groaned and appeared to be trying to push.

"Don't push too hard now Seraphina, you just let this baby come when it's ready. Don't be rushing it."

Seraphina opened her eyes and looked up at Elijah, wide-eyed with fear. He bent down and kissed her forehead, then forced a smile. "It's gonna be okay, Sera. We're all here, and we're gonna help you through this."

Micah returned with a bunch of rags, and Ella began putting them underneath Seraphina. When one filled with blood, she removed it and replaced it with another.

"Where's that water?" Ella tried to keep the panic from her voice. "I need to rinse her off so I can see what's happening."

Another contraction sent a bolt of pain through Seraphina's body. Too tired to scream, she continued to look into Elijah's face. Tears streamed down her cheeks.

"It's okay Sera, our baby's on the way. You gonna be pickin' out that name any minute now."

Seraphina looked away from Elijah and searched for her Bible on the ground. She reached out for it, and Elijah picked it up and put it in her hands. Seraphina clutched it to her chest, then let out a weak moan as another contraction caused her to convulse.

"Set it down there." Ella motioned to a spot beside her as a man arrived with the bucket of water. She wet one of the rags and used it to clean Seraphina. Again, the rag came back full of blood.

"This baby's coming Sera. One more big push."

Seraphina closed her eyes. The pain was unbearable. "Oh Lord, help me!" she cried. Then she pushed and her agony ended. It flooded out of her like water bursting from a cracked damn.

A baby's cry, low and weak, filled the air. Ella took a clean rag from Micah and gently wrapped the baby. She gave it to Elijah, who held it in his arms where Seraphina could see it.

"It's a boy," Ella told her. "A beautiful baby boy."

Seraphina looked at the baby, then smiled and turned her eyes to Elijah.

"We have a boy, Sera," he said. "A boy just like you wanted."

Seraphina's smile broadened as she looked from her husband to her son. Elijah felt a tear run down his cheek at the sight of her joy; he thought he had never seen her look so happy.

She started to speak, but before she could, a pain much worse than before overtook her. She arched her back and curled her hands into fists. Her Bible fell to the ground in front of Elijah. Seraphina's breath was forced from her lungs, and it brought with it a sound that was not quite a scream but more like the moan of a dying animal. She took one final look at Elijah and the baby, then her eyes closed.

Elijah felt her body go limp. "Sera! Sera, honey! *No!*"

The baby started to cry again. Micah, Ella, and the others looked on, unable to help, as Elijah held Sera in his arms. He gently rocked her lifeless body and their new baby boy.

* * *

The morning sun cast long shadows over the field. The workers stood in a loose group encircling Elijah and Micah, watching while they put the final shovels of dirt on

Seraphina's grave. Elijah had picked a spot at the base of the tree where they had been sitting the night before, the last time they had been happy.

The men bowed their heads with their hats in their hands; the women all wept, drying their eyes with handkerchiefs. Ella held the newborn wrapped in a blanket. She sang a hymn in low whispered tones as Micah secured a cross he had made from small limbs and vines. He pushed it into the dirt at the head of the grave.

People slowly turned and began to walk away, their silence a fitting end to an unexpected funeral. Elijah gave Micah his shovel and used his handkerchief to wipe his forehead and face before taking the baby from Ella. Micah looked over Elijah's shoulder and smiled down at the newborn.

"That's a fine boy you got there, Elijah. I just know Seraphina is lookin' down from heaven smilin' right now." He squeezed Elijah's shoulder, then turned and walked away.

"Did Seraphina have a name picked out for the baby?" Ella asked.

"She said she had been studying the Good Book lookin' for one, but never could find one that she liked. I don't know nothin' about that book, but I do know she smiled mighty big when she saw him. He made her last minute on the earth a happy one, so I'm just gonna call him Happy."

Ella smiled. "That's nice, Elijah. Sera would have liked that. Are you sure you can't stay? We could all help out watching the baby."

Elijah looked down at Ella, considering it, then shook his head. "I can't work the field with a baby on my back. I gotta try and find somethin' else."

An old carpetbag was sitting on the ground near Ella. She reached down and handed it to Elijah. "It ain't much, but everybody gave a little something. There's some food in there and a jug of goat's milk for the baby. Make sure you put that milk in a creek at night to keep it cool, so it don't spoil.

Ella leaned in to look at the sleeping baby. "You take good care of your Pappy now Happy." She smiled then looked up at Elijah. "And you take good care of that baby."

Stretching up on her toes, she kissed Elijah on the cheek, then walked away toward the nearby field. After a few steps, she stopped and turned back to see Elijah carrying the baby and the bag and leaving the grave site.

CHAPTER 2

As the sun started to set, Elijah and Happy made camp near a small stream. After a day of walking, carrying both the baby and the heavy bag, Elijah's arms and legs ached, and all he wanted to do was sit down and close his eyes.

Happy, still swaddled in the blanket Ella had wrapped him in, slept next to the fire as Elijah started to sort through the contents of the bag. He removed the jug of milk, which he gently placed in the cool creek water. A few pieces of clothing had been neatly placed inside, along with some bread and bacon.

At the bottom of the bag was Seraphina's Bible. Elijah trembled as he took the book out and turned it over in his hands. He looked at the worn spine, then used his fingers to trace the words *Holy Bible* on the front cover. Gently opening it, he found Seraphina's name carefully written in pencil on the cover page.

"Your momma sure was proud of this book," he said to the sleeping baby. "I remember the day she got it, just like it was yesterday."

He closed the book and placed it back into the carpetbag, then laid back with his head next to Happy's and closed his eyes.

* * *

FIVE YEARS EARLIER

The foreman wiped sweat from his forehead, then used his wide-brimmed hat as a fan before placing it back on his head to give his eyes some relief from the midday sun. Sweat stained the dress shirt he wore, and he could feel it run down his leg underneath his rough, home-spun trousers. He stood on the front porch of the plantation house, where not so many years ago his grandfather had worked as a slave master. A coiled whip—a remnant of those days—hung from his belt.

A small group of people, mostly black and dressed in dingy, worn clothing, were gathered in the yard in front of him. Some of the women were carrying young children on their hips while the older children were kept in line with a stern look from their fathers.

"So that's our offer," the foreman said. "Two weeks' work at thirty cents a day for adults and fifteen cents for children old enough to put in a day's work."

His grandfather would have never dreamed of paying people like this to work. The suggestion would have made him laugh out loud. But times had changed, and the plantation business had to change with them. That didn't mean he had to like it.

"We will supply you with meat, bread and coffee. Enough for one meal a day, and you can hold out enough of what you dig to round it out."

The sound of footfalls on gravel got the foreman's attention. Looking beyond the crowd, he saw a man walking up the farm road. He watched him as he fell in at the back of those gathered. The young black man was carrying an old carpetbag and had a worn-out guitar strapped on his back. The foreman knew his type just by looking at him: a troublemaker, young and cocky. His parents or grandparents might have been slaves, but he was free and he expected to be treated as an equal. The foreman spit a wad of chewing tobacco off the porch and into the dust. That's what he thought of equality.

"You lookin' for work, boy?" the foreman yelled to the new arrival.

The crowd turned and looked at Elijah.

"We need potato diggers not guitar pickers!" the foreman pressed.

Some folks laughed at this, but others just continued to stare at Elijah, wondering what he would do. Would he kowtow to the foreman or laugh at the man's joke to try to keep the peace?

"Yes, sir," Elijah answered in a strong clear voice. "My hands are plenty strong enough to do both."

"They better be."

Satisfied that that would be the end of it, the crowd turned back to face the foreman.

"All right, then," he continued. "You can make your camps in the field behind the house. There's a creek runs through it for water. Make your mark with Captain Mac at the table beside the house, then get settled in. Work starts tomorrow at first light."

Talking amongst themselves, the crowd began to make their way to the side of the house.

"Remember, it's a two-week job. You don't work fourteen days, you don't get paid."

The workers continued around the house with Elijah bringing up the rear. As he approached the porch, the foreman stepped down, blocking his way.

"I ain't gonna have any trouble out of you, am I, boy?" he asked.

"No, sir." Elijah made sure to keep his tone respectful. He could see the whip coiled at the foreman's side, and he doubted it would take much for the man to put that whip to work.

The foreman took a minute to look Elijah up and down, taking his measure, then spit a gob of tobacco juice at Elijah's feet. If he had expected Elijah to jump back to avoid the stream, he was disappointed. Elijah didn't move and looked the foreman straight in the eye.

"Just you see to it that I don't." The foreman stepped to one side to make room for Elijah to pass. "We got a lot of families in that group, and I don't want to hear nothing about you catting around. You understand what I'm saying to you?"

Elijah gave the foreman a slow nod before stepping around him to join the others.

A crowd had gathered around the small table at the side of the house where Captain Mac was sitting with paper and pencil making a list of everyone who was signing on for the job.

Captain Mac was another descendant of the plantation system. Hunched over and skinny, his clothes hung off him like overalls on an under-stuffed scarecrow. With contempt, he eyed each man that stepped up to his table. The black ones didn't deserve to be treated like humans, and the few white ones that were willing to work alongside the blacks were beneath him. None of them were good for anything but hard labor, except for the occasional young girl who passed through. He was always glad to show them just how to better themselves.

"Step up!" he called out to the next man in line. "If you people don't work any faster than this, them taters gonna go to rot in the field."

Elijah fell in line behind a family of five. The father was a massive black man whose muscular body towered over his small and frail-looking wife. Behind them were two little boys playfully pushing and roughhousing with each other. With practiced accuracy, their older sister reached over and slapped the boy closest to her in the back of the head.

"Straighten up," she whispered just loud enough for the boys to hear.

They immediately snapped to attention. After a minute, the boy who got slapped looked to see if his sister was watching before reaching up and rubbing the back of his head.

Seeing this, Elijah let out a quick laugh. The girl shyly turned and looked back at him, giving him an embarrassed smile. Their eyes met, and Elijah smiled back. He was immediately struck by her dark eyes, so deep and full of life. She obviously felt the intensity of his stare and looked away again, but almost immediately locked her gaze with his once more, and her smile grew.

"Seraphina!" her father barked, interrupting the moment.

"Yes, Daddy?" She spun around to face him and secretly hoped he hadn't noticed her making eyes at the stranger.

The big man looked from Seraphina to Elijah. The harsh expression on his face caused Elijah to take a step back.

"Next!" Captain Mac called out. "Hey, big boy! That's you!"

Seraphina and her family stepped up to the table.

"What's your name?" Captain Mac asked.

"Jessie Ischa," the big man replied. "This is my wife, Naamah. The children are Abraham, David, and Seraphina."

Captain Mac looked over the family and his eyes lingered on Seraphina. "How old's the girl?"

Jessie saw how the man watched his daughter and resisted the urge to snap his neck.

"Seraphina be fifteen, the boys is eight and nine."

"Fifteen, huh? Never would have guessed that." Captain Mac was still eyeing Seraphina when Jessie stepped in front of him and blocked his view. Captain Mac shifted his gaze from Seraphina to Jessie's face and smirked.

"Half wages for them two, full pay for you, your wife and daughter. You see to it that she earns it." Captain Mac slid a piece of paper and pencil across the table to Jessie. "Sign here."

Jessie stood still as a statue and stared down at the paper.

"Let me guess, you can't write?"

Jessie slowly shook his head.

"Can you make an *X*?"

Jessie nodded.

Captain Mac leaned across the table and pointed to Jessie's name written on the paper. "This is your name." He spoke like he would to a child. "Make your mark next to it."

Jessie bent low over the table and carefully put an X on the line.

"Good enough. Next!"

Seraphina and her family moved off to the side, and Elijah watched them walk away. For just a split second, Elijah and Seraphina's eyes met again before she turned away.

"Name?" Captain Mac asked.

Elijah, caught up in the moment, didn't hear him.

"Hey, boy! I said what's your name?"

Captain Mac's raised voice got Elijah's attention, and he stepped up to the table.

"Sorry sir, it's Elijah Parker."

Captain Mac laughed and looked over at Seraphina.

"Yeah, I could get a little lost looking at that, too."

Captain Mac turned his attention back to the job at hand and wrote *Elijah Parker* on the paper before turning it back around for Elijah to sign.

"This is your name," he said in his condescending tone. He pointed to where he had written it. "Put your mark next to it."

Elijah looked the captain in the eyes. "I can read and write my name."

"Well, ain't you a smart one. Write it next to where I did and move on."

Elijah did as he was told, then stepped to the side.

He looked up and saw Seraphina turn back toward him. He smiled and pretended to tip his hat to her, and that made her giggle.

Sensing trouble, the way only a father can, Jessie turned back around in time to see Elijah walking in the opposite direction.

* * *

A night filled with thunder and heavy rain caused the first day of work on the farm to be a particularly nasty one. Muddy fields were filled with grumbling laborers that had been kept awake by the loud rumbles and the flashes of lightning.

The first day's food rations had come too late for most of the folks to eat breakfast. Captain Mac made a show of dropping the small packages of coffee, bacon, and bread at each camp site. He lingered at the ones where the families with young girls were trying to get ready for the day's work.

Seraphina had seen him coming and left in the opposite direction. She chose to get an early start in the potato field rather than taking the chance of having to smile and speak nicely to him. Her father had told her that if she wasn't polite, she could cause them trouble with the captain. He had also *promised* her that the first time Captain Mac laid a hand on her, it would be the last time he laid a hand on anyone. She wasn't sure if her father was capable of taking another man's life, but she didn't want to find out.

Digging potatoes was hard work, made harder by the mud that had become caked on her shoes. Seraphina constantly had to shake the mud off them and also from the hoe she was using.

Elijah was working on the opposite side of the same field as Seraphina. He couldn't help but laugh as he watched her in her long dress, shaking mud from her boots. He also noticed that she would sometimes take those opportunities to steal a glance in his direction.

The man working the row next to Seraphina walked over to Elijah's side of the field to get a drink from the water bucket. He was an older white man with a chin full of salt-and-pepper whiskers and a patch over one eye. Seeing a chance to better his situation, Elijah left his row and met the man at the bucket.

"Excuse me, sir," Elijah said. "I was wonderin' if you would mind switchin' rows with me. That girl you're workin' next to is my sister, and I think our daddy would feel better if I was up there to watch after her."

The man reached for the dipper that hung off the side of the bucket, then filled it with water and took a long drink. "She ain't your sister," he said matter-of-factly, peering at Elijah with his one good eye. "I seen you come in late yesterday and you weren't with 'em." Elijah could see that the man was missing most of his teeth to the point that his mouth had begun to draw in. A jagged scar ran from under the eyepatch and ended just below the man's ear.

"You just wantin' to go sniff up around that girl and see if she's ripe for pickin'." The man snorted a laugh at his own joke that made his toothless mouth quiver. This was followed by a sucking sound as he tried to keep his spit from spraying all over Elijah's face.

Elijah smiled. "Fair enough. So do you mind?"

"Makes no difference to me. Taters is taters. But if you know what's good for ya, you'll leave that little girl alone. Her pappy's big as a barn and strong as a mule. Little twig like you liable to get broke in two and put on the fire." He let out another lip quaking laugh, this time not worrying about the spit.

"Guess that could happen." Elijah wiped at his now-damp shirt. "But I think I'll take my chances all the same."

"Good enough for ya' then." The man snatched the hoe Elijah was using out of his hands and went back to work.

Elijah took the long way around the field to get to the row next to Seraphina, hoping to surprise her. He quietly walked up to where the man had left off. Elijah started working, drawing ever closer to Seraphina. After a few minutes of fast work, he managed to catch up to her, but before he could say anything, she beat him to it.

"My daddy says to stay clear of you." She never looked up from the row of potatoes stretching out before her.

"Your daddy's a big man."

"He's stubborn and mean-tempered, too. Snap a little twig like you in two with one hand."

Elijah straightened up and looked down at himself. Being called a twig twice in less than an hour had him worried that he might be looking sickly.

"But I wouldn't let him do it," Seraphina said. She glanced over at Elijah and gave him a sly smile, then went back to digging potatoes.

* * *

1930

Elijah sat up and added a few sticks to the dwindling fire before opening the carpetbag again and reaching inside. He pulled the Bible out and reverently looked at it, watching the colors from the fire dance across its surface. Gently, he laid back down beside the sleeping baby. Elijah clutched the Bible to his chest, crossing his arms over it.

"Tomorrow we gotta do somethin' about findin' work. That little bit of bacon and jug of milk ain't gonna last us long. If your momma was here she'd be prayin' about it, but I'm guessin' that old man up yonder wouldn't listen even if I tried."

Elijah stared up at the stars in the cloudless sky. "Can't blame him really. I never gave him much thought, truth be told."

Happy stirred in his blanket, and Elijah reached over to gently touch the baby's face.

"What do you think?" Elijah smiled down at Happy. "Think maybe Sera will put a good word in for us with the man upstairs? I hope so 'cause we gonna need all the help we can get."

With his son sleeping beside him and his beloved wife's prized Bible close to his heart, he closed his eyes and drifted off to sleep.

CHAPTER 3

Small clouds of dust rose behind Elijah as he walked down a deserted dirt road. The Mississippi midday sun beat down on him while Happy wiggled uncomfortably in the makeshift sling that he had made from the blanket and hung around his neck.

Elijah tried his best to stay in the slight bit of shade coming from the trees that lined his path, but with the noon sun hot overhead there was very little shade to be found. A kind of lethargy came over him brought on by the heat and the rhythmic sound of his footfalls.

At first, he failed to hear the old truck's engine as it turned onto the road behind him. The truck backfired, and its unseen driver gunned the engine in an attempt to keep it running. Startled, Elijah turned to face the oncoming vehicle and stuck out his thumb in hopes of getting a ride. The truck swung wide and never slowed down. Elijah stopped and just stood still, watching as the truck moved away.

"That's the first person we've seen all day, Happy, and he didn't even give us a second look." With a deep breath and a loud sigh, Elijah began walking again.

About an hour later, he rounded a curve and noticed some buildings in the distance.

The first one he came to had Flanigan's General Store painted on the window. He stepped up on the porch and took a moment to knock some of the dust off his pants before going in.

The heat from outside was nothing compared to the stifling temperature inside the store. Elijah was immediately struck by the smell of garbage. Then, hearing flies buzzing, he spotted the source of the odor. A small display of apples just inside the front window had gone bad, and a swarm of fruit flies were feasting on their newfound treat.

A short, heavyset white man, wearing long sleeves and an apron, stepped out from the back room and hurried toward the apple bin carrying a tin pail. Seeing Elijah, he smiled hesitantly and raised a hand. "Didn't hear you come in. I was just in the back looking for something to clean up those bad apples with."

The little man waddled up to the display and used a trowel he pulled out of his apron to move the rotten fruit into the pail.

"Damn flies. Once they get a taste, they never leave. I'll be fighting these pests the rest of the summer now."

Elijah watched him work for a minute, then took a step closer. "Looks like you could use a little help around here. I'm new in town and I sure could use the—"

"Let me stop you right there." The little man quit what he was doing and looked over at Elijah. "I can't hire you. I can't hire anybody, but I especially can't hire *you*."

"Oh, I see. Thank you." Elijah turned to leave.

"It's not me," the man explained. "I'd hire you in a second, but I don't own this place. The Flanigan brothers do, and to be honest, if they find out that I let you in here, I'll be out there trying to find work right alongside of you."

Happy kicked and began to cry.

"Is that a baby you got wrapped up in there?" The little man leaned in to look as Elijah loosened the wrap around Happy.

"Yes, sir. Name's Happy but he ain't livin' up to it right now. I'm afraid he's hungry."

A concerned look came over the little man's face. "I tell you what, you take little Happy and go back out on the porch, and I'll see if I can find a little something for him and you both. But then you gotta go. Okay?"

Elijah smiled and nodded his understanding. "Much appreciated."

The shopkeeper waddled quickly toward the back of the store as Elijah went out on the porch. A moment later, the man stepped out and handed Elijah a small cloth-wrapped bundle. "I'm afraid it's not much, just some hardtack and little bit of milk for the baby."

Elijah looked down at the bundle then back up at the man. "It may not be much, but it's more'n anyone else has offered us in the last few days. Seems like ain't nobody interested in helpin' out a wanderin' fella with a baby. I can't thank you enough."

"I wish I could do more, but…" The man just shrugged.

"I understand. Things is tough all over."

Elijah turned and stepped off the porch, thinking that he needed to find a shady spot for him and Happy to have a meal. With a little something in their stomachs, Happy would calm down, and *he* would be able to think straighter.

"You might try the church up the street," the man said, pointing in the direction of some more buildings. "There's a new minister, and I understand he's shaking things up a little. Maybe he can help or knows someone who could use you."

Elijah nodded his thanks and turned to walk in the direction the man had pointed.

As he made his way up the street, he saw an elderly woman sweeping her front porch, while two small children played in the yard. When she saw him, she stopped sweeping and watched as he drew closer. Seeing that she'd taken notice of him, Elijah gave her a friendly nod and waved hello with his free hand. The woman, without ever taking her eyes off him, gathered the children to her and hurried them inside.

"Guess they don't cotton to our kind here much," Elijah said and smiled down at Happy. "Startin' to feel like nobody does."

He looked up just as two dogs came running from behind the old woman's house. The larger of the two was black, and its muscular body writhed under its skin. Its eyes looked cold over its angry, bared teeth. The second smaller dog was no less worrisome; what it lacked in size it made up for in pure aggression.

Elijah stopped. Then, without turning away from the dogs, he slowly walked backward across the dusty street. A movement from the porch caught his eye, and he spotted the old woman peeking out through a window.

"She done turned the dogs loose on us," he whispered and instinctively pulled Happy closer to him.

He was still keeping an eye on the dogs when he bumped into a white picket fence. Startled and afraid that he had run into someone, he turned quickly, ready to apologize. Realizing his error, Elijah took a deep breath, pulled his handkerchief from his pocket and used it to wipe the sweat off his face.

"I swear these folks done got me plumb jumpy."

A sharp whistling sound came from across the street. An old man in worn overalls stood at the side of the house watching Elijah. The dogs stopped barking, trotted over, and sat quietly at his side.

Feeling the man's cold stare following him, Elijah made his way to the front of the tall brick church. It stood like a monument on an expanse of green lawn behind the fence he had just bumped into.

A hand painted sign inside a white wooden frame read:

St. Castulus Methodist Church

Below that in dainty, hand-painted white letters someone had added:

Feel safe all who enter here

Elijah set his carpetbag down in front of the sign and reached out to touch the writing. He looked from the sign to the entry way of the church. Happy made a gurgling noise and began to stir inside the sling. Elijah smiled and gently rubbed Happy's chest to try and calm him down.

"This ain't no life for you little one, beggin' for scraps and havin' the dogs set on you. If I was a prayin' man, I'd ask that fella up yonder to help us out, but I don't much guess he looks out for the likes of us. So, it's up to me to do what I think's best for you."

Elijah reached into the sling, took the wide-eyed baby out and nestled him into the crook of his arm. He removed the sling from around his neck and placed it inside the carpetbag. He saw Sera's Bible there at the bottom of the bag and picked it up. Was he really about to do what he was considering? If

Sera had survived, he wouldn't be making this decision. Instead, they would be making their way through life together, the three of them.

Elijah read the sign again, *Feel safe all who enter here*, and hoped that applied to babies as well as sinners. With the slow heavy pace of a man being led to the gallows, he walked up to the church.

As he stepped into the church's shadow, a cooling breeze blew gently across the sweat that had formed on the back of his neck. Elijah shivered. Happy made one of those soft cooing noises that only an infant can make and Elijah knew his boy felt the coolness, too.

Elijah stepped up onto the small stone porch that formed the church entryway and stood facing two heavy wooden doors. He expected them to be locked, and that the welcoming invitation on the church sign was really just empty words. Surely, no one like him and Happy would ever be welcome there.

He turned and looked back across the street, fully expecting to see the old man and his dogs still standing there watching his every move. But the yard was empty. In fact, the whole town appeared to be deserted. He faced the church again, grasped the old brass door handle, and gave the door a push. To his surprise it opened easily, letting a shaft of light into the room. He stepped inside and allowed the door to close softly behind him.

The large sanctuary had a slight musty smell and was bathed in shadows caused by the filtered light coming in through the frosted glass windows. After being outside in the bright sunlight, it took a moment for his eyes to adjust to the dimmer light. Wooden pews stood in two columns down the length of the sanctuary, leading to an altar table behind which was a simple pulpit. A small statue of Jesus stood on the altar table with its hands reaching out in a welcoming gesture.

Elijah walked up the aisle, his feet and legs passing through the shadows cast by the pews. As he drew close to the altar, his heart started to race. He wanted to turn and run.

Happy began to cry, and Elijah tried to calm him by touching his finger to the baby's mouth. Happy's small hands reached up and grasped Elijah's finger, and that connection seemed to ease him.

Elijah stepped up to the altar table and looked down at the statue of Jesus standing there. He took a deep breath to steady his nerves, and before he had a chance to rethink his decision, Elijah gently placed Happy on one side of the statue and Seraphina's Bible on the other.

"Always remember that your Daddy and Momma loved you," he whispered to the baby, then turned and spoke to the statue of Jesus. "We ain't never talked before, but my Sera put mighty stock in you and your book. So, I'm trustin' you to take care of little Happy. Don't let me down, all right?"

Elijah leaned in and kissed Happy on the forehead, then turned to leave, pulling his finger out of the baby's grasp. Without Elijah's finger for comfort, Happy began crying again. Elijah lowered his head in determination and began to walk away. As the baby's cries got louder, Elijah concentrated on the approaching doors and tried to convince himself that he was doing the right thing.

What do I know about raisin' babies? he thought to himself. *Happy's damn near starved to death already. I can't do this without Sera, and she's dead!*

As he reached out for the door, Happy's cries suddenly stopped. Shocked by the silence, Elijah spun around.

A pinched-faced older woman wearing a high collared black dress stood beside the altar holding Happy in her arms. A door off the sanctuary opened with a creak of old hinges, and a minister wearing clerical robes and collar stepped into the room. Without a word to Elijah the minister crossed to the woman and gazed down at Happy cradled in her arms.

"This is a mighty beautiful child," the minister said as he looked across the sanctuary to Elijah. "Are you sure this is what you want to do?"

Tears started to burn in the corner of Elijah's eyes, and he wiped at them with the back of his hand. "No sir, but Seraphina—that was my wife—she always had faith in the church and in that there book."

The minister reached down and picked up Seraphina's Bible.

"Now that's she dead," Elijah continued. "I can't figure how to go on. So, I thought that this would be the best place for little Happy."

The matronly woman's face softened as she looked down at Happy and smiled. "*Happy*. That seems to suit him." Her voice sounded much kinder than her apparent demeanor.

"Come on back up here, son," the minister said. "Mrs. Jones will fix us some refreshments, and then maybe we can figure out something better than leaving little Happy here with strangers."

Elijah hesitated, quickly glanced at the doors, then turned and walked back to the front of the sanctuary.

* * *

The church parsonage was in the back of the building, and Elijah soon discovered that the minister was a bachelor, and that Mrs. Jones was an employee of the church hired to cook and clean for him.

Elijah sat at a large table that took up most of the dining room. He held Happy in his lap and fed the baby from a proper baby bottle. At the head of the table sat his host. The remains of a large meal covered the table in front of them, and Elijah realized that this had been the first full meal that he had eaten since Seraphina's death almost two weeks prior.

Mrs. Jones, with an apron added over her high-necked dress, came into the room carrying a pie. She set it down in front of the minister who began slicing and serving it.

She took her place at the table and placed a cloth napkin in her lap. With a smile and a *no-nonsense* nod, she accepted the piece of pie that the minister sat in front of her, then cleared her throat. "Now that you and that sweet baby are done eating, why don't you finish telling us your story?"

Happy took the last drop of milk that the bottle had to offer, and Elijah placed him on his shoulder and gently patted him on the back.

"Well ma'am, there's ain't much more to tell."

Happy let out a burp any grown man would have been proud of, and Elijah settled him back down in his arms.

"Ever since Sera passed, me and Happy have been ridin' our thumbs tryin' to find work and a place to settle down. We've met some nice enough folks that have helped out with a penny or two, but that's about it. This is the first real meal we've had in well over a week."

"Well, Elijah," the minister said in his warm comfortable voice. "I think that was because the Lord was leading you in our direction. Mrs. Jones and I were just saying yesterday that we could use a man to take care of the grounds and do handyman work here at the church."

Mrs. Jones shot him a confused look, but the minister just smiled and nodded, acknowledging her concern

"We can't pay you but we can keep you and little Happy fed. There's a shed out back that you can clean up that would make a nice room for you two to stay in."

Elijah looked from the minister to Mrs. Jones, determined not to let them see the whirlwind of emotions that their offer had stirred up inside of him.

"That would be just fine, sir, and thank you, ma'am. I really can't tell you what this means to us."

"There's no need to thank us," Mrs. Jones said. "This is a job we are offering you, not charity. You need a place to stay, and we need your help. It's simply a solution to a problem. But understand I will not put up with any foolishness. There will be no smoking or drinking on the church grounds, and I am the housekeeper—not a nanny—so do not expect me to take care of that baby. He is *your* responsibility and yours alone."

The minister used his napkin to cover the smile on his face. Mrs. Jones noticed and gave him a harsh look. He cleared his throat and placed the napkin back on his lap.

"Well now that that's settled, what say we try this delicious looking pie?" The minister took a forkful of the flaky crust filled with blueberries and placed it in his mouth.

"I have some cold milk out in the kitchen, it will go well with the pie," Mrs. Jones informed them. She got to her feet and left the room.

The minister watched her go, then in a conspiratorial fashion, leaned over toward Elijah. "Don't let Mrs. Jones bother you," he whispered. "She's gruff on the outside, but inside beats a heart of gold. She lost her husband last year and has since devoted herself to the upkeep of this church, and its minister." He took another bite of pie and chewed it slowly, enjoying the tart taste of the berries and buttery crust. "And she makes the best blueberry pie in the county."

* * *

A small, but welcoming, parlor sat off the dining room of the parsonage. In it, a leather couch and wingback chair sat facing a small fireplace. The walls were covered in shelves filled to overflowing with old books. Elijah couldn't believe his eyes. The minister carried the carpetbag for Elijah while he held Happy, who was sleeping comfortably tucked into the bend of his arm.

"Really Pastor, you don't have to go to all this trouble for us. Happy and me don't mind sleepin' outside till we get that shed cleaned out. We're kinda used to it."

"Nonsense," the minister overruled him. "What kind of a man of God would I be if I let you and that beautiful child sleep out in the damp when there is a perfectly good sofa right here in the parsonage?"

As if on cue, Mrs. Jones came in carrying a stack of blankets and set them on the couch. "Well, I can't say that this couch is comfortable." Mrs. Jones wiped a speck of dust off a small wooden end table with the hem of her apron. "But it will beat sleeping on the cold ground."

Elijah looked around the room, and for the second time that day fought back a wave of emotions. "I don't know how to thank you folks enough."

He began to unpack his bag and was about to place some things on the end table when Mrs. Jones stopped him. She turned and removed a lace doily from a small compartment in one of the shelves and placed it on the end table, then took the sleeping baby from him. She gave him a nod indicating that he should continue.

"Don't mention it," she instructed him. "Just work hard for us and remember, no foolishness."

"Yes, ma'am, I won't forget." Elijah couldn't help but smile at the serious tone in her voice.

"This poor child is in desperate need of a good bath," Mrs. Jones announced and left the room with Happy.

When she was gone, the minister walked over to the end table and picked up Seraphina's Bible. He turned it over in his hands, then opened the cover and looked at the printed inscription there. "I always love seeing a well-worn Bible."

"Yes, sir. It is that." Elijah took the final items from the bag.

"It also looks very well *read*, as a Bible should."

Elijah turned and faced the minister, who was gently leafing through the book. For some reason he didn't understand, Elijah reached out and took the Bible from him.

"That was all my Sera's doin'," Elijah said. "She read this book like her very life depended on it. Can't say it did her much good." He started to put the Bible back in his bag.

"Elijah, have you read Sera's Bible much?"

Elijah stood and stared down at the book's worn cover and cracked spine. "I've tried. I really have. But to be honest, I can't make much of it."

The minister took the Bible back from Elijah and sat on the couch. He motioned for Elijah to join him.

"Do you remember how you told me that Sera reached for this Bible when things started going wrong?" he asked.

"Yes, sir, that's what she did."

The minister looked up into Elijah's eyes, then reached out and put a comforting hand on his knee. "Then I believe it may have done her more good than you give it credit."

"Not meaning no offense sir, but she's still dead," Elijah said with a small shake of his head.

The minister turned to a dog-eared page and straightened the bend.

"Sera done that every time she stopped readin'," Elijah said. "I used to tell her that if she kept up bendin' them pages, she was gonna have to get another book 'cause that one was gonna get all worn out."

The minister looked at the marked page, then up at Elijah. "So, do you think this was where she was reading before she passed?"

Elijah nodded. "Most likely."

"Looks like she was reading in the fourth chapter of Philippians," the minister told him, then began to read aloud. "*I know what it is to be in need, and I know what it is to have plenty. I have learned the secret of being content in any and every situation, whether well fed or hungry, whether living in plenty or in want, I can do all this through Him who gives me strength.*"

The minister closed the Bible. "She's dead on this earth, Elijah, but let me tell you where I think she is."

He began telling Elijah of heaven and of God's promises made to those who believe, and for the first time that night— for the first time since Seraphina's death—Elijah allowed all his emotions to freely be released.

* * *

The next day, Elijah woke early feeling refreshed from a good night's sleep. He sat up on the sofa and looked around the parlor. He found it hard to believe the turn his and Happy's lives had taken in the last twenty-four hours.

He looked over at the chair where he had made Happy a bed out of blankets and was shocked to see that the baby wasn't there. Struck with fear that Happy could have fallen out and gotten hurt, he dropped to his knees and looked under the chair. Not finding him there he searched under the sofa, then crawled around the floor. He still couldn't find little Happy.

The sound of metal hitting metal came from the other room and caught his attention. Elijah jumped to his feet and ran toward the sound.

"Happy, Happy!"

Elijah raced into the kitchen at a full sprint, then skidded to a stop, not believing what he was seeing. Mrs. Jones was already there making breakfast with Happy tucked safely in her arms.

"Good morning, Mr. Parker," she said, never turning around. "Coffee's ready, so just have a seat."

She motioned Elijah to a chair at the small kitchen table and placed a steaming cup of hot coffee in front of him.

"My husband and I had four boys, Mr. Parker." She returned to the stove. "I became very accustomed to cooking with a baby in my arms. To tell the truth, I quite miss it."

Elijah had never been served by a white woman before, and he wasn't quite sure what to do. Mrs. Jones turned back to the stove and returned moments later with a plate stacked high with eggs, corn cakes, and sausages. She set the plate down in front of Elijah, then noticed the strange look on his face.

"Is there something wrong with your coffee, Mr. Parker?"

"Oh, no, ma'am." Elijah quickly lifted the cup to his lips and took a drink of the strong black coffee. "It's real nice."

Mrs. Jones motioned to the plate of food she had set in front of him. "Eat your breakfast. You have a busy day ahead of you if you intend to get that shed cleaned out and habitable."

"Is this *all* for me?"

"Of course, it is. Now you best eat before it gets stone cold."

Not needing to be told twice, Elijah began eating. It was the most amazing breakfast he had ever eaten, and even though he quickly began to feel full, he could not make himself leave one crumb remaining on the plate. As he used the last piece of corn cake to mop up the remains of the eggs, the minister came into the kitchen.

Instead of his robes today, he was dressed in a simple black suit and tie. His suit coat was draped over his arm, and he transferred it to the back of the kitchen chair before sitting down. "Good morning, Mrs. Jones, Mr. Parker. Looks like the good Lord has blessed us with a perfect summer day."

"That it does," Mrs. Jones agreed. She turned from the stove with the minister's morning coffee.

He saw Happy in her arms, and a great smile crossed his face. "And good morning to you, young Master Happy!"

Happy gurgled in response, making the minister's smile all the wider.

"How has our Mrs. Jones been treating you this morning, Mr. Parker? From the look of that empty plate in front of you, I assume she has fed you well."

"Oh yes, sir. Yes, sir!" Elijah pushed himself away from the table and stood. "But I would like to ask a favor of the two of you if that's all right?"

Mrs. Jones turned from the stove and placed the minister's breakfast on the table. "No need to be so formal, Mr. Parker, just speak up."

"Thank you, ma'am." Elijah swallowed nervously, then pushed on. "If it's all the same to you, could you just call me

Elijah? I mean, I just ain't never gonna get used to white folks callin' me mister."

"Elijah it is," the minister agreed. "But it is my fervent prayer that the day will come when we can all equally call each other mister and ma'am without feeling anything other than pride and brotherly love."

"Amen," Mrs. Jones said, bringing the discussion to a close. "Now, Mr. Parker...er, *Elijah*. It's time for you to take possession of this little man as I have dishes to do and bedding to wash." She handed Happy to his father, turned her back on the men and began addressing the stack of pots and pans in the sink.

"What's your plan for the day, Elijah?" the minister asked around a mouth full of egg.

"Guess me and little Happy here gonna go check out that shed you told us about. See if we can't get it cleaned out and cleaned up."

"It's a yeoman's task, but I do believe you can make a comfortable place out of it with a little hard work and elbow grease."

"Yes, sir. I'm gonna give it my best." Elijah started to leave, then remembered his manners. "Thank you so much for that wonderful breakfast, Mrs. Jones. A man could get mighty spoiled eating like that every day."

"You're very welcome, Elijah. Now you best get to work before the heat of the day turns that shed into an oven."

"Yes'm." Elijah and Happy headed out of the kitchen, then out through the back door and into the yard.

Mrs. Jones watched them through the kitchen window until they reached the shed at the back of the property. Once she was sure they were out of earshot she joined the minister at the table.

"Elijah seems like a good man," the minister said and sipped his coffee.

"That he does, but good man or not, the Flanigan brothers are not going to like the fact that you're letting him work here. And God help us if they get word that you let them spend the night in the parsonage."

The minister set his coffee cup down on the table, took the napkin from his lap, and wiped his mouth before laying it on top of his empty breakfast plate. "The Flanigan brothers do not run the church, I do."

A look of worry darkened Mrs. Jones's face. "But they are on the church council, and they have the ear of quite a few of the other members."

The minister stood and pulled on his coat. "Matthew seven and twelve says, *Therefore all things whatsoever ye would that men should do to you, do ye even so to them. For this is the law of the prophets.* I do believe I have just decided on the text for my message next Sunday." He smiled and winked at Mrs. Jones, then turned and left the kitchen.

Watching him go, Mrs. Jones tilted her face toward the celling and prayed, "Lord, please make it that easy. Amen."

* * *

Elijah was sweeping out the old storage shed after spending most of the morning emptying it of odd pieces of broken tools, cleaning rags, and furniture that had seen better days. Some of the old furniture and other junk were sitting beside the building waiting for Mr. Bradley, the local junk man, to come by and haul it off. Whatever Elijah was sure Mr. Bradley wouldn't want, he burned in an old barrel down by the creek.

He had made Happy a swing out of ropes and an old wash tub he had found inside the shed. The baby was currently spending his morning sleeping and enjoying the warm breezes that blew up the valley from the creek below.

Elijah stopped sweeping just long enough to stretch and try to work a knot out of his back. He looked over at Happy, then back at the church, just in time to see Mrs. Jones watching him from the kitchen window.

"I bet that lady don't miss nothin' that goes on around here," he muttered to himself.

He returned to his sweeping and began whistling an old tune he remembered his momma singing to him when he was a baby. Caught up in the work and his childhood memories, he didn't notice when an older man, thin and bent-over, came into the shed.

"Just what do you think you're doin', boy?" The old man's words came out slightly garbled because of a plug of chewing tobacco in his jaw.

Surprised, Elijah faced the man and squinted, trying to make out his features. The bright sunshine outside the shed partially blinded Elijah. "Good Lord man, you 'bout scared the livin' daylights out of me!" Elijah leaned the broom against the wall of the building and walked toward the man, offering to shake his hand.

"The name's Elijah. The minister and Mrs. Jones brought me on to do some upkeep around the place. It's a pleasure to meet you Mr. . . . ." He questioned the man with his eyes.

The old man looked at Elijah's outstretched hand and didn't say anything. He just turned and spat a stream of tobacco juice on the floor at Elijah's feet, and walked away. Shocked, Elijah just watched the man leave.

A moment later, Mrs. Jones appeared at the shed door. "I see you met our Mr. Flanigan. *Jim* Flanigan. He and his brother Jasper are charter members at the church, and two of the wealthiest men in town."

She noticed the tobacco juice on the floor of the room. "I do not care much for them, but as I am a Christian, I will pray for their continued health and prosperity." A stiff tone resonated in her voice. "Just not very often."

She flashed Elijah a sarcastic smile, then curtly turned and walked away.

Laughing, Elijah got the broom and swept dust over the tobacco juice to soak it up.

* * *

That evening, Mrs. Jones cooked a meal fit for a king. Baked ham, mashed potatoes and gravy, pinto beans and cornbread had been served, and they had all eaten well. Happy had just finished a warm bottle of milk, and Elijah was trying to get him to take a taste of the mashed potatoes when the minister cleared his throat and let out a groan.

"Many more meals like this Mrs. Jones and you're going to have to start letting out the waistline of my preaching pants." He patted his small belly then turned his attention to Elijah. "I hear you had a run in with the illustrious Mr. Flanigan today."

"Yes, sir." Elijah smiled and a nodded. "But I've been around folks like him most of my life. I don't pay it no never mind."

"All the same I think I'll have a word with him and his brother."

"You will do no such thing," Mrs. Jones said with concern in her voice. "The Flanigan brothers are influential members of this community and this church. If you cross them, they will have you run out of town on a rail, just like they did the minister before you. You have worked hard and made a position for yourself in this community. People are coming to church like never before, and we are all better for it."

"Now Mrs. Jones just calm down."

"No. I will not calm down. You know full well what the Bible says in Luke six and twenty-seven. *Love your enemies, do good to those who hate you, bless those who curse you, pray for those who mistreat you.* I dislike the Flanigan brothers as much, if not more, than you do, but that is what I plan to do, and I expect nothing less from you."

Mrs. Jones, having said her last on the subject, stood and took Happy from Elijah. "The baby needs changing and made ready for bed, so I will say good evening gentlemen."

After she left the room, the minister cleared his throat again, stood, and walked over to a china cabinet that sat against one wall. He opened a drawer and removed a flask and a cigar. He poured himself a small glass of amber liquid, then turned to Elijah.

"If you're sure Mr. Flanigan didn't bother you," the minister said, striking a match and bringing it up to the tip of the cigar, "then it might be best if we do as she says."

"No, sir, he didn't bother me none." Elijah watched as the minister exhaled a large plume of cigar smoke. The pungent smell filled the room and immediately, Elijah's mouth watered.

Noticing Elijah's shocked expression, the minister turned and took another glass from the cabinet. He poured a small amount of the contents of the flask into it and held it out to Elijah. "It's medicinal, but just to be safe, let's not mention this to Mrs. Jones."

Elijah joined him at the cabinet and took the glass.

"You give me one of them there cigars, and you got a deal."

The minister nodded and raised his glass in a salute. "To the Flanigan brothers. May the Lord forgive them because I don't know if I can."

He and Elijah touched glasses and drank.

* * *

Elijah's first week at the church had been an absolute joy. He spent his days repairing the little problems that were always popping up in a building as old as St. Castulus: a wobbly pew here, a squeaking door there, and there was always upkeep to do on the exterior of the building and grounds.

It was Friday, the day Elijah had set aside for working at the front of the building. He had started his day early, clipping the weeds growing at the sides of the church. He was not a fan of the weed shears he used to do the job. They left his hands tired and sore, but when he was finished, he stood back and was proud of himself for what he had accomplished.

He returned the shears to the storage cabinet he had built at the side of his shed and picked up a rake, then he made his way back to the front of the church to gather all the clippings for burning.

After a few minutes, he had gathered an impressive pile of debris and was about to go get a wheelbarrow to cart it off when Mrs. Jones stepped out on the stoop. She was cradling Happy in one arm and holding a glass of lemonade in the other hand.

"Elijah, come take this and rest a minute. You won't do anyone any good if you fall out dead in the churchyard from heatstroke."

He stopped his work and joined her in the cool shade of the church entrance. He took a deep drink of the cold bitter lemonade and immediately felt refreshed. "Thank you, ma'am." He used the sleeve of his shirt to wipe sweat from his forehead. "That sure hits the spot."

Mrs. Jones looked around the yard then back to Elijah, who was finishing off his lemonade. "You have done an impeccable job cleaning up the church yard. Much better than the man the Flanigan brothers had do it last season. He was a drunkard and quite lazy."

"Ma'am, tell me if I'm out of line, but these Flanigan fellas don't seem all that Christian to me. They just seem *mean*."

Mrs. Jones smiled at this and nodded her head in agreement. "The Good Book tells us that all have sinned and fallen short of the glory of God. I can only assume that in the Flanigan's case, some have fallen further than others."

"Yes'm, but why do y'all put up with them?"

"The book of Matthew tells us that we must love our enemies and pray for them which use and persecute us. That is reason enough, but if I may be brutally honest, Elijah, it takes money to run a church, and in this town, the Flanigans have all of it. So, if it means condoning these men in order for the church to survive and accomplish all the good things it does for the folks around here, then so be it."

"Yes'm." Elijah handed the empty glass back to Mrs. Jones and picked up his rake from where he had leaned it against the wall of the church. "Thanks for the lemonade. I guess I best get back to these clippings."

"Elijah," Mrs. Jones said. He stopped to give her his attention. "The Lord works in mysterious ways, and they are not ours to questions or understand. We take the bad with the good as He sees fit to send it our way because we all know it's part of His larger plan. Do you understand?"

Elijah considered the question, then shook his head. "No, ma'am, I can't say that I do."

"Truth be told, sometimes neither do I. Maybe someday, when we stand before Him in Glory, He will explain it to us. Until then, we will just have to accept it by faith."

Mrs. Jones turned and stepped back inside. Elijah watched her disappear into the building, then started again raking up the clippings in the yard.

An unexpected cold breeze whistled around the building. The hairs on the back of his neck stood at attention and a chill ran down his spine. The wind carried with it whispers of a conversation, and Elijah looked around for the source of the muffled voices.

Across the street from the church, he saw two older white men who stood with their backs to the feed store. They were looking at him. Elijah immediately recognized one of them as Jim Flanigan, the man who had spit tobacco juice at him rather than shake his hand. He figured the other must be his brother, Jasper. They were talking quietly, each taking a turn looking at Elijah.

Half out of spite and half in an attempt at being neighborly, Elijah raised his rake in greeting. He gave them his best smile and nodded, then started back to work. The old men studied him for a moment, then turned and walked away. Elijah chanced a glance up from his work and watched them leave. He had a good thing here, and he feared that those two men could be the ruin of it.

CHAPTER 4

FIVE YEARS EARLIER

Just four days in, and Elijah was already tired of potatoes. He spent his days either digging or hauling them. Today he was hauling potatoes from the field to one of the many storage sheds built around the plantation. These wooden sheds were small, their dirt floors covered in a deep bed of straw to keep the potatoes off the ground, until they were shipped out or put to use.

Each day Captain Mac would pick a few of the stronger men to push wooden wheelbarrows of potatoes from the field to the sheds, and today was Elijah's lucky day. In fact, it was his third *lucky* day so far. Elijah suspected that Captain Mac had seen him and Seraphina talking in the field the first day, and he had been sentenced to hard labor ever since. He made a mental note to keep an eye on her when her daddy wasn't around.

Rumor had it that Captain Mac had an eye for young girls, especially the black ones. He had been talking to a couple of the men the night before who had worked this farm in the past, and they said that Captain Mac had *had his way* and *gotten rough* with a young black girl the year before. They had also said that when the foreman got word of it, he had covered it up. He had sent the girl's family on their way early and empty-handed.

Once a plantation, always a plantation and once a slave, always a slave, Elijah thought. *All that Lincoln man done was make rich folks pay their niggers with coins instead of with a leather strap across their backs. But the master is still the master and the slave's still the slave all the same.*

Caught up in his thoughts, Elijah wasn't watching where he was going and was surprised when the hard wooden wheel of the wheelbarrow struck a large rock, causing it to tilt drastically to one side. He did his best to regain control but only managed to overcompensate and dump his load all the same.

Just as the potatoes started rolling out of the wheelbarrow, Captain Mac rounded the corner of the house in a hurry. Elijah spotted him, and with a sigh, prepared himself for the tongue-lashing that was sure to be coming his way. Oddly, the captain paid him no attention and hurried off. Relieved, Elijah got to the task of reloading the wheelbarrow.

Ten minutes later, with the wheelbarrow once again full, Elijah continued on to the storage shed, this time keeping his eye on the path and his mind on business. He parked his load beside the shed. The door was kept closed by a metal clasp with a tapered wooden spike in it. Elijah pulled the spike out and stuck it in his pants pocket.

Inside, the shed was dark and the heat made it feel like an oven; the smell of hot straw and earth was almost overwhelming. A few loads of potatoes had been offloaded earlier in the day, so the ground was already covered. Elijah was tempted to upend the wheelbarrow at the door and let the potatoes just fall inside, but he knew if he did that he would only be making more work for himself. Taking the easy way now would only mean having to take the time to distribute them around the shed later, so he set about the task of gently pitching each potato toward the rear of the shed, making sure not to let them hit the back wall and get cut and bruised.

By the time he was finished, he was dripping wet with sweat, and his hands were caked with dirt. He pushed the shed door closed and started back toward the fields. There was a bucket of water just inside the first gate, and Elijah stopped and took a long drink from the dipper. The water was warm and tasted like the inside of the barrel, but it quenched his thirst and brought relief to his dry throat, and that was good enough. He poured a second dipperful over each hand, then reached for the kerchief he kept in his pocket to dry them off.

When he pulled the kerchief free, the wooden spike from the door fell to the ground. He dried his hands, stooped over and picked up the spike, and started to put it back in his pocket, thinking he could just take it back with him on the next wheelbarrow load. Then he remembered that he had seen Captain Mac up in the area of the shed. Leaving the shed door unfastened was just the sort of thing that would set Captain Mac off, and the man was angry enough as it was. No need to make things worse.

He left his wheelbarrow beside the water bucket and made his way back to the storage shed, keeping an eye peeled for Captain Mac along the way. He made it to the shed without incident and placed the spike back into its home in the clasp. As he turned to leave, he heard a rustling sound come from behind the shed. Probably a fox or an opossum looking for a potato to add to his lunch of table scraps and stolen eggs. The rustlings came again then a voice, and not just any voice. He immediately recognized it as Seraphina's. She sounded scared and panicked.

"No . . . *don't*. Stop that!"

Elijah rushed around to the other side of the building and discovered Captain Mac holding Seraphina by the upper arms and trying to kiss her. He had pinned her against the back wall of the shed, and she was struggling and turning her head to keep her face from his. It was obvious that she was no match for the older man's strength, and before he knew what he was doing, Elijah blurted out. "Captain Mac, sir!"

Captain Mac's head jerked up and he looked over at Elijah without letting go of Seraphina. "What's the matter with you boy? Can't you see I'm busy?"

"Oh yes, sir," Elijah said thinking fast. "You do seem to have your hands full, but the foreman, he says to me, he says, *find Captain Mac and tell him to drop what he's doin' and get his ass down to the south field.* And that's just what I'm doin'. There's a problem with one of the horses, and he needs your help."

Captain Mac scowled, and with a huff, he let go of Seraphina. She fell to her knees beside the wall of the shed and sobbed. He looked back at her, then turned and walked up to Elijah. The captain stood about three inches taller than Elijah in his work boots, and Elijah was very aware of the slapjack that hung off the man's belt. Captain Mac leaned down to be eye to eye with Elijah.

"If you are lying to me boy," the man hissed. "I will kill you. You hear me?" As he spoke, Elijah could smell the stale chewing tobacco that stained his teeth.

Elijah nodded slowly, all the while the muscles on the back of neck tightened and his hands curled into fists.

"Then," Captain Mac continued, "I'll come back and take what I want from that one all the same. Now why don't you think about what you just said and tell me again what the foreman told you."

Elijah stared into Captain Mac's eyes, not blinking. He refused to give the man the satisfaction of seeing him falter in any way. "He said, *hey boy, go find Captain Mac and tell him to get his ass down to the south field.*"

Captain Mac looked deep into Elijah's eyes, trying to decide if he's being lied to. "Right."

Captain Mac pushed him out of the way and stormed off. Elijah watched till he was out of sight before rushing over to check on Seraphina.

"You all right?"

Seraphina nodded, but Elijah could see the tears welling up in her eyes. He knelt down next to her and placed a comforting hand on her arm. She burst into tears, and he pulled her close.

"It's okay, it's gonna be okay," he whispered, stroking her hair.

Jessie had been looking for Seraphina ever since she had failed to return to the field in a reasonable amount of time. As he came around the shed, he saw them sitting there together with Seraphina's head resting against Elijah's chest.

Jessie rushed in and grabbed Elijah by the shoulders. His hands were like iron as he tore Elijah away from Seraphina and threw him to the ground. Elijah rolled to a stop, and before he could wrap his mind around what was happening, Jessie came toward him like an angry bull. The big man's fists were raised as he covered the distance that he had just thrown Elijah.

Trying to buy himself some time, Elijah scrambled backward and attempted to get to his feet, but in his panic, he only fell again, then Jessie was on him. One big iron fist reached down and lifted Elijah off the ground by his shirt collar as the other pulled back in order to cave in his head.

"No, Daddy, don't!" Seraphina jumped up and wrapped herself around her father's cocked arm. "Elijah didn't do nothin'! It was Captain Mac. Elijah *stopped* him."

Jessie turned and looked at Seraphina for the first time. He saw her red eyes and tear-streaked cheeks, and he dropped Elijah back to the ground. Then he gently used his big hand to wipe away her tears.

"He grabbed me, Daddy," Seraphina explained and started to cry again. "I was walkin' back out to the field, and he just come up and grabbed me from behind. He said awful things to me Daddy, then turned me around and pushed me up against the shed wall. He tried to put his mouth on mine."

Watching from his place on the ground, Elijah saw the muscles of Jessie's back and neck start to tense as his breathing became harder and faster with anger.

"I was so scared . . ." Seraphina let go of her father and walked over to where Elijah was sitting. "Then I heard Elijah's voice, and he told Captain Mac that the foreman needed him and Captain Mac went running."

Jessie stepped up to his daughter and wiped another tear from her cheek before turning to Elijah and offering him his hand. Elijah hesitantly took it and allowed himself to be pulled into a standing position.

"Captain Mac said if I was lyin', he'd kill me and take what he wanted from her." Elijah brushed away the dirt and leaves from his clothing. "I sent him to the south field, but still, it won't be long before he figures out what I did. After that..." Elijah shook his head, then looked down at the ground.

"Sera, go find your momma." Jessie's voice rumbled like an earthquake, and Elijah heard the anger and hurt buried deep within it.

"Yes, Daddy," Seraphina said and ran off toward the field where they had been working.

Jessie started toward the fields, then stopped and turned back to Elijah. "Ain't you got work to do?"

"Yeah, but you ain't gonna just—"

Jessie stopped Elijah with a hard look. "Don't you make no never mind about what I'm gonna do."

Jessie turned and followed Seraphina toward the fields. As he went, Elijah heard a low rumble come again from the big man. The sound reminded him of distant thunder, and he wondered if the lightning was far behind.

* * *

Later that night, Elijah was smoking and playing his guitar by the campfire. He strummed an old song his father had taught him when he was just a kid and quietly hummed the words. Across the fire, Seraphina and her parents sat together quietly talking to each other. Other folks from the camp milled around taking care of their evening chores in preparation for bed. The sound of a stick breaking in the dark got Jessie's attention and caused Elijah to stop playing.

The foreman stepped into the light from the fire and didn't waste any time getting down to business. "Listen up!"

The conversations stopped as the workers gathered around.

"Captain Mac's gone missing," the foreman said. "I need to know where he is, and I suspect some of you know."

A low murmur of whispered conversations filled the air. Elijah made eye contact with Jessie who just stared back at him, unmoving.

"So that's how it's going to be," the foreman continued. "Nobody knows nothing. I expected as much."

He looked around at the blank faces staring at him over the fire. "Maybe an extra day's wages will loosen your tongues and jog your memories. If it does and you decide that you have something to tell me, you come find me."

The foreman left the camp, and Elijah began to play again, never taking his eyes off Jessie. Abraham and David, Seraphina's little brothers, came in laughing and roughhousing, stopping only long enough to take their father's hands. They led him away to play with them.

Seraphina's mother whispered something to her, then kissed her cheek and followed her husband and sons off into the darkness. Seraphina watched her go, then stood and rounded the fire to sit next to Elijah.

"You play awful pretty," she said shyly.

Elijah just smiled, nodded, and kept on playing.

"I never said thank you for what you done this afternoon."

"I should be thankin' *you* for not lettin' your daddy flatten me out behind that shed."

Seraphina looked up at the stars, quietly listening to Elijah play. "Daddy's a good man. It's just that two summers ago, a man we were working with forced himself on Momma. Daddy nearly beat him to death before the foreman and his hands could stop him."

Elijah quit playing and turned his full attention to Seraphina.

"When Daddy told him what happened, the foreman had that other man hauled off and we never seen him again. But

Daddy's still mad, and he says he'll kill any man what touches any of us."

Firelight reflected in the tears that started to roll down her cheeks, and Elijah gently wiped them away. She put her hand over his and leaned in for a kiss. Elijah began to lean in as well, then abruptly pulled back.

"I ain't ready to die tonight," he said and got to his feet. He picked up his guitar. "You best go catch up to your momma."

* * *

A summer thunderstorm overnight turned the fields to mud and made Elijah's job pushing wheelbarrow loads of potatoes from field to shed that much harder. The sheds closest to the fields had filled up quickly, so he was having to go farther each trip as well. His boots quickly became caked with mud and he had to watch his footing to keep from slipping.

As he passed each field, he looked for Seraphina. He finally spotted her and her family working in a small area near the creek. They worked like a well-oiled machine. Seraphina and her mother would dig up the potatoes, then the two boys followed behind them putting the spuds into bushel baskets that had been placed at intervals along each row. As the baskets filled, Jessie would carry them, one on each arm, to the waiting wheelbarrow, then place the basket farther up on the row, ready to be filled again.

Sensing that he was being watched, Jessie stopped and looked up the hill at Elijah. Making eye contact with the giant man made a shiver run down Elijah's back. Those eyes carried a world of emotions. Anger and hate mixed with compassion and fear for his family's safety, but most especially distrust of him. Elijah nodded a greeting that was not returned. Thinking it best to keep moving, Elijah lifted his load by the wheelbarrow's handles and continued on.

His shed for the day was located about three-hundred yards from the field where Seraphina was working. As he covered the distance, he tried to imagine what Jessie was going through. What it would be like having to move a family from farm to farm, trying to earn enough money to keep them fed through the winter when jobs were hard to come by. Trying hard to keep them safe in one strange situation after another.

He thought about his own father. Born a slave on a plantation much like this one, his father had gained his freedom after the Civil War when he was just five years old.

Memories of the man's stories rushed back to him: Elijah's father had been a young man with a new world of freedom ahead of him, but he soon learned that the freedom they had prayed for came at a price. They may have been free, but they were still black, and being black in the post-Civil War South was not freedom.

His father's family had left the plantation with the intent to go north where rumor had it there were more opportunities to find work and to be treated like human beings. Their trip was cut short when Elijah's grandfather, Amos, was arrested and accused of stealing a loaf of bread from a nearby farmhouse. The county sheriff and two deputies rode up on horseback, threw a rope around Amos and pulled him away from his family.

Elijah remembered *vividly* his father telling him the story —that they couldn't hear what the men said, but Amos had shaken his head *no.* The sheriff and his men had laughed at him, then one of the deputies broke away and rode over to them and used his horse to block their view.

Elijah shook his own head to push away the memory. He moved the wheelbarrow into the shade of the shed and stopped. He hadn't thought about the story his father had told him for years but seeing Jessie's dedication to his family had brought it all back. As he mopped the sweat off his head with his handkerchief, he could picture the blank faraway look that had come over his father's face as he told it.

Just like before, more memories flooded his mind:

The deputy's horse had startled when two pistol shots rang out. His mule-like laugh had mixed with his grand-mother's screams when the sheriff rode by at full speed dragging Amos's body behind him. They eventually found his grandfather's body broken and mangled in a ditch a few miles down the road, and his grandmother had frantically tried to dress the gunshot wounds to the man's knees even though he was obviously dead. They had buried Amos in that same ditch an hour later before continuing their journey.

That night as they had huddled together to stay warm around a tiny campfire, Elijah's grandmother had removed a loaf of fresh baked bread from inside her coat. Her tears fell on the crusty outside of the loaf, making it taste slightly salty when Elijah's father had eaten it.

Elijah had asked his father why his grandmother had not admitted to stealing the bread, why she had let Amos die for what she had done. His father told him that Amos knew she had the loaf all the time, and he also knew that if the deputy found it, the punishment inflicted on his grandmother would have been much worse than anything they would have done to him. He also figured that when they had finished with her, they more than likely would have killed them *both*.

"It wasn't about the bread," his father had told him. "It was about the power. The power to control people that these men felt were beneath them. Mr. Lincoln had stripped them of that power, and then they had gone to war to get the power back that they had lost. So, now people like the sheriff and his deputies corrupted the law and pretended that the law gave them their power."

His father had sat there quietly for a long while that night after telling Elijah the story. He turned, looked his son in the eye, and told him something that Elijah would never forget: "Your grandfather knew the value of family because he had seen it ripped away. He had seen families bought and sold. He had seen them torn apart for profit with no regard for the human cost. Your grandfather knew that family was worth protecting. It was worth *dying* for."

Elijah let out a long breath.

He guessed that Jessie knew that as well. The man was protecting his family, and Elijah respected him for that.

The potato shed was just like all the others on the plantation; its door held closed by a metal clasp and wooden spike. Elijah reached up to remove the spike but it wasn't in the clasp. He looked around on the ground, thinking that the last person to open the shed might have dropped it, but it wasn't there.

"How hard is it to remember to put the spike in the door?" he asked no one in particular. "That's just great. Now I'm gonna have to whittle out another one before I can get back to work."

He decided to empty his wheelbarrow first, then he would walk to the nearby trees and try to find a small branch that would become his new spike. He pulled open the door and was immediately overrun by potatoes. A small avalanche of spuds rolled out the door and onto the ground. He jumped back out of their way, hitting his shin on the wheelbarrow in the process.

Elijah yelped and grabbed at his leg, furiously trying to rub the pain away. When it subsided, he put his hands on his hips and looked down at the mess he was now going to have to clean up. This was why he always took the time to toss his potatoes to the back of the shed, so that the next man who came to unload would not have this mess to deal with.

Reluctantly, he started picking up the spilled potatoes and tossed them to the back of the shed. It was slow work, but he finally managed to get them all back in. Now he was faced with another problem: the literal wall of potatoes that blocked the door. He would have to start at the top and work his way down, until the door was clear enough to off-load his wheelbarrow without recreating the mess he had just cleaned up.

He dove in with both hands, picking up potatoes and tossing them to the back. Just as he was starting to make progress, the wall gave way and another avalanche dumped more out onto the ground. He tried to jump out of the way, but this time he was too slow. The rolling potatoes got under his feet and caused him to fall headfirst into the shed. He landed spread eagle, face down on a lumpy bed of dirt-covered spuds.

He spit dirt out of his mouth and placed his hands palm down to try and push himself out. This only caused more of the potatoes to roll out of the way, taking his arms with them in opposite directions. For the second time in less than a minute, he found himself face down, but this time, it wasn't potatoes he was looking at. Instead, another face was looking back at him.

Elijah got up in a flash, scrambling backward like a mouse trying to escape a hawk. His only thought was to get out of that shed and away from whoever was buried under the potatoes.

When he touched solid ground, he jumped to his feet and quickly put some distance between himself and the shed. Panic had overtaken him. His breath was coming in short bursts, so he bent down and placed his hands on his knees to try and get it under control. His head swam with too many thoughts to come to terms with. *What do I do now? Who was that? How did they get there? Who do I tell? Do I tell anyone? What if they think I did it?*

His thoughts were interrupted by the foreman who had seen him standing there on his way back to the main house.

"You all right, boy?" the foreman called from across the small yard in front of the sheds.

Elijah snapped to attention and turned to face the foreman. "Oh yes, sir, I'm fine. It's mighty hot out here, and I was just catchin' my breath."

"I didn't hire you to breathe. I hired you to move potatoes. Now quit fooling around over there and get busy! Those potatoes aren't going to store themselves."

"Yes, sir, I'm on it!"

The foreman moved away, and Elijah crept over to the shed. Back at the open door he leaned in, secretly hoping that he had imagined everything and wouldn't see anyone lying there. But there it was; part of a face sticking up out of the potatoes. The longer he looked at the partially uncovered face, the more he recognized it.

Elijah slowly sank to his knees and crawled back over the potatoes to the man lying there. He began moving potatoes one by one until he had uncovered the face fully. It was Captain Mac, just as he had expected, and he had also found the missing wooden spike, buried in Captain Mac's temple almost to the hilt. It would have taken a mighty force to plunge that dull wooden spike all the way through the man's skull, and there was only one man in camp that Elijah thought would have had the strength to do it.

Elijah's panic returned. If the foreman were to catch him in the shed with the dead captain, it would not only mean the end of his working there, but it would probably mean him hanging from a rope somewhere back in the woods.

Elijah frantically picked up potatoes and piled them back over Captain Mac's face. Once he felt secure that anyone casually looking in the shed wouldn't see the dead man, he backed out and gathered the remaining potatoes that had rolled out and flung them back into the shed. Then he pushed his wheelbarrow up to the door and dumped that load of potatoes inside, rebuilding the wall he had worked so hard to disassemble. Finally, he closed the shed door and the clasp.

A quick search of the area produced a small fat piece of wood that Elijah forced into the clasp to keep it shut. Next, he found a rock with a sharp edge and used it to carve the word *FULL* into the wood of the door. He hoped that would keep anybody else from trying to load their potatoes into the shed until he could figure out what to do next.

CHAPTER 5

St. Castulus was beginning to feel like home to Elijah. He and Happy had been there for almost two months and had gotten settled into the shed. Mrs. Jones had brought them a crib that her children used when they were babies, and Happy had taken to it right away. That little crib was a bed fit for a prince compared to the hard, cold ground where Happy had spent his first few weeks sleeping. Elijah had made himself a bed box from some scrap wood he had found cleaning out the shed. A local farmer had provided some feed sacks that Elijah stuffed with straw and clippings from the church yard and used them to make a mattress. It was possibly the most comfortable place where he had laid his head since becoming an adult and heading out on his own.

Summer was changing into fall, and the nights were starting to get cooler. Elijah wrapped a second blanket around Happy, then sat at his small table and began making plans as to how to create a working fireplace in the shed to provide heat for the colder winter months. It would mean cutting a hole for a chimney in the roof, but that shouldn't be any harder than it was to cut out the small window he had made in the wall.

A rustling sound outside caught his attention, and he walked over to the window and looked out. The church was dark, except for a light in the kitchen. The minister had been meeting with the church committee that evening, and the gathering had gone later than expected. So, even at this late hour, Mrs. Jones was still finishing up the dishes and preparing for tomorrow's morning meal.

Elijah had developed a deep respect for Mrs. Jones over the last few months. She worked harder than almost any woman he had ever known. In many ways, she reminded him of Seraphina, or rather, what he thought Seraphina would have become if she had lived to be Mrs. Jones's age. She was fiercely loyal to the church and its minister, and he was sure she had been equally loyal to her sons and recently departed husband. Mrs. Jones was a very proper person, who never spoke out of turn but was always quick to speak her mind when she felt her opinion was warranted. Much like Seraphina, she knew her Bible and often quoted it chapter and verse. Elijah had been studying the Book with the minister almost every night since he arrived at St. Castulus, but he doubted he would ever come to know it the way Mrs. Jones did.

The rustling noise came again, and Elijah thought he saw someone moving between the shed and the parsonage. He strained his eyes to try and make out anything in the pitch black of the church yard and was caught off guard when flames burst from the side of the shed.

"Lord Jesus!"

He grabbed the bucket of water he kept in the shed for washing and raced out the door.

The tool storage cabinet he had built beside the shed was ablaze. The old wood he had made it from had caught fast and burned like paper. If he didn't get the flames under control soon, they would quickly move to the roof.

He took careful aim for what he figured to be the source of the fire and hurled the water from the bucket at the cabinet. Steam erupted with a loud hiss and most of the flames died immediately. Elijah kicked at the cabinet and brought what remained of it to the ground so he could stomp out any remaining embers. Before he could do that, someone grabbed him from behind and slung him to the ground.

A hard boot caught Elijah in the ribs and his breath left his body in a rush. He tried to roll away from whoever had kicked him but was met with another hard boot to the ribs from the other side.

Elijah tried to scramble to his feet, but a sharp pain ran through him, doubling him over. A strong arm wrapped around his throat and put him in a headlock. Whoever held him pulled him to his feet. He attempted to fight back, but every time he tried to make contact with the man behind him, the arm would tighten around his neck. He felt himself being pulled toward the shed door. His head swam from a lack of air. His ribs sent lightning bolts of pain throughout his body as his feet were dragged across the ground.

The person holding him reached the door to the shed. He brutally pushed Elijah inside where he landed in a pile on the floor next to the table. He reached up and grabbed the edge of it in an attempt to get to his feet and received another kick in the ribs. All he could do was fall back and try to stay conscious.

"I guess you think you're pretty smart, don't you boy?"

Elijah heard the voice through the ringing in his ears and turned in the direction from where it had come. His eyes didn't want to focus or stay still. He blinked over and over in an attempt to see the face of the man speaking. When he finally did come into focus, he was horrified to see a large man in overalls holding Happy in his arms. The man's face was covered in a hood made from an old feed sack with eye holes cut in it and a slit for the mouth.

"Little black babies shore is cute." The man tickled Happy's chin with his finger. "Be a damn shame to hafta mess this little fella's face all up."

This time Elijah *did* make it to his feet, but before he could move toward the man holding Happy, he again felt the muscular arm close around his throat and begin to squeeze.

"Yeah, you're a smart one all right," the other man said. "You just sashayed in here like you owned the place and buffaloed the preacher and that old, hired witch of his into treating you like you was a proper white man."

The man took one of Happy's ankles in his beefy fist and slowly raised the baby up in the air. Elijah lunged, trying to break the other man's grip. He was met with a fist to the ribs. The pain was so intense that his knees buckled. I If not for the arm around his neck, he would have landed back on the shed floor.

Happy shrieked in fear and pain as the man dangled him over the hard dirt of the shed floor. Through the baby's cries, Elijah heard the man who held him, laughing. He felt his chest rise and fall against his back with each breath. The man that had Happy laughed as well.

"Here's what's going to happen, boy," the man said. "You're gonna take this here little squealing black pig and you're gonna hit the road. If you don't, we'll be back and see to it that this little piggy don't never squeal again. As for you, I'm sure we could—"

The click of a pistol hammer locking into place stopped the man short, and the arm around Elijah's neck dropped away. He lunged forward and nearly fell but was able to grab the dangling baby from the other man, who never took his eyes off the other side of the shed.

Elijah cradled Happy in his arms then collapsed against the wall for support. He looked up to see Mrs. Jones holding a pocket-sized Colt revolver to the temple of the man who had been holding him. The gun's barrel puckered the feed sack he wore over his head, just behind the man's ear.

"The Good Book says thou shalt not kill," she said. "Lucky for you men I take what that book says seriously, but it doesn't say anything about not blowing this fool's ear clean off his head." She pushed the barrel forward till it connected with the man's ear. "My late husband was a crackerjack shot, and he taught me all he knew." She turned her attention to the other man. "So have no doubt that before the ringing even starts in this man's head, I'll have at least one bullet in you as well."

Mrs. Jones took the man nearest her by the back of his hood. She used the gun for leverage and turned him toward the door of the shed. Then she motioned with her head for the other man to move. He looked over at Elijah and the baby, then did as Mrs. Jones had directed. Walking past her, he stepped out of the shed door. Mrs. Jones shoved the back of her captive's head in the same direction, and he stumbled out as well. Once outside, he turned back and pointed a finger at her.

"Nobody puts a gun to my head you stupid bi—"

The Colt jumped and a portion of the man's hood tore away in a spray of blood and burlap.

"*Damn,* woman!" he cried out and pressed his hand to the side of his head. His partner grabbed his arm and drug him along as they ran from the yard.

Mrs. Jones slowly lowered the gun and turned to Elijah, whose eyes began to roll back in his head. She rushed across the room just in time to take Happy from him before he passed out and fell to the floor. She heard a commotion outside the shed and feared the men were coming back, so she raised the gun and pointed it toward the door just as the minister stepped into the light. Relieved, Mrs. Jones lowered the gun and dropped to the floor beside Elijah.

"Jesus, God help us," the minister whispered, trying to understand what he was seeing. Gun smoke hung heavy in the air as he crossed over to Mrs. Jones, Elijah, and the crying baby.

* * *

The minister turned from the stove with two steaming hot cups of coffee and carried them over to the table where Elijah and Mrs. Jones were sitting. Mrs. Jones was holding Happy and massaging his bruised ankle while Elijah held an ice pack to his bruised ribs.

"I sent word for Doc Mayberry over two hours ago," the minister said as he paced beside the table. "I don't know what could be keeping him."

"You didn't need to do that on my account." Elijah grunted as the effort to talk sent another bolt of pain through him.

"Look at you," Mrs. Jones said. "You can't even talk without hurting, but yet you don't want any help." She shook her head, then pointed her finger in Elijah's direction. "That's just arrogant male pride. The scriptures say that God opposes the proud but gives grace to the humble, so humble you will be and quiet also, until the doctor gets here to examine you."

"I still don't understand what happened out there," the minister said, still pacing. "Who were those men, and why did they want to hurt you and Happy?"

Elijah started to speak but Mrs. Jones silenced him with a look.

"As I was approaching the shed, I heard one of the men tell Elijah that they wanted them to leave, and if they didn't, then they would return and hurt the baby. Now Reverend, I don't know who that sounds like to you, but I'd wager my eternal soul that those horrible Flanigan brothers were behind this." Mrs. Jones reached into the pocket of her apron and removed a lace handkerchief to dry the tears. "The very thought of grown men threatening the life of an innocent like little Happy here, I just don't understand it."

"Hatred and bigotry know no bounds, I'm afraid." The minister sat down next to Mrs. Jones and took Happy from her. "And as much as I agree with you that it does sound like something the Flanigan's could be a part of, unfortunately, they do not have a monopoly on these types of feelings and beliefs. So, without some concrete proof, I'm afraid we can't accuse them."

A loud knocking came from the parsonage door, startling all three of them.

"That should be Doc Mayberry," the minister said. "I'll go let him in." He took Happy with him and left the room.

With much effort Elijah turned to face Mrs. Jones. "I can't thank you enough for what you done tonight." He managed a smile. "I might not be sittin' here if you hadn't showed up."

"Don't mention it. I'm just glad I heard the baby crying when I did."

Elijah started to laugh. Even with the intense pain, he couldn't stop himself. Tears rolled down his cheeks.

"Whatever has come over you Elijah? Stop this foolishness before you do irreparable damage to yourself."

"I, I, I can't help it." Elijah tried to pull himself together, but the laughter came over him again, and he clutched at his sides in pain. "I just keep seein' you out yonder with your gun, threatenin' to shoot off that man's ear. It was about the most frightenin' thing I've ever seen in my life."

Mrs. Jones looked at Elijah—nearly doubled over with pain and laughter—and started laughing herself. Shuddering, deep laughter overtook her, and she dabbed at her eyes to collect the tears forming there.

Having heard the noise the two were making all the way down the hall, the minister and Doc Mayberry rushed into the room. They found Elijah laughing with his head on the table while Mrs. Jones sat next to him, shaking and covering her face with her handkerchief.

Doc Mayberry placed his black bag on the kitchen table.

"Looks like if I was any later I might have missed all the fun." He took his round, wire-rimmed glasses from his coat pocket and pulled the chair out next to Elijah.

"I'm sorry, Doctor," Mrs. Jones said, pulling herself together. "It's been a difficult night, and I'm afraid Mr. Parker and I let it get the best of us for a moment." She stood and walked across the room to the stove. "I believe you like your coffee with cream, am I correct?"

"Yes, you are, and thank you," the doctor said before turning to Elijah. "I hear you had a little run-in with some of our less open-minded citizens tonight, young man." The doctor helped Elijah to sit up straight in the chair, then looked at the bruises forming around his neck before placing his hand on

Elijah's side. At his touch, Elijah sucked in air in an attempt to not cry out at the pain.

"Feels like you've got some broken ribs. Whoever did this to you did a thorough job of it." The doctor looked back at the minister. "I'll have to wrap his ribs, and then he's going to need at least a couple of weeks of bed rest." He turned back to Elijah. "And I mean *rest*, no work and no lifting, not even that little fella over there." He pointed at Happy, who was asleep in the minister's arms.

Mrs. Jones returned to the table with the doctor's coffee. "That won't be a problem. We'll keep Mr. Parker under observation and make sure that little Happy there is well cared for."

"Good, then I best get to applying this wrap." The doctor first took a sip of the coffee, then reached into his bag for a roll of bandages. "You always have the best coffee, Mrs. Jones. Beats the swill they gave me over at Jasper Flanigan's place. But I guess you can't expect anything good to come from the kitchen of a lifelong bachelor."

Mrs. Jones and the minister exchanged a quick glance.

"Were you over at Jasper's tonight, Doctor? I do hope no one is ill," Mrs. Jones said in her most concerned tone.

"Well, nothing they're gonna die from anyway." The doctor wrapped the bandage around Elijah's midsection. "One of his hired men managed to get his head caught up in some barbed wire. Damn near tore off his ear." Realizing he had let a four-letter word slip, he looked sheepishly up at Mrs. Jones and the minister. "Sorry, I didn't mean to offend."

"No offense taken," Mrs. Jones answered. She glanced again at the minister who had an expression on his face she had never seen before. She suspected it was anger mixed with concern and disappointment.

* * *

A week passed, and Elijah had had enough. If he had to sit in that shed or on the minister's couch for another minute, he would lose his mind.

He carefully stayed out of sight of the kitchen window and Mrs. Jones and made his way to the front of the church and stepped inside. It was cool and quiet in the sanctuary, and using the pews for support, Elijah went to the front where the welcoming statue of Jesus still stood on the altar table.

Elijah took a seat on the front row and looked closely at the statue. Jesus's arms were outstretched, but Elijah thought his eyes had a sadness to them. He figured if he had a church and it happened to have folks like the Flanigans in it, he would be sad, too.

"Lord, it's Elijah," he prayed. "I want to thank you for takin' such good care of Happy and me and for bringin' us to the minister and Mrs. Jones. But I'm afraid we may be bringin' some heat down on them that they don't deserve. They're good people." He tried to think of something else to say, but couldn't, so he guessed he'd said enough and pushed himself up out of the pew.

A tingle of pain ran across his chest as a reminder that he still wasn't completely healed, but he chose to ignore it and move on. As he came to the sanctuary door, a thought struck him, and he stopped and turned back to the statue.

"One more thing. If you think we've worn out our welcome here, could you let me know? The minister says you have a plan for all of us, and if that's so, I sure would appreciate you lettin' me in on what it is." Elijah nodded and smiled —thinking that he had gotten his point across—and walked out of the room.

Classrooms were located down a short hallway off the sanctuary, and as Elijah looked down its length, he saw that some dust and dirt had been tracked in during services the previous Sunday. Mrs. Jones kept a broom and dustpan behind the sanctuary door for just such an occasion. He took a deep breath to test his ribs. The pain was minor, so he figured he was at least in good enough shape to sweep up. He had begun to take a bit of pride in how nice the church looked since his arrival, and he didn't want folks to think he was slacking in his duties.

He swept his way down the hall, making sure to get in every nook and cranny. He thought that the dirt was like the devil. It would find a crack to get in through, and before long, that dirt would fill the whole building.

A small alcove with a window was located halfway down the length of the hall. Elijah took a minute there to rest and get his breath back. He looked out the window and was surprised to see an old Willy's Whippet sitting beside the building. Dirt and dust covered its black paint, one headlight was obviously broken, and the tires appeared threadbare. A big man stood beside the car smoking a hand-rolled cigarette. He stopped occasionally to pick a bit of tobacco leaf off his tongue, or to touch the bandage that wrapped around his head and over his ear.

Bile started to rise up from Elijah's stomach, and it touched his throat. He swallowed it back down, along with the anger that was building inside him. Was this the man who had come into the shed, into his *home* to threaten him and Happy and had lost part of his ear for his trouble? He recognized the car as well. It belonged to Jim Flanigan. Elijah had overheard many whispered conversations after services about what a disgrace that car was and how the Flanigans should be ashamed to drive such a car, considering they had all the money in the county and could easily afford better.

Elijah got to his feet and started to leave the alcove. He planned to go have a few words with the man standing next to the car, when he heard the door at the end of the hallway open. He peeked around the corner and saw the minister step inside and carry a stack of books into the church library.

"Jim, Jasper, what a surprise. I didn't expect to see you here today," the minister said from inside the room.

Elijah picked up his broom and started sweeping again, drawing ever closer to the library door. The minister had not closed it completely, and as Elijah approached, he could hear every word being said.

"I can only guess that you have come to discuss Elijah and his employment by the church."

Elijah recognized the sarcasm in the minister's voice but doubted that either of the two men in the library with him had the self-awareness to tell that they were being mocked.

"Reverend, I ain't sayin' that what you're doin' letting the nigg—um—*black* feller work here is wrong, but—"

"What Jim is trying to say," Jasper said, interrupting his brother. "Is that it's all well and good to give one of them a handout, but takin' them in like you would a white man is just wrong."

"Folks in town are talkin' about not coming to services next Sunday," Jasper said, continuing his brother's thought. "They're afraid to bring their kids here. I don't think you have any choice but to get rid of that boy."

Elijah risked a look into the room. The Flanigans were seated in chairs better suited to children and were facing the minister's back while he was shelving the books he had just brought in. The minister started to turn away from the shelves, so Elijah ducked quickly out of sight.

"And how much of this fear is because you two are telling folks that they have something to be afraid of?" the pastor said pointedly.

"You know, Pastor," Jim said. The anger in his voice was evident to Elijah, listening outside the door. "The last man that preached here got a little too big for his britches and ended up havin' to leave town."

"And your britches are startin' to look a little strained to me," Jasper added.

"Jim, Jasper, that is enough!" A harshness had come into the minister's voice that sounded completely alien compared to his usually calm tone. No doubt, he had reached the end of his patience. "I will not be threatened in my own church! You may not like that Elijah is working here, and you may disapprove of my letting him and his baby sleep in the shed out back. But I don't answer to *you*, I answer to the good Lord above. You remember Him, don't you? He's the one that said to love thy neighbor as thy self and to suffer the little children to come unto me. And in the book of Galatians, it says *There is neither Jew nor Greek, neither bond nor free, neither male nor female for ye all are one in Christ Jesus.*"

Elijah risked another look into the room and had to stifle a little laugh as he saw the minister pick up a Bible and wave it at them as he spoke.

"Now I know His word, and I promise you nowhere in this book does it say to love your *white* neighbor as yourself, or to suffer the *white* children to come unto me."

The minister slammed the Bible back down on the table, causing Jasper to jump.

"Now you go tell anybody that will listen that these doors will be open on Sunday morning as they are every Sunday morning, and if they want to learn what else God has to say, then they are welcome. And if they don't, then they can just stay home! And that goes for you two, as well!"

"Come on Reverend, we ain't tryin' to stir anythin' up but you just got to understand..."

Trying not to laugh at the way the minister took the wind out of the Flanigan's sails, Elijah turned and went back down the hallway toward the sanctuary door. He returned the broom and dustpan to their resting place, then stepped inside the sanctuary. As he closed the door softly behind him, he turned and was surprised to see the man with the bandaged ear standing at the altar table with the statue of Jesus in his hands.

Elijah put his back to the closed door. Memories of the beating he had taken a week earlier rushed into his mind. His heart started to thump fast in his chest and a cold sweat formed on his brow.

The man seemed equally surprised to see Elijah and took a step toward him. Just then, he heard the minister's voice come from down the hallway, along with Jim's and Jasper's voices still trying to argue with him. The man stopped, then with a look of pure hatred, he held the statue out toward Elijah in one big meaty hand, and with the other, he reached out and snapped the head off it. He stared, unmoving, at Elijah for what felt like a lifetime before he dropped the broken Christ back on the table, turned, and left the building.

Elijah approached the altar table with his heart still pounding in his chest. With gentle reverence, he reached down and picked up the two pieces of the broken statue. He held the small head up and looked at its sad eyes, which detached from its welcoming body, now made total sense.

* * *

Lost and confused, Elijah paced around the small shed that he and Happy called *home*. He had hoped that the church would be a *good* home for them. A place where Happy could grow up and he could grow old. For the fourth or fifth time in the last hour, he sat down at the small table and held the two parts of the Jesus statue, staring at it and trying to come to a decision.

He loved the life he and Happy were living here at the church. The minister and Mrs. Jones had quickly become like family, and that was part of the problem. The story his father had told him years ago kept coming back to him. Family was worth protecting, even *dying* for if the situation called for it.

If he and Happy stayed at the church, they might very well die. But what good would their deaths do the minister and Mrs. Jones? *None*. In fact, if they stayed, the minister might lose his job, and Mrs. Jones might be forced to leave her place at the church as well.

He looked again into the sad eyes of the Savior.

"Are you tryin' to tell me somethin'?" he asked the head of Jesus. He picked up the body of the figurine and placed the head back on it. In one piece, with its arms outstretched toward him, he felt welcome and loved. Then he let the body fall away, and it was as if he was being accused of something—like his actions had brought great harm to the folks who had taken him in.

From the cradle, Happy sighed and let out a weak little cry before falling back asleep. Elijah walked over and looked down at the small form lying there. So innocent and so dependent on him for everything. The weight of those responsibilities lay heavy on his shoulders. Now he felt that the safety of his new-found friends was another weight being placed there as well.

A loud crash startled him out of his thoughts, and he turned to face the door, prepared to defend himself and his son. But no one was there. Instead, he saw that the body of the statue had rolled off the table and broken on the floor of the shed, leaving only the head sitting there, looking at him with its sad eyes.

"Okay, Lord. I get it."

Elijah found his old carpetbag under his bed. Again, he looked over at Happy. Was he making a mistake taking the child from the only stable home he had ever had? What choice did he have? After the actions of the men a week before, he and Happy would probably be safer on the road.

He pulled the bag out and started filling it with what few things they had acquired during their stay at the church. The baby began to stir, so Elijah picked him up out of the cradle and nestled him into the crook of his arm.

"I heard the minister tell them fellas that they were to love us, but I don't much think they believed him. And I know them fellas that whooped up on us the other night ain't feelin' the love. So, I think it's time that Happy and his Pappy head for the hills."

Happy squirmed in his arm, trying to get comfortable, then he looked up into Elijah's eyes, and for the first time, Elijah thought that Happy just might have an idea of what was going on.

"I'm shore gonna miss Mrs. Jones's cookin', and I know you gonna miss that fresh milk she brung you every mornin'. But it's gonna be okay."

He picked up the last thing he had to pack—Seraphina's Bible—and gently kissed it.

"You know, me and the minister been studyin' this book." He showed the Bible to the baby. "It says in here to trust God with all your heart and not lean on your own understandin'. Well, I sure as hell don't understand why folks gotta be the way they are, but your momma trusted God, and if it was good enough for her, it's gonna be good enough for us."

Elijah looked again at the small figurine's head sitting next to his bag, then down at the broken pieces on the floor. He then packed the Bible in the bag. When he picked it up, he was surprised at how much heavier the bag felt now, compared to when they had first come to the church.

On his way out, he stopped and looked one more time at what they were leaving behind, then he blew out the candle and stepped outside, closing the door behind him.

It was dark in the church yard except for a dim light coming from the window in the minister's study. As Elijah and Happy made their way past the church, he looked up at that lighted window just in time to see the minister pass by. Elijah smiled, said a silent thank you to the shadow behind the curtain, then turned and walked down the moon-lit street.

"Don't you worry none, Happy," he whispered. "Just up the road, I bet we find us another nice house, a good job, and an even nicer lady to help tend you."

Taking care to stay in the shadows, Elijah moved away from the church and into the darkness.

Chapter 6

Five Years Earlier

By the light of the full moon, Elijah started for the woods with the body of Captain Mac. He tried to move as silently as he could, knowing full well that if he were caught carrying a dead white man, no jury would ever believe he had nothing to do with the death.

Who was he kidding? Men like him never had the luxury of being brought before a jury. If he was caught with Captain Mac's dead body, he would be hanging from the limb of a tree before sunup.

Relief washed over him when he stepped into the cover of the trees. Just after dark, he had scouted this area and used a shovel he had borrowed from the farm's tool shed to dig a hole large enough to bury the body. Once he had dug the hole, he made his way back to the shed and had carefully pulled the dead man from his resting place beneath a hundred pounds of potatoes. It had been a risk crossing the open field between the potato shed and the tree line, but now that he had reached the woods, he could breathe a little easier. With any luck this would be the end of the mess, and all concerned could go back to life as usual.

Seraphina watched him approach from behind a large tree. She had seen Elijah steal into the woods earlier, and when her parents weren't looking, she slipped away to follow him. She thought that maybe he was meeting another girl, or maybe he had something hidden that he didn't want anybody else to see. She was naturally curious, and her mother had told her many times that her curiosity would one day get her in trouble.

When she came to where his trail ended, she was disappointed that he wasn't there. All she found was a *hole*.

Nothing exciting about that, she thought.

She was turning to go back to camp, when she heard heavy steps walking through the debris on the forest floor. Someone was coming, and she didn't want to be caught in the woods alone.

She ducked behind the biggest tree she could find.

Seraphina watched, wide eyed, as Elijah entered the small clearing. For a moment, she couldn't make out what he was carrying, then he passed through a pool of moonlight and she recognized Captain Mac lying dead in Elijah's arms.

She came out from behind the tree and confronted him. "Did you kill that man 'cause of what he done to me?"

Elijah dropped the body into the hole, grabbed the shovel, and raised it in a defensive manner.

"My God, girl!" he exclaimed, seeing who it was. "How long have you been standin' there?"

"Long enough. Did you kill him on account of me?"

"I didn't *kill* him." Elijah lowered the shovel. Without saying anything else he started covering the body with dirt.

"Then why are you buryin' him? You know what the fore-man will do if he catches you?"

"I know, but he's at the cat house in town. I heard some of his boys talkin' about it. Now go on, I need to finish what I'm doin' before somebody else comes sniffin' around."

Seraphina watched as Elijah went back to work. She saw how his sweat had soaked through the back of his shirt and watched as the muscles in his arms expanded and contracted with each shovel full of dirt he threw over the dead man's body.

"It was my daddy, wasn't it?"

Elijah stopped shoveling and looked up at her.

"Yeah, it was."

Seraphina looked from Elijah to the mound of dirt at his feet. "So, you're buryin' him to protect Daddy, then," she said flatly.

Elijah just chuckled at that and went back to work. He used the back of the shovel to tamp down the loose earth, then gathered sticks and leaves to try and make the new grave blend in with the forest floor around it.

"Why?" she asked him. "Daddy never been nothin' to you but mean."

Elijah again stopped what he was doing, stepped up to her, and looked her in the eye. "I'm not doin' it to protect him. I'm doin' it to protect *you*. Where would you and your ma and your little brothers be if somethin' happened to Jessie? And besides, I don't blame him for killin' Captain Mac. If he hadn't, I might have."

His last words surprised Seraphina. She studied his face and saw nothing but honesty there. A warm sensation washed over her; it was a feeling she had never felt before. It made her want to turn and run, but at the same time, it kept her from doing just that.

"You would've done that for me?"

Elijah didn't answer. Instead, he just shook his head, picked up the shovel, and walked out of the clearing.

Seraphina stood there and watched him leave. When she realized that he had left her alone in the woods, she ran after him.

* * *

Later that night, Elijah walked into the campfire's light and over to a bucket of water, warming by the fire. Seraphina and her family were there finishing up their dinner, and she watched him as he pulled up a dipperful of warm water and poured it over one hand and then the other to wash off some of the dirt remaining on them. Then he took another dipperful and poured it over his head. He shook it to get some of the water out of his hair, and when he stopped, her daddy was towering over him.

Elijah straightened but still had to look up to see Jessie's face. For a tense moment they just stood there, one taking the measure of the other. Elijah expected that at any moment the big man would swing his fist and smash it into the side of his head. But that didn't happen. Instead, Jessie nodded once, turned, and walked away. Elijah watched as he circled the campfire to where his wife was waiting for him. They joined hands and stepped into the darkness, leaving Seraphina behind. Elijah, still unsure about what just happened, walked over and sat next to her.

"What was that all about?" he asked, looking past her into the darkness.

"I told Daddy what you done for us. That was him sayin' thank you."

"He's got a heck of a way about him, don't he?" Elijah laughed, feeling relief spill over him.

"I guess he do."

They sat in silence for a few minutes just staring into the flames, then Seraphina reached over and took Elijah's hand. He gazed down at their hands clasped together—hers young and soft, and his rough and scarred—then he looked up into Seraphina's face. This time, when she leaned in for a kiss, he gladly responded in kind.

* * *

The rest of their time at the potato farm passed quickly and without further incident. Elijah spent his days hauling potatoes back and forth to the different sheds and his evenings with Seraphina. Jessie still kept a close eye on them, and Elijah made a point to give him plenty of distance.

Their final day on the farm was payday, and the workers all gathered around the table where just two weeks before they had signed on for the job. As Elijah came upon the growing crowd, he spotted Seraphina and her family. Just as he was about to call out to her, the foreman called their name and they stepped up to the table to get their pay.

Elijah knew that they planned to move on immediately, and the thought of being away from her had kept him up most of the night. As they sat by the fire the night before, Seraphina had suggested that he come with them. Jessie had heard of a farm in Tennessee that was going to be looking for tobacco hands, and she was sure they would be needing every able-bodied person they could get. Elijah had considered it, but in the end, he thought that tagging along behind her family like some little lost puppy was not the way he wanted things to go.

Seraphina had called him stubborn and pigheaded, but she had still held his hand and kissed him goodnight. She was something special. He loved her, and surely, she felt the same way about him. That's part of what had kept him awake the night before.

If he had any sense, he would ask her to marry him, but what did he have to offer? All he could promise her was a life traveling from farm to farm, working all day in the hot sun and sleeping on the hard ground at night. He didn't have a home to take her back to or even a place to stay during the cold months. He just followed the sun and tried to keep working, sometimes going a week without any real food. It was no life for a young woman, especially one as beautiful as Seraphina. He had made up his mind to try and forget her, to just let her go north with her family to Tennessee, and he would head west and hope that time and distance would keep him from missing her.

Jessie made his mark on a piece of paper, and the foreman handed him an envelope. They stepped off to the side of the table, and Jessie handed the envelope to Seraphina, who began to count the money inside it. As she was counting, her mother saw Elijah watching her and walked over to him. Naamah was a small, frail-looking woman with light skin and a splash of freckles across her nose. Her hair was starting to gray, and it gave her an air of authority and pride. When she stepped up to Elijah, she took his face in her hands and gently pulled him down to where she could kiss his cheek. Naamah had never even spoken to him before, and this sudden familiarity left him speechless.

"I know what you did," she said in a soft, immediately soothing voice. "Jessie tried to deny it, but I know all the same. For my family, I say *thank you*."

Elijah saw so much of Seraphina in her mother, and it broke his heart to think of continuing on without her. All of his plans, everything he had decided the night before, disappeared in a rush of emotions.

"Mrs. Ischa, I uh... It's about Seraphina... You see, I uh..."

Naamah reached out and hushed him with a finger gently placed on his lips. "I know that too, so hush your foolishness and get on with it."

Naamah gave him a knowing smile, turned, and rejoined her family.

* * *

By the time Elijah had picked up his pay envelope and gathered his things, most of the workers had begun leaving the farm. He had made up his mind that he would ask Jessie's permission to court Seraphina. If Jessie agreed, then he would travel with them to Tennessee, and after an appropriate time had passed, he and Seraphina would be married.

Jessie and his family were standing together with a group of other workers making plans and preparing to leave. Elijah stepped up behind Jessie, who was kneeling down placing supplies in a burlap bag. Elijah was nervous, and he couldn't seem to find the right words. He started to speak but nothing came out, so he cleared his throat and tried again.

"Excuse me, Mr. Ischa." Elijah hated the quiver he heard in his own voice. "I would like a word."

Jessie looked around at him, then stood up to his full height. He stared at Elijah with his arms crossed and his face like a stone statue. He didn't speak, but Elijah read volumes into his silence, and it made him that much more nervous. To make matters worse, Seraphina and her family, as well as the others they had been talking to, stopped what they were doing, and all turned to see what was about to happen.

Elijah took a deep breath in an attempt to slow his racing heart, then stepped back from the towering figure before him.

"Sir, I know this is unexpected, but over the last two weeks I have grown very fond of Seraphina." He paused, then decided that he better not beat around the bush. "No, that ain't right. I've grown to *love* her."

A peep of excitement escaped from Seraphina, who had been hanging on Elijah's every word. She covered her mouth with her hands to make sure nothing else slipped out. Her mother cleared her throat and gave Seraphina a hard look. She knew from experience what that look meant, and she pulled herself together.

"Sir," Elijah continued. "It would be an honor to make Seraphina my wife, but I will only ask her if I first have your blessin'."

Jessie remained still as a statue and did not answer. Naamah stepped up beside her husband and laced her arm in his. The big man looked down at her, and she gave him a quick nod, then released his arm and stepped back beside her daughter. Jessie turned his head and looked back at his wife and daughter, then without speaking, he gave Elijah a slight nod and stepped to the side, leaving him an open path to Seraphina.

Her excitement was almost too much to bear. With a smile so big it made her lips ache, she began to bounce on her toes with her hands clasped together at her chest. Again, her mother cleared her throat and again, Seraphina contained herself. At least a little bit.

Elijah stepped forward and looked into her dark brown eyes as Naamah stepped away from her daughter and moved near Jessie.

"Seraphina," his voice squeaked with nervous energy. He stopped, swallowed hard and began again. "Seraphina, I know we've not known each other that long, but in that time, I've come to see what an amazin' person you are. Sera, ah Seraphina, would you give me the honor…"

She could no longer hold in her excitement. She rushed to Elijah, jumped into his arms, and knocked him to the ground. She landed, straddled, on top of him. "Yes!" was all she managed to say before kissing him all over his face.

"Sera." Jessie's voice cut through all her excitement, and she jumped off Elijah.

Having had the breath knocked out of him, Elijah wasn't as quick to get to his feet. Next to Jessie stood the small, old white man with the eye patch and scruffy beard. The man that Elijah had met early on in the field. This time instead of getting water from a bucket, he was carrying a Bible.

"Uh, hello," the man said. He looked uncomfortable and made a sucking sound as he fought to keep spit from running out of his mostly toothless mouth. He kept stealing glances up at Jessie as he spoke. "I'm Jonas Wright, but most folks call me Joe. Naamah told me last night that you folks might want to get married, and I guess I'm the closest thing to a preacher around here."

"What?" Elijah asked, confused. "*Now*?"

Joe looked up at Jessie again, and with a single nod, Jessie made his wishes clear.

"Yes," Joe confirmed. "Now."

"I guess we're gettin' married now." Elijah stepped closer to Seraphina, took her arm in his, and they turned to face Joe.

"Do you…" Joe hesitated then looked up at Jessie.

"Seraphina."

With a smile and a nod Joe turned back to face the couple. "Seraphina," he continued. "Take …."

"*Elijah*," Jessie inserted.

"Right." Joe smiled and continued. "Do you Seraphina take Elijah to be your husband?"

"Yes," Seraphina answered before the words had completely left Joe's mouth. Her excitement was so great that she could hardly stand still, and she wiggled just a little.

Joe looked again up at Jessie, who again only nodded.

"What about you Elijah?" Joe continued. "Do you take Seraphina to be your—"

"Yes," Elijah interrupted. "Yes, I do."

"Well, alrighty then. Kiss her already."

Elijah pulled Seraphina into his arms and started to kiss her, but stopped and looked up at Jessie. The big man's hard face broke into a smile, and he nodded. Seraphina let out a squeal, grabbed Elijah's face, and kissed him hard.

"I know it ain't much, but I'd like you folks to have this." Joe handed Elijah the Bible he had been carrying. "Make it the beginnin' and end of each day, and you will have a long, happy life."

With that said, Joe smiled at them, then turned to Jessie. He reached out and shook the big man's hand, smiled again, then with a shake of his head, moved away and got lost in the crowd.

Naamah stepped in and gave Seraphina a big hug, then turned and hugged Elijah as well.

"Welcome to the family," she whispered in his ear.

Jessie stepped over, then reached down and took the Bible from Elijah. He looked around, and then stopped another man who happened to be walking by. With one large hand, Jessie reached down and took a pencil out of the man's shirt pocket. Carefully, he opened the Bible to the front cover, and with much concentration and effort, began to write.

Confused, Seraphina looked from her mother to Elijah, then back to her father. Jessie closed the Bible, then reached out and took Seraphina's hand. Elijah wasn't sure, but he thought he saw a tear fall from the big man's eye as he pressed his lips to the back of his daughter's hand, then gave her the Bible. Seraphina opened it, and on the cover page in big block letters, Jessie had written her name.

When Jessie turned to go back and finish making plans with the other workers Naamah laced her arms through Elijah's and Seraphina's and pulled them close. "I told your father last night that I had a feelin' this was gonna happen. He wanted to do somethin' special for you, so he worked all night to learn to write your name." She looked over at Seraphina and smiled when she saw a tear run down her daughter's cheek. "Your daddy loves you so much, he give that preacher man a day's wages for his Bible just so he could write your name in it and give it to you."

Elijah was fighting back tears himself when Naamah turned to him and said, "It's hard for a man to give up his only daughter so you best treat her right, you hear me?"

"You ain't gotta worry about that, Mrs. Ischa. I'm gonna take good care of her."

Naamah furrowed her brow and pursed her lips. "Who you calling Mrs. Ischa? From now on you best be calling me Momma!"

CHAPTER 7

The blistering sun was directly overhead, and Elijah could see the heat rising as he shuffled along the shoulder of a narrow dirt road. He was exhausted. Between the heat, the long days walking, and the even longer nights sleeping on the hard ground, Elijah had reached his limit.

With Happy cradled in one arm and carrying the carpetbag in the other, he began to daydream about life at the church. Had he been hasty to run away like he had? Should he have left a note for the minister or said a final thank you to Mrs. Jones? Would he and Happy even still be alive if he had stayed?

Happy began to cry and Elijah stopped to try and comfort him. He rearranged the baby in his arms and started humming an old tune he remembered from his childhood.

"Shhh, baby, I know you're hungry. I'm hungry, too." Elijah looked up and down the deserted road. "I'm hungry and tired of walkin' this damnable dirt road. Mile after mile, town after town, and nothin'. No food, no job..." Elijah's head started to spin and his vision blurred. If he didn't get something to eat soon, he was going to die out here on the road and take the baby with him.

A warm wind blew road dust over them, and Elijah did his best to cover Happy's face with the cloth he had him bundled in. The wind carried with it a strange sound like the beating of a distant drum, then it changed direction and Elijah thought he heard the low angry growl of a bobcat.

He scanned the road again first to his left, and he saw nothing, then back to his right, and still the road was empty.

This is it, he thought. He was losing his mind, hallucinating from hunger and exhaustion. The sound continued to grow louder and took on a more mechanical tone. Elijah looked again to his left. A black object started to take shape from the waves of heat rising from the hard-packed dirt. Happy began to cry again, and Elijah took his eyes off the wavering shape to check on the baby. Before he could say *hush,* a black car pulled to a stop beside him, and the passenger side window rolled down.

"Boy, oh boy, did you pick a bad day to go for a walk," a man said from inside the car.

Elijah blinked away the dust the car had stirred up. When his vision cleared, he leaned in and looked across the interior of the car. A large white man wearing a black felt hat, a black coat, and a pressed white shirt was sitting behind the wheel. Around his neck was a black leather string tie with a set of gold bull's horns keeping it tight.

The man leaned his head out the window and looked up into the cloudless sky. "It must be a hundred and five degrees in the shade."

Elijah looked at the man, amazed that, although he had been inside the car with the windows up, he didn't appear to be hot. The car was brand new, immaculate, without a single bit of dust or road dirt anywhere to be seen.

Happy let out a loud cry and kicked at the cloth Elijah had him wrapped in.

"Is that a baby you've got all bundled up in there?" the man asked. "You gonna melt him away to nothing."

Elijah couldn't think of anything to say. This just didn't feel right to him. All his senses were telling him to run, to get away, but he was just so tired. Like before, his head began to swim from the heat and his confusion. He felt like his knees might give way at any minute. He just needed to think. If he could just *think* he would figure out what to do.

He took a small step away from the car, hoping that some distance might help him see things more clearly. The sun glinted off the window, causing him to blink and turn away. When he turned back, for a split second, the car had changed to a pale horse with a hooded rider. He shook his head, and when he looked again, it was just a car. A big, black, shiny car.

"Elijah, that boy of yours shore looks hungry," the man said in an almost fatherly manner that brought Elijah out of his stupor. He moved back up to the car and bent down to better see the man inside. Any man who drove a car like this was probably well-off and might feel sorry enough for him and Happy to help them out a little.

"Uh, yes, sir, he is a mite hungry, and to be honest, so am I." He put on what he hoped was his most needy face. "Could you maybe spare a little change to help us out?"

"I can do better than that." The man smiled. He never took his eyes off Elijah as he reached into his coat pocket and produced a crisp new ten-dollar bill and handed it out the window. Elijah could not believe what he was seeing.

"There's a lot more where that came from if you want it."

Elijah took the bill and looked closely at it before tucking it into his pants pocket. "Yes, sir, I believe I might."

"Well then, you are in luck. It just so happens that I have a little supper club that I run just up the ways a bit, and I shore could use a man of your many talents." The man leaned over, pulled the handle of the passenger door and pushed it open.

Elijah stepped back and just stood there on the side of the road not believing what was happening.

"Well get in boy," the man persisted. "That is, if you want some more of that green to stuff in your pocket."

Elijah reached for the car door to get in, then stopped and looked back in at the man. "I'm sorry mister, but I gotta ask. How do you know my name? Have we met somewhere before?"

"No Elijah, we never met before, but I know plenty about you and little Happy there. I've had my eye on you ever since Sera died."

Elijah looked uneasily down at the man in the car, and Happy cried harder.

Think, Elijah thought to himself. *Think, think, think. This is too easy. Somethin's not right. Think before you do somethin' you're gonna regret.*

Elijah looked over the car, searching the empty road, wishing for someone or something else to come along. Something or someone to stop him from getting in the car with this man. *Please Lord, let somebody,* anybody, *come by and get me out of this mess.*

The man in the car started to chuckle. It was a hoarse, gurgling sound that made Elijah's mouth go dry.

"The answer to your prayers doesn't come this way very often, Elijah," the man said with a slight lilt to his voice. Then, as if someone had thrown a switch, his voice became deadly serious. "Now *get* in the car."

Elijah breathed deeply and blew it out again. He took a long look at Happy's crying face, then against his better judgement, he got in. Before he could even get the door closed, the man dropped the car into gear, and with gravel shooting out from under the wheels, they sped away.

* * *

Elijah followed the man in the black suit into a dimly lit bar. Its main room was large with wood paneled walls, high ceilings, and a stage in one corner. A massive bar took up all the space along the wall on the opposite side. In between, were twenty or more tables all with their chairs placed upside down on them, their legs pointed to the sky. The floors were made of old wooden planks, some of which had begun to warp. Elijah had to watch his step to make sure he didn't trip and wake up Happy.

One table in the back of the room near the bar had its chairs properly underneath it, and the man in the black suit motioned Elijah toward it. Elijah took a seat at the round table and set his carpetbag on the floor beside him. The table's top was scarred from many years of use, and its finish discolored by one too many spilled drinks. Happy squirmed a bit in his arms but went back to sleep.

"It don't look like much right now, but after dark this place comes alive," the man said in a sprawling southern accent from behind Elijah.

"Good music, good food," he bent down low and whispered in Elijah's ear like he was telling a secret that no one else should hear, "and other good stuff, if you know what I mean."

The man removed his hat and carefully placed it upside down on the table before sitting next to Elijah. "Elijah, you look hungry. Can I get you something to eat?"

"I'd be much obliged. And maybe some milk for the baby?"

The man clapped his hands and the sound echoed around the empty room. A split second later, a heavy-set white woman wearing a loose-fitting dress that struggled to contain her large breasts came from behind the bar carrying a plate. It held a large steak sitting next to a heaping pile of fried potatoes.

The woman placed the plate in front of Elijah. The smell coming from it drifted up to his nose, and without thinking, he licked his lips.

Before he could stop her, the woman grabbed Happy from him and took a seat across the table. Without any sign of modesty, she used her free hand to slip one side of her dress off her shoulder and set the baby to her breast. Happy immediately took to her and began to silently nurse.

The man found that entertaining and laughed as he turned back to Elijah, who was staring at the woman.

"Elijah, Elijah, look at *me* boy!"

Elijah slowly pivoted away from the woman nursing his child and faced him.

"Elijah I'm gonna make you a deal," the man said. He winked and gave him a quick nod of assurance. "I'm going to keep you and that boy of yours fat and happy. I'll give you a place to live, food on the table, and a little spending money. All you gotta do is play guitar for me."

For the second time that day, Elijah thought that what he was hearing was too good to be true. The urge to grab Happy and run flooded over him again. He looked over at the woman nursing Happy, and he was surprised to see that she was staring back at him. Their eyes met. Hers were a deep soft brown, and to Elijah it looked as if twenty lifetimes were hiding behind them, but there was something else. Was it fear or sadness, maybe a little of both? Elijah couldn't tell, but it made him all the more apprehensive.

The man cleared his throat, and Elijah forced himself to refocus his attention on his host.

"I know a few chords, sir, but I ain't really played in a long time. I'm not very good."

"You don't have to be very good, just good enough," the man replied.

At that moment the oil lamps encircling the stage blazed to life. From the back-stage area, a scantily clad Asian woman stepped out through the curtains and into the light, carrying a guitar case. She was wearing a sheer flesh-colored dress that hugged her hips and chest with a bit of lace on the low neckline to provide a touch of mystery as to what lay beneath.

Barefooted, she stepped down from the stage and brought the guitar case to the table. She opened it and removed a beautiful new acoustic guitar. The polished spruce body caught the light and reflected it back, highlighting her face and giving it an angelic glow. She bent over more deeply than she needed to and placed the guitar in Elijah's lap, before turning and walking away. He watched her every move. His eyes hung on every ripple the material made, hypnotized by its flow over her hips and around her legs.

"Uh, excuse me Elijah," the man said, sarcasm dripping from every word. "If you can stop staring at my woman's ass for a minute, I'd shore enough like to hear you play."

Elijah snapped back to attention; his face flushed with embarrassment.

"Yes, sir. Sorry about that."

He started strumming the guitar. As he warmed up, everything he had learned from his father began to come back to him. He started playing using four of his fingers to pick out a rhythm as his thumb played an accompaniment on the lowest string. The man clapped his hands to the rhythm which encouraged Elijah to play faster and stronger.

The man abruptly stood up, knocking over the chair he was sitting in. "Enough!"

Startled, Elijah stopped playing and looked up at the imposing figure standing next to him. The man clapped twice, and the Asian woman returned. This time, she came from behind the bar carrying a feather quill pen, an inkwell, and a rolled piece of paper. The man took the pen and handed it to Elijah as the woman placed the inkwell on the table, then leaned over and slid the paper in front him.

The man looked down at her and slowly ran his fingers along her back, leaving little marks on her dress. He righted his chair and sat next to Elijah. The man's black eyes bore into Elijah as he guided him to put pen to paper.

"I believe in you, Elijah, and that makes you good enough. You just put your mark on the line at the bottom of this page, and you will be on your way."

Elijah stared at the paper spread out before him, then laid the pen on the table beside it. He picked up the paper, preparing to read it, but before he could finish the first line, the man reached over and pushed his arm down till the paper was once again flat on the table.

"What's the matter Elijah, don't you trust me?"

"Do I have a choice?"

"You always have a choice, Elijah. It's called *free will*. The question is *will* you sign my little contract and be *free*?"

Elijah met the man's eyes for a moment, then he turned to face the Asian woman. The way she was leaning across the table revealed everything the lace of her dress tried to hide. He looked up into her face, and she bit her lip, then let it slowly pull away, revealing an inviting smile. Happy began to cry softly, and the woman nursing him started humming a comforting song. It sounded familiar, and Elijah realized it was the same song that he had hummed to Happy earlier in the day at the side of the road.

Elijah turned back to the paper and signed it. His hand shook so badly that it made his signature unreadable.

A big smile crossed the man's face as he took the paper from in front of Elijah. He rolled it neatly and handed it and the pen to the Asian woman, who quietly returned to her place behind the bar. He turned and scooped up Happy, pulling him away from the woman sitting at the table. He lifted the baby high over his head then brought him back down, cradled him in one of his massive arms and gently rubbed his belly.

"Ha ha!" the man laughed. "Looks like this little one is full enough to pop!" He returned his attention to Elijah. "Come with me." He offered him his hand. When Elijah took it, the man lifted him from the table. "You can call me Mr. Give 'cause today is your lucky day!"

Mr. Give, still holding the baby, took his hat from the table, and with a flip of the wrist, twirled it to its correct position on his head, then turned and walked toward the door. Elijah stuffed a forkful of food into his mouth and followed closely behind.

* * *

The dirt road Elijah and Happy had been walking on just an hour before looked completely different from the front seat of Mr. Give's car. Elijah marveled at the soft leather upholstery and how that even on such a hot day, the inside of the car was actually cool and comfortable. He reached out and touched an open area in the car's dashboard where a stream of cold air blew out. The air traveled up his arm and caused goosebumps to form there.

"That's a little something I dreamed up a while back," Mr. Give said proudly. "Suspect it will be a big thing in a few years, but for now I just keep it for myself."

Elijah smiled and nodded in agreement before turning his attention to the road ahead. They rounded a curve, and he spotted a car off to the side of the road with a man and woman standing behind it. The man was down on one knee trying to remove a flat tire, and the woman stood over him fanning herself. He had seen that car before, or one like it. It was an old Willy's Whippet like the Flanigan brothers drove. As they drew nearer to the car, he recognized Mrs. Jones and the minister.

What were they doing all the way out here in the Flanigan's rattle trap?

"Mr. Give, can we pull over? I know those folks, and it looks like they're havin' trouble."

Mr. Give never let off the gas. They drove past the car, leaving it in a cloud of dust.

"Let's get one thing straight Elijah, your new life began today when you signed our little agreement. Anything that happened before that, you would be best to forget."

Through the car's rear-view mirror, he saw the minister stand and kick the tire, then they were out of sight as the car went around the next curve in the road.

Elijah thought about Sera and her Bible that was buried at the bottom of his case. He could never forget her, no matter how good or bad things went going forward. His heart and soul belonged to Seraphina and that was one thing that would never change.

A short time later, a small cottage appeared to his left. It sat in the middle of a field and was painted white with light blue trim and shutters.

Looks just like somethin' out of a storybook, Elijah thought to himself.

Maybe someday, if Mr. Give paid him like he said he was going to, he would be able to afford a place like that for him and little Happy. It didn't look like a house to him, it looked like a *home*. A perfect place for a little fella to grow up, a happy place. Happy's happy place. He smiled at that thought and looked down at his son, who slept contentedly in his arms.

The car turned off the main road, and loose gravel rumbled under the wheels. Elijah looked up to see where they were. To his surprise they were pulling up to the white and blue cottage. Closer now, he could see the little porch, complete with a rocking chair and welcome mat at the door. The mat was well-placed as the little house did in fact feel very welcoming.

Mr. Give pulled the car to a stop outside the cottage and retrieved his hat from the back seat. "Don't just sit there, get out!" he boomed. The big man opened his door, stepped out into the hot summer sun, and walked to the front of the car. Hesitantly, Elijah followed and stopped beside him. "Well, there she is boy. What do you think?"

"I think it's just about the most beautiful place I ever seen! Is this *your* house?"

Mr. Give laughed, a growling hyena-like bray that echoed across the field. He took off his hat and used it like a fan to shoo away a pesky fly. "Me live here? Now that's funny. No Elijah, I don't live here, *you* do."

Elijah looked from Mr. Give to the house, then back again before taking a hesitant step toward the welcoming porch. He stopped short of setting foot on the painted boards, turned, and stepped back beside Mr. Give.

"It's too much," Elijah told him. "You don't even know if folks will like my playin'."

"You let me worry about that. Now why don't you and Happy go on in and get settled." He used his hat to point Elijah toward the house. "My man will be back here to pick you up just after dark on Saturday night. That's just three days from now, so you best spend your time picking that guitar and getting ready. There's a black suit of clothes hanging in there and matching hat. You have them on and be ready to play next time I see you."

"But—"

"No buts, you just go on now and do as I tell you." Mr. Give gave him a gentle push.

Elijah stepped up on the porch. The white paint on the house shimmered in the summer sun so much it looked like light reflections on a still lake. Happy woke up and began to twist and turn in Elijah's arms.

"It's okay baby, we're home," Elijah whispered. He reached for the doorknob but realized that he had not properly told Mr. Give thank you. To his surprise, when he turned back around, Mr. Give and the car had disappeared. Surely, he would have heard the car's engine start or its wheels rolling over the gravel. A sense of deep worry flooded over Elijah as he turned and stepped into the house.

The inside was as nice as the outside. The house consisted of one large room with a new stove on one wall and a table in the middle. A bed and cradle sat opposite the stove, and a small couch with an end table sat under the room's only window.

The heavy-set woman who had nursed Happy at the bar was standing at the stove cooking. She had traded in her faded dress for a more stylish one and had added a bright flowered apron to complete the outfit. She turned from the stove and smiled as she walked over to Elijah and extended her arms to take Happy.

Elijah stepped back from her and she lowered her arms, tipping her head in confusion.

"What are you doin' here?" he asked.

She turned to the table where there was a pencil and a pad of paper. She quickly scribbled a note and handed it to him.

My name is Marie I am here to take care of you.

Elijah looked up from the note and watched Marie as she went over to the guitar case that was lying on the bed, opened it, and handed him the instrument from inside. He took the guitar with his free hand, and then surrendered Happy to her care.

She began to hum that same familiar tune to the baby and took him outside. Elijah's head was spinning from everything that had happened to him in the last two hours, and he took a seat at the table to try and steady his nerves. Could this be real?

The smell of whatever Marie had left simmering in a pot on the stove drifted to him. The meaty, salty odor gave the little house a warm and inviting feel. He watched as the sheer curtains that hung in front of the window rose and fell with a warm summer breeze. From out on the porch the sound of Marie's humming came to his ears, and he began to relax. He took a deep breath and wrapped his fingers around the neck of the guitar. Using the fingers of his other hand, he gently plucked the strings and played along with her as the sun slowly started to set.

* * *

Elijah looked in the mirror next to the door and straightened his tie, then he placed his hat on his head, making sure to get the angle just right. He had decided to make the best of this weird situation that he found himself in. If Mr. Give wanted a sharp-dressed guitar player to entertain at his club, then Elijah would give him just that. Happy deserved some good things in life, and Mr. Give seemed to be just the man to make those things happen.

Elijah gave himself a wink in the mirror, picked up the guitar case, and stepped out on the porch.

Mr. Give's car pulled to a stop outside the house, and the back passenger door opened on its own. Elijah took a few tentative steps in the direction of the car, then stopped and looked back when he heard the screen door on the house open. Marie came out on the porch carrying Happy and waved him on with a flick of the wrist. Happy looked contented in her arms, which brought a smile to Elijah's face. Confident that his son would be well cared for while he was gone, Elijah turned back to the car.

A very large man stood beside the open door. He wore sunglasses and a black suit similar to Elijah's, and he was smoking a fat cigar. "Get in. The boss says I'm to bring you to the club."

Elijah got into the back of the car, then watched the man closely as he circled and got in behind the wheel. He took one last long draw off the cigar before tossing it out of the car window. Elijah hated the smell of cigars and reached over to crack the window next to him but discovered that there was no crank mounted in the door panel.

The car's engine roared to life. The driver put it in gear and stomped the gas, causing the tires to spin in the gravel. Elijah didn't say anything, but he felt like the man should have more respect for his driveway and decided that he would let Mr. Give know about the man's behavior. Skidding in the loose gravel, the car fishtailed onto the hard-packed dirt road and threw Elijah against the door.

He sat back up and straightened his jacket. He had just about decided to give the driver a piece of his mind when he looked up and saw the man staring at him in the rearview mirror. The driver had removed his sunglasses, and his eyes were a pale, albino blue. The man took the first turn in the road without ever taking his eyes off Elijah. He just stared at him— *through* him—with those cold, almost dead-looking eyes.

Elijah couldn't stand the way the man was looking at him, so he leaned into the corner of the back seat, hoping to get far enough over so he wouldn't be visible. The man in turn reached up and adjusted the mirror in order to keep Elijah in sight.

"How long you been workin' for Mr. Give?" Elijah asked, hoping to divert the man's attention.

He continued to look at Elijah for another full minute before answering him. "I guess you could say I've always worked for the boss." He turned his attention back to the road.

Elijah breathed a sigh of relief. "Like, since you was a kid?"

"Yeah, something like that."

"He seems like a nice enough fella, give me a new suit and a new guitar. Give me a *house*."

"He certainly seems that way, doesn't he?"

Elijah didn't know how to take that and went on the defensive. "Well, he do to me."

The man looked back at Elijah and smirked, then turned back to watch the road.

Elijah put his attention on the car he was riding in. He felt the quality of the leather seat, opened and closed the ashtray mounted on the back of the seat in front of him, and wiggled a little, enjoying the feel of the soft seat underneath him. "This sure is a fine car. Is it new?"

"Yeah, it's new."

"I've never been in a car like this before." Elijah couldn't hide the amazement in his voice. "Man, I would really love to have me a car like this someday. Maybe if I tell the boss that I need a car like this to get around in, he'll give me one like he give me the house."

The man in the front seat rolled down his window just a little and went about the process of lighting another cigar before turning his attention back to Elijah. "Look, you seem like a nice enough guy so I'm going to give you a piece of advice." As he spoke, he again made eye contact with Elijah in the rearview mirror. "The boss knows full well you don't need a car, so don't lie to him and act like you do. Whatever you do, never lie to the boss. It's the one thing he will not tolerate. He can't stand a liar. You got that?"

"Yeah, I got it." Elijah looked away from the man's cold eyes. "So, the boss don't like folks to tell him one, not even as a joke?"

"The only jokes the boss likes are his own. You could say he has a dark sense of humor. So, if I were you, I wouldn't put it to the test. Be smart and never lie to the boss even if you think it's going to be funny."

Elijah nodded as silence filled the car again. He needed to do something to take his mind off the driver and his dead eyes, so he opened the guitar case and took out Seraphina's Bible. The instant he opened the book, the driver slammed on the brakes. The car skidded to a stop and threw Elijah into the back of the driver's seat.

The man twisted around to face Elijah directly. His face was red with anger, and the smoke from the cigar hung like a curtain around his head. "What the hell is that?"

"It ain't nothin'." Elijah pushed himself back into the seat. "Just an old book my wife give me." He tossed the Bible back into the guitar case and latched it shut.

"Bullshit! That was not just some old book, that was a Bible, and if you know what's good for you, you won't ever let the boss see you with it. In fact, when you get home tonight, you best burn it."

"I can't do that. My wife give me that on the night she died, it's all of her I got."

The driver turned back around and tossed his cigar out the window. He took a couple of deep breaths, then looked up at Elijah in the mirror again. "Bury it then. But whatever you do, don't let the boss know you've got it, understand?"

"Yes, sir." Elijah nodded and looked away.

"I mean it," the driver continued. "Bury it, burn it, hide it, whatever you have to do to make sure the boss never sees it or even suspects that you have it."

"Yes, sir, I'll do that."

Elijah slowly reached over and laid his hand on the guitar case as the driver put the car back in gear and pulled out on the road.

* * *

The parking lot of Mr. Give's supper club was packed as the car pulled up next to the awning over the front entrance. The driver opened Elijah's door, and the car was immediately filled with the sound of muffled music coming from inside, as well as the smell of fried food, stale beer, and cigarettes. Nervousness suddenly struck Elijah, and he found that his feet didn't want to step out of the car.

"Well come on," the driver said. "What's the holdup? You don't want to keep the boss waiting."

Elijah didn't answer he just swallowed his nerves and forced himself to get out.

"Come on, you gotta get inside."

It was all Elijah could do to keep from throwing up all over his new shoes, so he just stood there, eyes down, trying to pull himself together. With great effort and all his senses telling him not to, Elijah took a few tentative steps toward the door and stopped again. He looked up at the driver, hoping to see some compassion in his face, hoping the man would tell him it was okay if he just went back to the house and tried this again tomorrow. Instead, all he saw were the man's cold eyes and an impatient expression.

"It's just that I ain't never played in front of a bunch of strangers before," Elijah explained. "I don't even know how to start."

"Don't worry, the boss has it all under control."

The beautiful Asian woman, who had brought Elijah his contract a few days before, opened the door and the crowd noise got louder.

"What's the holdup out here Apollyon?" Her voice was nasally and high pitched, her accent sharp. "The boss is waiting."

Elijah stepped up to the door next to Apollyon and the woman. "I'm sorry ma'am, it's my fault. I'm just a little nervous I guess."

She looked Elijah up and down. Her face was tight and her lips pressed together so hard that they showed white even under her bright red lipstick. Elijah found it hard to believe that this was the same woman from before whom he had found so attractive.

"We don't have time for you to be nervous." She practically spit the words at him. "Now get your ass in here and play that guitar."

Apollyon put one large hand on Elijah's back and gently pushed him forward through the door and into the dark club. The Asian woman gave Apollyon a concerned look, then they turned and followed Elijah through the door.

It took a few seconds for Elijah's eyes to adjust to the dim, smoky atmosphere. The air was warm with the heat coming off all the bodies crowded in there like sardines in a can. Elijah stopped just inside the door and tried to take it all in. A topless woman was dancing on the stage while the men in the first few rows hooted and hollered for her to *take it off* and to *shake it*.

There were roulette wheels spinning on some of the tables, others were crowded with men playing cards. The back bar was *standing room only* as two bartenders tried to keep up with the onslaught of orders for beer and whiskey.

A waitress in a very short skirt and halter top passed by Elijah carrying a tray full of plates piled high with steaks and potatoes. She stopped at a table full of old men in suits and set a plate in front of each one. She received a pat on her rear as a tip.

Elijah's heart beat hard in his chest. He tried to take a deep breath to calm his nerves, but the heavy smoke hanging thick in the air only caused him to cough and his eyes to water. *What am I doing here?* he thought to himself for the hundredth time in the last few days. *I can't do this. I can't go up on that stage after that girl and play guitar for these people, they'll tear me apart.*

Elijah looked back over his shoulder toward the door and saw Apollyon and the woman standing there blocking his escape. There had to be another way out.

As he scanned the room, the girl on stage turned her back on the audience, spread her legs wide and did a deep bend at the waist. The crowd went wild as she looked at them between her legs and gave them a little wave goodbye. The spotlight dimmed and she disappeared behind a curtain on the right-hand side.

Bingo, he thought and took a step in the direction of the stage. A heavy hand landed on his shoulder, stopping him.

Mr. Give stepped beside him. "You're on, Elijah. Now go up there and make me proud."

"Yes, sir," was all Elijah managed to say.

When he didn't move, Mr. Give snapped his fingers and the Asian woman appeared and took Elijah by the arm. Her grip on his bicep was like iron, and when she started moving him forward he couldn't resist. She guided him to the stage in that fashion then changed her demeanor. She took his arm in hers—like two lovers on a midnight stroll—brought him on stage, and introduced him to the crowd.

CHAPTER 8

Sunrise had become Elijah's favorite time of day since moving into the little cottage with Happy and Marie. He tried to wake early and have those few peaceful minutes to himself before Marie started in on him to do this or fix that, and before Happy's first cry of the morning.

Often this was when he would sit on the front porch and read Seraphina's Bible. It still didn't make a lot of sense to him, but with the lessons he had received from the minister, he was starting to pick up on some of the teachings it held inside its covers. Sometimes he would just let the book fall open on his lap, and he would read a random passage. This morning it had fallen open to the book of Psalms:

But I will sing of your strength.
I will sing aloud of your steadfast love in the morning.
For you have been to me a fortress
and a refuge in the day of my distress.

That got him thinking about Sera, how she had reached for the book while she lay there dying on the cold ground. No matter how much he had tried to comfort her, she seemed to only find peace when she held this book close to her chest.

A tear rolled down his cheek, and he pulled the Bible close, holding it over his heart. He blinked away the tears and as his vision cleared, he thought that he saw Sera walking toward him. She was holding her hand out to him like she wanted him to come away with her. As she drew closer, he heard her footsteps, and a breeze brought her smell to his nose—a clean scent of soap with a touch of vanilla.

The front door opened and Seraphina faded into the morning sun. Marie stepped out and joined him on the porch with Happy in her arms. She placed him at Elijah's feet then went back into the house and returned with a basket filled with wet laundry.

Marie reached out and gently touched Elijah's shoulder as she made her way past him. She stepped off the porch and headed for the clothesline he had strung for her between two poles in the side yard.

Elijah watched her as she moved away. Marie was a strange one, she never spoke but she made her intentions known through the way she looked at him. If that didn't work, she would write a note for him with the pad and pencil that she always kept with her. He had grown to care for her over the last few weeks, and she took good care of the baby, but he still wasn't sure he could trust her. Sometimes he would catch her staring at him, and he would get the same uneasy feeling he had gotten when the driver was looking at him in the car's mirror.

Marie hung the last piece of clothing on the line and came back to the porch. A curl of black hair hung loose on her forehead, and she stopped long enough to push it back in place. Her smile faltered when she saw the Bible he was holding, then it was back again, but this time it felt forced. He returned her smile and placed the Bible in the basket beside Happy.

Marie stepped up on the porch and went into the house. A minute later, she came back out holding a glass of water. She took a sip, then handed it to Elijah. She looked down at him and smiled again, and this time he felt the warmth of it and knew it was real.

He took a long drink of the cold water and felt the chill spread out through his chest. What was he worried about? His dreams were coming true—he just needed to accept it. *Enjoy* it.

He gave the glass back to Marie, and their hands brushed together during the exchange. He let his hand linger against hers, enjoying the warmth of her fingers. He thought he saw her blush, but then she pulled her hand away and turned to go back inside.

It truly was a beautiful morning, and he felt sure it was going to be a beautiful day.

* * *

It had been a beautiful day. After a breakfast of bacon, eggs, and Marie's amazing biscuits, Elijah had taken Happy for a walk down to a small stream that ran behind the cottage. Happy laughed when Elijah dipped his toes in the cold water, then they sat there on the bank as Elijah told him stories about his momma and pointed out the occasional deer or rabbit.

He thought more about Sera and how she would have loved it here. Before he knew it, the morning had passed them by. Happy started getting hungry and fussy, so they made their way back to the cabin.

Marie was sitting on the front porch pulling the last feathers off the carcass of one of the chickens that ran loose in the back yard. This could only mean one thing: that she was planning to make her world-famous fried chicken for dinner.

One night after the baby was asleep, he asked her where she had learned to cook so well. She had written back, *In another life, I ran a restaurant*. He thought back to when they had first met and how he felt that there were a thousand lifetimes hiding behind her eyes. What else had she done in her life? He would have loved to know but guessed he never would.

The fried chicken was the best he had ever tasted. He had eaten his fill and then some, savoring the spices she had added to the breading and the sweetness of the buttermilk she had soaked it in. While he ate, she fed Happy, and with his tummy full, he had fallen asleep in her arms. Marie had put him to bed and started in washing the dishes.

Elijah pulled out Seraphina's Bible and began reading it by the oil lamp that they kept in the middle of the table.

Marie dried her hands and stepped up behind him. She ran her hands through his hair, then let them trail down to his back. This sent a chill through Elijah, and as she began to massage his shoulders, he arched his back, giving her more area to work with.

"Mmm, that's nice," he said just above a whisper as he closed his eyes and enjoyed the feel of her hands on him.

Marie reached down over him and closed the Bible. Surprised, Elijah turned and peered up at her.

She gave him a look that sent another chill through him. As she stepped around the chair to stand in front of him, she slowly undid the buttons of her shirt. She leaned in and brushed her lips against his ear while lifting his hand and placing it against her breast.

Elijah reached up with his other hand, and with the slightest touch, Marie's shirt fell off her shoulders and down around her feet. His heart raced when she took his hand and placed it against her lips. Her hot breath on his palm sent shivers rushing down his spine.

Elijah's hands traveled along the length of her body; its heat radiated through his fingers as he caressed her skin, and a low moan came from deep within her.

He looked up at Marie, and with a nod, she let him know that she wanted him to stand. He did, and she gently caressed his cheek with the back of her hand before she knelt in front of him.

* * *

The next morning, Elijah was up early as usual and was surprised to find the cottage empty. He stepped to the window and saw Marie and Happy sitting on a blanket in the front yard. She was lying on her side watching as Happy tried to roll over. Satisfied that everything was right in the world, Elijah went to get Seraphina's Bible off the table where he had left it the night before.

The Bible wasn't there.

He thought back over the previous night and was sure that the last thing he remembered—at least about the book—was Marie leaning down over him and closing it. So why wasn't it on the table?

Panic crept up inside of him. That Bible was the only thing of Seraphina's that he still had, and if it was lost, he didn't know what he would do.

He pulled out the chairs and looked under the table, thinking that in the rush of the evening he had knocked it off, but nothing was there. He rushed over to the little counter by the sink, but it was empty as well. Maybe it was in the carpet-bag under the bed. How it would have gotten there was beyond him, but he was well past rational thinking at this point. If he had to, he would tear the cottage apart until he found it.

Elijah went over to their little sofa and looked under the cushions. He dropped them back in place and was just about to turn the sofa over to look underneath when he saw Marie standing there with Happy, watching him.

"Where is it?" he demanded.

Marie placed Happy down on the bed, then went to Elijah and reached out in a gesture of comfort.

Elijah grabbed her by the upper arms, and his fingers dug into the muscle there like claws. "I said, where is it?"

Marie shook her head as if she didn't know what he was talking about.

"Don't act stupid!" Elijah shook her, causing her head to snap back and her hair to fall in her face. "You know what I'm lookin' for. Sera's Bible. What did you do with it?"

Again, she shook her head, then tried to turn her face away from Elijah.

"Don't lie to me!" Elijah yelled as the anger built up inside of him and threatened to spill out. "Give me the book or so help me I will beat the livin' daylights out of you until you do!" He raised a hand and started to bring it down on her.

Marie jerked out of his grip and fell cowering on the bed next to Happy. The baby started to cry.

Elijah took a step toward her with his hand still raised, but before he could strike out, she reached in the pocket of her apron and extended the Bible toward him. He snatched it away from her and went back to the table. Still angry, he yanked out one of the chairs, sat down hard, and buried his head in his hands.

What had he just done? Where had all that anger come from? This wasn't like him. He was the calm one always thinking on his feet, always able to avoid a confrontation. A shudder passed through him as the adrenalin drained from his system, leaving him feeling tired and achy.

Marie walked over to the table where just the night before they had been so intimate. She tentatively touched his shoulder. He flinched, and she drew her hand back. Elijah looked up at her. Tears ran down her cheek, and he saw for the first time how his anger had affected her. Embarrassed, he stood and faced her. She stepped back, keeping a space between them.

"I'm sorry I came at you like that," he said sincerely. "It's just I was scared when I couldn't find Sera's Bible. It's all I have left of her and losing it would be like losing a part of my-self."

Marie's fear drained from her face and a look of empathy replaced it. She reached out and took his hand as they both walked back over to the table and sat down. She pressed Elijah's hand to her face. With her eyes closed, she rubbed her cheek against the back of his hand, then opened her eyes and looked up at him.

"So that's how it is, is it?" Elijah peered deep into her soft brown eyes, felt her warmth, and saw her feelings for him and Happy all laid out there. "Well, I guess I feel that way, too. You've been so kind, taking care of me and Happy, that I just don't know how I could feel any other way. But you got to understand, Sera and me was together for a long time, and she was Happy's ma."

Tears welled up in Marie's eyes as she let go of his hand and stood to leave. Elijah grabbed her arm and stopped her. He pulled her to him and wiped the tears from her eyes with the sleeve of his shirt.

"Don't cry, it's okay," he whispered and used his thumb to wipe away another tear. "If it upsets you that much, then I'll never mention Sera again."

Marie's face brightened, then she looked over at the Bible on the table. Elijah picked it up and held it in both hands, considering.

"Is that what it's gonna take?" he asked her.

Her eyes never left his, and she gave him a single affirmative nod.

"Okay, then." Elijah walked with the Bible to the bed, reached under, and pulled out the old carpetbag. He placed it on the bed, opened it, and put Seraphina's Bible inside. Latching the case shut felt very final to him, and he took a moment to get his emotions under control before sliding it back under the bed.

Marie smiled, took his face in her hands, and kissed him.

* * *

Another week passed, and Elijah was going through his last-minute preparations inside the cottage as Marie sat in the rocking chair on the porch with Happy, who quietly slept in her arms.

Mr. Give's car pulled to a stop, and Apollyon stepped out from behind the wheel. He took a moment to light a cigar before making his way to the porch.

"Well, ain't that just the sweetest thing I've ever laid eyes on," he said.

Marie smiled and continued to gently rock the baby as she eased one hand out from under Happy and showed the big man her middle finger.

"Well, that's not very motherly," Apollyon continued unfazed. "Were you able to get rid of the book?"

Marie nodded while keeping a smile glued to her face. She had many reasons for hating Apollyon, but he was Mr. Give's right-hand man, and it was always best to try and stay on his good side.

"Good," Apollyon said, stepping up on the porch. "We like to keep the boss's folks good and stupid when it comes to their other options. No sense letting them get ideas."

Again, Marie nodded her agreement. Her smile never faltered, but when Apollyon tried to reach down and touch little Happy, she pulled the baby away in a protective manner.

"Careful now, don't go and get attached to these two," Apollyon warned. "You have one job here and that is to keep an eye on Elijah. The boss wants him kept happy and willing." He stepped down off the porch and looked up at the full moon.

"Just remember, there's a bunch more where you came from." He turned and looked Marie in the eye. "And every single one of them would love to be where you are right now."

Marie's plastic smile melted into concern.

Elijah stepped out on the porch, wearing the black suit and carrying the guitar case. "I'm ready and raring to go! How do I look?" He set the case down and took a couple of strutting steps across the porch and back.

Marie stood up, and holding the baby in one arm, used her other hand to brush a couple of flecks of dust off his shoulder.

"'Bout time you got out here" Apollyon grumbled. "Let's go. It ain't good to keep the crowd waiting."

Elijah picked up the guitar case and was just about to step off the porch when Marie stopped him. She reached up and straightened his tie, then used it to pull his face down to hers and kissed him goodbye.

Tears stung the backs of her eyes, so she quickly turned and took the baby inside, closing the door behind her.

She hurried to the window and peeked out, watching until the car had disappeared around a turn in the road. When she was sure they were gone, Marie put Happy in the crib and covered him with a blanket. She took the lamp from the table beside the couch and crossed over to the bed. She had to move the light around to overcome the shadows underneath it and find what she was looking for: Elijah's carpetbag. It was pushed back against the wall, so she had to lie on her stomach and wiggle part way in to reach it. A loose spring on the bed-frame caught the back of her dress. It tore the material and opened a small cut on her skin, but she paid it no mind.

Her outstretched fingers barely reached a corner of the bag, but it was enough for her to move it in her direction until she could get a good grip and pull it out from under the bed. She sat spread-legged on the floor, placed the bag in front of her, and pulled it open. Inside, she only found some old clothes. Panicking, she turned the bag upside down and shook it, but nothing else came out. Tears welled up in her eyes and spilled over her cheeks. She punched the bag over and over with her fists before throwing it across the room.

* * *

Elijah finished his set, and the crowd's reaction was overwhelming. Applause like thunder filled the club, and he gave a final wave to the crowd as he made his way to the dressing room. People standing in the back hallway stopped him along the way to shake his hand or pat him on the back. He took his time, enjoying the attention, and made sure to shake every hand offered him.

By the time he reached his dressing room door, he was feeling fine. He was high as a kite on adrenalin and the roar of the crowd, but all that came to a sudden stop when he opened the door to see Apollyon standing in the middle of the room holding Seraphina's Bible.

"Ain't this some shit." Apollyon slapped the Bible against his hand, then pointed it at Elijah. "I told you to burn this and never let me see it again."

"And I told you I couldn't do that," Elijah answered.

Apollyon threw the Bible down on the ground at Elijah's feet and started pacing around the room.

"That stupid bitch," he whispered to himself before turning and getting up in Elijah's face. "She had one job, just one job. Just keep you happy and distracted. That was it and could she do that? *NO!*"

Apollyon's face was turning red and Elijah took a step back, unsure of how far Apollyon's anger would take him.

"I'm going to have to let the boss know about this. It's my ass or hers." He opened and closed his fist as he stormed around the room. "I'm not taking the fall for this one. He let her off easy once but not this time."

He suddenly stopped pacing and looked at Elijah who had backed himself into one corner of the room.

"Let this be a lesson to you. Remember what I told you about lying to the boss?"

Elijah nodded, afraid to speak.

"I told her the same thing. But did she believe me? Hell no she didn't. She was possibly the best singer that ever lived. She signed a contract just like you, and just like you the boss gave her everything she wanted. Fame, money, you name it, she had it. Then she screwed up, she fell in love with a preacher, of all things, and told him about her little deal with the boss. Then to make matters worse, when he asked her about it, she lied and said she didn't even know the man. The boss asked her again, and she lied again. In fact, she kept lying right up to the minute that the boss ripped the tongue out of her mouth."

Apollyon stopped pacing and smiled a little. "Then he made her watch as he had two fellas break every bone in that preacher's body."

Apollyon's anger returned, and he snatched the guitar out of Elijah's hand and put it back in the case. He closed the latches, then threw the guitar case at Elijah. "I've got to talk to the boss, so you start walking, and you think about what I told you. Straighten up, or it could be you next time."

Apollyon crossed the dressing room, and the door opened for him without being touched, then slammed itself behind him.

Elijah realized that he had forgotten to breathe the whole time Apollyon was ranting, and he took a deep breath and waited for his heart to slow down before leaving the dressing room. The once-busy hallway was deserted and dark. As Elijah stepped out and started toward the back door, he saw a rat scurry from one dark shadow to another, and he picked up his pace.

The dimly lit parking lot was equally empty, but Elijah felt a weight lift off him all the same as he breathed in the cool night air. He stopped and looked back to see if he was being watched, making sure Apollyon wasn't following him. Confident that he was alone, he reached behind him and underneath his jacket to pull Seraphina's Bible from the waist band of his pants. He held it tight to his chest and walked off into the darkness.

* * *

It was a long walk from the club to Elijah's house, and he was feeling every step of it. It had turned cold overnight, and his breath formed into clouds that floated away into the crisp morning air. The cold didn't seem to bother the birds, who had started singing with the dawn, but it bothered Elijah. His joints were aching and he had to keep switching the guitar case from hand to hand in order to keep the blood flowing to his fingers.

As he rounded the last curve in the road, he thought the birds' singing had changed. Their short bursts of notes had become a longer sound. Not a song so much as a cry. As the house came into view, he realized that it was not a bird's cry he was hearing, it was a baby's. *His* baby's. His fear at the sound of Happy crying made him forget his stiffness and pain. He dropped the guitar case and ran toward the house.

Elijah burst through the front door to find Happy sitting in the middle of the floor. His full diaper had leaked, forming a puddle, and Happy slapped his hand against the floor as he cried. It caused little splashes of urine to rise around him like some kind of filthy fountain.

Elijah rushed over, scooped Happy up in his arms, and tried to comfort him.

"Marie!" Elijah called out. He walked in a small circle around the puddle in the floor, bouncing the baby and making soothing shushing noises into Happy's ear. "Where in the Hell is that woman?"

Happy started to calm down, so Elijah took him over to the bed and changed the nasty diaper and got a clean shirt for himself. With both of them feeling better, they went back out on the porch to see if Marie was anywhere to be found. The laundry hanging on the line got his attention. One of the sheets had a large red stain on it.

He sat Happy down to play in the grass and made his way toward the drying laundry. As he drew nearer, he saw Marie standing next to the pole of the clothesline, facing away from him. Anger began to well up inside of him. What was wrong with her, she couldn't talk, but her hearing was fine. How could she just stay out here hanging laundry out to dry while the baby was inside crying and pissing all over himself?

"Marie, what the devil's gotten into you?" Elijah demanded.

When she didn't react to the sound of his voice, his anger turned to dread and he picked up his pace. He drew closer to her and was shocked to see that she wasn't standing with her back to the pole, she was hanging from it. A rope had been placed over the crossbeam of the pole, then used to tie her hands. She was short enough that this left her feet dangling above the ground.

He had to get her down. It had to be hard to breathe like that.

Just as he reached her, he slipped in the wet grass and fell, landing flat on his back. To his horror, he realized that the grass wasn't wet from morning dew but from Marie's blood. He looked up at her—his friend, his lover, the closest thing Happy had ever had to a real mother—and saw a sharp piece of wood protruding from her neck just below the jaw line.

Her left shoulder and the side of her dress were matted with blood that was still dripping and forming a pool on the ground at her feet. The front of her dress has been torn open, and Elijah could see scratches on her chest. He stepped up to Marie and moved a limp curl of hair off her forehead, leaving a red streak.

He didn't want to see more, but he had to know . . .Slowly, he pulled aside the flap in her dress.

"*No!*" Anger and pain washed over him.

At the sound of his desperate wail, Happy began to cry again. The pitiful noise echoed off the nearby foothills, doubling, then tripling the sadness in its sound before fading away.

Elijah stood and wiped his mouth with the back of his trembling hand. This was his fault and the proof had been carved into Marie's chest. The accusation and condemnation were all right there: in her delicate skin, someone had slashed the word, *LIAR.*

* * *

For the second time in less than a year, Elijah shoveled dirt onto the grave of a woman he loved. He realized as he had struggled to cut the ropes that bound Marie that he had indeed loved her. Not in the same way he had loved Seraphina, but it was love all the same.

As he carried her lifeless body away from the pole where it had met its untimely end, he forgave her. Maybe what Apollyon said was true, that she had been working for Mr. Give when she first set foot in their little cottage, but Elijah felt sure that she had loved him in the end. Stranger situations had brought people together in the past.

The midday sun was directly overhead and shining down on him as he shoveled the last of the dirt onto the grave. He reached into his pocket and removed a kerchief to wipe away the sweat and perhaps, a tear.

Happy was sitting on the ground playing as Elijah stepped away from the mound of dirt that would be Marie's final resting place.

"What a waste."

The sun momentarily blinded Elijah. He raised a hand to shield his eyes and saw Apollyon standing there holding Happy.

Elijah jumped back and raised the shovel in a defensive gesture. Apollyon paid him no mind. He just stood there looking at the grave and shaking his head like he felt some loss in Marie's death.

"She knew better than to cross the boss, and now so do you." Apollyon looked down at Happy, scrunched his face up, and made a cooing sound that immediately caused the confused baby to start crying. The man acted disappointed.He walked over to Elijah, ignoring the raised shovel, and held out his son.

Elijah dropped the shovel and took the baby.

"Guess you are going to have some adjusting to do now that she's gone." Apollyon dusted his hands like they were covered in dirt. "Boss said to tell you that the little fella there will be okay by himself when you come to the club to play. You can just leave him here at the house, and the boss will watch out for him."

Apollyon turned to go. He took a few steps, then stopped, turned back to Elijah, and snapped his fingers like he had just remembered something terribly important. "Oh yeah, and don't think you pulled one over on me the other night when you hid that Bible in your britches, 'cause you didn't."

Elijah's heart began beating faster, and panic rose up inside of him like acid from his stomach.

"I asked the boss if he wanted me to take it from you, because you know, I could." Apollyon winked at Elijah like they were two old friends sharing a joke that only they got the punchline to. "He said no, for now. But let me warn you one more time—not that I think it will do any good. If you have any sense of self-preservation anywhere inside of you, you will burn that book and scatter the ashes on her grave, 'cause it ain't gonna do you no good."

Apollyon walked toward the house. "Oh, I brought you a little present from the boss," he continued, never looking back at Elijah. "It's parked out front. Seems he has another job for me, so you're gonna have to drive yourself to the club from now on."

With a few more steps, Apollyon disappeared around the side of the house. Elijah waited to make sure he was actually gone before he picked up his shovel and went that way himself.

In the front yard sat an old truck. He leaned his shovel against the porch and slowly circled the worn-out vehicle, letting his hand trail along the peeling red paint and rust that appeared to cover every surface of it. He kicked one of the bald tires, then tried to adjust the mirror attached to the passenger's side door. It promptly broke off in his hand. When he got back around to the front, he noticed a note on the window. Carefully, he raised the windshield wiper just enough to free the piece of paper. On it was written in a smooth flowing hand:

Every Saturday night at midnight. Never be late.

* * *

Elijah sat at the small table as Happy slept quietly across from him on the couch. He was trying very hard to pray, but the words just wouldn't come. How do you pray for forgiveness for causing a person's death, when what you did to cause that person to die was to refuse to burn the Word of the God who you need to pray to in order to get forgiveness?

He flipped randomly through the pages of Seraphina's Bible, hoping that some great wisdom would come flying out of it. When that didn't happen, he closed the book—a little harder than he planned to—stood, and walked over to the door. Looking out at the pristine countryside as the sun began to set, the weight of the decision he had made when he signed Mr. Give's contract sat heavy on his shoulders. Had it been worth it?

When Sera died, he didn't know how he was going to care for his son. Those first few days on the road nearly broke him. If it weren't for the kindness of the minister and Mrs. Jones, he felt sure that he would have eventually left little Happy somewhere with someone more capable of tending him. Elijah also knew that doing that would have been the end of him. The only reason he had the power to go on after Sera's death was because of Happy.

He remembered part of a passage that the minister had talked to him about. Something about the Lord being a safe place. Elijah racked his brain to put it together but couldn't come up with it. Then he remembered that the minister had marked it for him, so he could find it when he needed to. Elijah turned back to the table and picked up the Bible. This time he flipped through the pages more slowly. As they fluttered past, a dark smudge caught his eye. He sat the book down and pulled the oil lamp over closer to him.

There it was: a simple black cross at the top of a page in the book of Psalms. He trailed his finger down the page until he found the underlined section. He turned the book more toward the light and the underlined words came into better focus:

The Lord also will be a refuge for the oppressed,
a refuge in times of trouble.
And they that know thy name will put their trust in thee.
For thou, Lord, has not forsaken them that seek thee.

Elijah read the words again and again until Happy started to stir.

"I bet you're hungry, ain't ya?"

Happy answered him with a smile and a spit bubble. That made Elijah laugh. He carried the boy over to the stove where Marie had left the cereal she had made for him that morning. He lit the fire and stirred the thick white mixture of ground corn, butter and a little sugar. Marie had fed Happy the same thing every morning since she had weaned him from the breast.

"Enjoy this while we got it," he told the baby. "I ain't the cook Marie was."

With the cereal warm, Elijah banked the fire and covered the pot. He fed Happy with a little silver spoon that had been in the cottage cupboard when they had arrived. The baby ate like he had not been fed all day, and in truth, he hadn't.

Elijah tasted a little of the bland mixture.

"I guess it's all right if it's all you got." He fed another bite to the baby, then looked back over at Sera's Bible.

"I think I messed up, Happy. After we left the church, I just let everythin' that minister told me fade away. Instead of trustin' the Lord, like your momma did, I jumped at the first thing that come along. Now look at the mess we're in."

Happy burped and a little of the cereal ran down his chin. Elijah used his shirt sleeve to mop it up and gave the baby another spoonful.

"Now it may be too late."

The sun set, leaving the cottage dark, except for the light from the oil lamp. Elijah looked around him at the deep shadows thrown by the flickering flame, and a chill came over him. Marie was gone. He and Happy were alone for the first time since they had met Mr. Give on that old dirt road. He looked back at the open Bible lying in front of him on the table, adjusted the lamp's flame, and began to read.

* * *

Saturday night came quickly. It hadn't taken Elijah long to realize how much he had depended on Marie. Between doing housework, taking care of the baby, and tending his little garden, Elijah had little time to sleep much less practice his guitar.

He had gotten in the habit of playing for Happy at bedtime. It soothed the baby to sleep and got him a precious few minutes of practice all at the same time. Tonight, that had worked like a charm, and Happy was sleeping soundly in his crib.

Elijah was dressed for the club except for his hat, coat, and tie. He stepped up to the mirror next to the door and slipped the thin black string tie around his neck and tightened it with the shiny tie clasp that held it all together.

Happy rolled over and made a gurgling noise. Elijah turned to check on him and straightened the sheet that covered the baby.

"I'll be back just as soon as I can," he whispered. "Apollyon said Mr. Give promised that nothing would happen to you while I was workin', and I've gotta trust him, but I'll rush back all the same."

A soft snore escaped the baby, and Elijah leaned in and brushed his lips against Happy's cheek.

"Pappy loves you, little man."

With that, he turned and pulled his jacket off the back of one of the chairs. The jacket's tail caught around the back of the chair and pulled it over. It hit the floor with a sharp bang, instantly waking Happy who began to shriek with fear. Elijah tossed the jacket on the bed and rushed over to comfort the baby. Happy was not living up to his name. His cries filled the small cottage and carried outside where they echoed in the darkness.

"Hush, hush now baby. Pappy's here."

Elijah started his nightly trip walking around the cottage, gently bouncing Happy and whisper=singing in his ear. He glanced at the clock. 9:45.

He had done a test drive in the old truck the day before. It ran, but just barely. He figured that if he pushed it, the truck would get him to the club in around half an hour, a trip that took ten minutes in Mr. Give's fancy black car. So, he was okay. He just needed to keep calm and get the baby back to sleep.

Happy was having none of it. The more Elijah bounced him, the louder Happy cried. Elijah took him out on the porch hoping the cool night air would calm the screaming child. Instead, a wolf pack running in the trees behind the house joined in howling to match Happy's cries. Elijah dampened a handkerchief with rainwater from the barrel at the side of the porch and wiped the baby's face, but that just caused him to sputter and cry even harder.

All he had left was the guitar, so he took Happy back inside and laid him in his crib. The baby cried out so loudly, Elijah was afraid he would choke. So, he rolled him over on his side. He grabbed the guitar out of the case and pulled a chair over by the crib where Happy could see him and began to play. After a few minutes it seemed to be working; Happy was actually starting to calm and take deep breaths. Elijah played *Turkey in the Straw* then *Old Dan Tucker*, next was *In the Jail House Now* and *Swanee*. He played every song he could think of and finally played Seraphina's favorite, *Amazing Grace*, and Happy went to sleep.

"Oh, thank God," Elijah whispered to the quiet room.

He leaned the guitar against the bed frame and stretched, the vertebrae in his back popping in protest. He ran his hand over his hair and chuckled to himself in disbelief. It was finally over, and after all this, he still had to go play to the crowd at the club. He leaned over and looked at the clock on the bed-side table. 11:40.

Panic raced through him. He jumped to his feet, almost knocking the chair over again. He managed to grab it just in time and set it to rights. With the guitar in one hand and his jacket in the other, he bolted out of the house and jumped in the old truck.

Never be late, the note had read, and Elijah repeated that to himself over and over as he stuck the key in the ignition and turned it. Nothing.

"Oh, Lord help me," he muttered and gave the key another turn. Still nothing.

"Start, you stupid piece of s..." He tried the key again, and this time the truck's engine fired to life with a loud backfire and a puff of black smoke from the tailpipe.

Elijah dropped the transmission into first gear and released the clutch too fast. The old truck shuddered and jumped until he could give it enough gas for the gears to fully engage. When it did, it threw a wave of gravel out from under the tires before finding solid ground and sending Elijah on his way.

He pushed the truck as hard as he dared to, and then some. All the way, he repeated the last three words of Mr. Give's note.

"Never be late, never be late, never be late."

At the intersection with the highway, he didn't even bother to look for oncoming cars, he just pressed the gas pedal to the floor and skidded onto the paved road.

"Never be late, never be late, never be late."

The town's single traffic light turned red as Elijah approached it. He never slowed down, just closed his eyes, locked his arms and hoped for the best.

"Never be late, never be late, never be late."

With a squeal of the tires, he jerked the wheel hard to the left and skidded into the gravel parking lot of the club, hit the brakes hard, and slid to a stop outside the main entrance.

The Asian woman was waiting for him with her arms crossed across her chest and a sour look on her face. "You're late."

"I'm sorry, the baby..." Elijah sputtered and jumped out of the truck. He rushed up to her, guitar in hand.

She slapped him across the face hard enough to turn his head, causing his cheek to burn and his eyes to water.

"Apollyon puts up with your crap. He's too soft, I'm not. You were told to never be late. I had to put someone on to cover for you."

Stunned, Elijah watched as she opened the door and led him inside. The crowd was booing and yelling at a young man on the stage. He was dressed in a lime green suit and wore a matching hat that sported a huge feather as an accent. A chalkboard sign on a stand at the side of the stage read, *Funny Larry*, and beside it sat a fat, nervous looking older man in a black and white striped shirt and black pants. A pair of suspenders that looked like they could give way at any moment completed his outfit. He sat on a wobbly looking stool with a snare drum between his legs, and after every joke the young comedian told, the drummer would do a rim shot for emphasis.

Elijah followed the Asian woman to the side of the stage where she stopped and directed him to watch the show.

"I'm sorry I was late," Elijah said over the roar of the crowd. "It was the baby. He was upset and I couldn't just—"

"Shut up and watch," she interrupted him. "It's your fault he's up there."

A crash of breaking glass came from the stage. An unhappy customer had thrown a beer bottle at the comedian and missed.

"All right, all right, all right." The man in green held his hands up to the crowd in a futile attempt to calm them down. "How do you make a handkerchief dance?" He put a hand to his ear and leaned out toward the crowd like he expected an answer. When he got nothing but boos, he stepped back to the microphone to deliver the punch line. "You put a little boogie in it!"

The drummer did his rim shot, Ba Da Bum, and the comedian danced a little jig on the stage before addressing the audience again.

"What's the matter, ain't you got no sense of humor?"

It was obvious to anyone listening that the crowd was getting tired of this man and his jokes, but he continued on all the same.

"Okay, okay, okay. How about this? How do you tell the difference in a bull frog and a horny toad?" Again, the hand goes up to his ear. "The bull frog says, *ribbit, ribbit* and the horny toad says, *rub it, rub it*!"

Ba Da bum.

The Asian woman had hit her limit, and grumbling under her breath, stepped up on the stage with Elijah following close behind. She walked up to the comedian and shoved him away from the mic. The crowd continued to boo and shout. Another beer bottle flew through the air. With uncanny speed, the Asian woman stepped to the side, letting the bottle fly past her and strike the comedian in the groin. He doubled over on the stage and got his only laugh of the night.

"Yes, I know," the Asian woman said, trying to calm the rowdy audience. "Don't worry, he will never be back."

Ba da bum.

The Asian woman gave the drummer a dirty look, and he hastily gathered his drum and stool and disappeared backstage.

"And now without further ado," she continued. "Our featured entertainer." She motioned to Elijah, who stepped up to the middle of the stage where he was met by the old drummer carrying a tall chair for Elijah to sit on while he played. Elijah raised a hand in welcome to the crowd and began to play *Old Dan Tucker.* The crowd went wild.

Elijah finished his second set and made his way back to the dressing room behind the stage. He lit a cigarette and poured himself a taste of whiskey to steady his nerves. He was exhausted, and he was afraid of what the Asian woman was going to do to him when he tried to leave. He smoked slowly and had a second taste of whiskey. When he finished the cigarette, he pulled himself together and decided to face what was coming to him.

He stepped out into the main room, expecting the worst, but he found it empty. The crowd was gone, the lights were on, and no one was left except the bartender, who was quietly placing the chairs on the tables in preparation for mopping.

Elijah walked across the dance floor, the sound of his shoes on the hard wood bouncing around the empty room. The bartender saw him and gave him a simple nod that Elijah returned. He stepped outside into the cool night air; it was a relief after being in the smoke-filled club for so long. The parking lot was as empty as the bar and Elijah crossed it to where his truck was parked beneath a yellowed streetlight.

He placed the key in the ignition and the truck roared to life on the first try.

"Now you start!"

Elijah pulled out onto the highway and turned toward home. He rolled down the old truck's window and welcomed the cold air blowing in his face. He took a deep breath, letting it fill his lungs fully before blowing it out. The night was over and he had survived. He wondered how many other people felt relieved when they managed to survive a day at work. He figured there must be a few.

He turned off the highway onto the dirt road, going at a much slower speed than when he had last made that turn. It grew darker the farther away from town he drove, and the old truck's headlights were only able to light the road ahead a few feet in front of him. This was the first time he had driven this way in the dark, and the road took on an ominous feeling. No sound but the wind blowing in the window and the short visibility made Elijah feel trapped.

He looked in the rearview mirror attached to the driver's side of the truck, remembering that the other mirror was still sitting on the porch back at the house. Two glowing red eyes were floating in the bed of the truck. Elijah whipped around in his seat to look directly out the rear window. The bed was empty, the eyes a trick of the light. With a sigh of relief, he turned back to face the road just as something massive landed on the hood.

"*Aaaah!*" Elijah screamed and snatched at the wheel. He turned it first left, then right, and put his full weight on the brake pedal trying to stop.

The truck skidded in the loose gravel, and the passenger side wheels slid off the road and into a low drainage ditch. Elijah hit his head on the steering wheel with the sudden stop, opening a small cut there that leaked blood into his eye.

He pulled his handkerchief out of his back pocket and wiped his eye clean before applying pressure to the cut. His heart raced as he looked around the cab of the truck, then outside. The weak headlights were shining on a mound on the side of the road. The dust that had stirred up when he stopped kept him from getting a good look at what it was, possibly a deer or a bobcat.

He pushed open the truck door and pulled himself out and into a standing position. His head swam, and little red fireworks burst in his vision. He closed his eyes tight, and when he reopened them, the fireworks were gone and his head felt more stable. He reached back into the cab and picked up a big stove length of wood that he kept there for emergencies. If that was a deer or bobcat lying over there and it wasn't dead, he would have to the do merciful thing and end it.

Stepping around the front of the truck, he started toward whatever it was. As he drew closer, he saw that it was green. *Lime* green. Realization hit him like a load of bricks, and he dropped the stick and ran over to the body of the comedian.

The man's legs were at odd angles to his body, and Elijah could see the dust collecting in a puddle of blood beneath his head. Tears welled up in Elijah's eyes, and he slapped them away.

"Oh Lord, what have I done?"

He rolled the young man over, so he could see his face, or what was left of it. A knife with a gold handle was sticking out of the center of the man's chest, and to Elijah's horror, he saw that it had been run through a piece of paper before it had been used to stab the comedian. With trembling hands, Elijah grasped the knife's handle and pulled it from its resting place. He slid the note free and turned it so that he could read it in the truck's headlights. Written in the smooth-flowing hand that Elijah had come to recognize as Mr. Give's, the note read:

This is what happens when you are late.

Elijah sat back on the ground and crushed the note in his hands.

* * *

The sun was rising over Elijah's cottage as he pulled the truck to a stop. The once-beautiful cottage had lost its luster in Elijah's eyes over the last week. Marie's death, the warning from Apollyon, and now the death of the comedian had caused the cottage to look sad and rundown. It had stopped feeling like a home, and now it was more of a nightmare prison where he and Happy were sentenced to spend eternity.

He made his way to the back of the truck and lowered the tailgate. The comedian's body lay there with its blood soaking into the rust of the bed, then running down and out a crack in the metal to drip onto the rocks of the driveway.

Taking it by the feet, Elijah pulled the body out of the truck, allowing it to fall to the ground with a dead *thump*. He dragged it around to the side yard and placed it next to the disturbed earth where he had so recently buried Marie. After he went inside to check on Happy and feed him breakfast, he would come back out and go about the business of making a second grave in the yard.

* * *

That night, Elijah dreamed that Seraphina came to him carrying her Bible. She was dressed in white, and a golden halo encircled her head. She knelt beside him as he lay in a field of wildflowers and whispered in his ear. "Be sober, be vigilant. Because your adversary the devil, as a roaring lion, walketh about, seeking whom he may devour."

In his dream, he reached up to touch her, but she pulled away, and then wings, white as snow, lifted her above him. Hovering there, she looked deep into his eyes. "Submit yourselves therefore to God. Resist the devil, and he will flee from you."

Her wings spread, and she was lifted away from him and out of his sight. Even in a dream his heart was broken with her departure. He felt all the loss and sadness that he had carried for the last few months well up in him all at once, and he thought that he would die from the pain.

He tried to scream, but a finger touched his lips and he looked up to see Happy, now a grown man, standing over him.

"Thus saith the Lord of hosts. Turn ye now from your evil ways, and from your evil doings. But they did not hear, nor hearken unto me, saith the Lord."

Happy then turned his back on Elijah, and he began to change. His back bent forward and his hair thinned and grayed around the edges. His hands drew up into claws, and his fingers trembled. Happy turned back to face Elijah and he was older still, wrinkles extended from the sides of his eyes, and his teeth were yellowed with dark patches where they met his gums. As Elijah watched in horror, Happy's eyes clouded over with cataracts then turned a pure white.

"*NO!*" Elijah sat up and reached out for Happy. He tried to touch his son's gnarled hand, but Mr. Give was standing beside Happy and knocked his hand away. Elijah recoiled as a burning pain flared where Mr. Give had touched him.

"Who sinned, this man or his parents, that he was born blind? Doth not the son bear the iniquity of the father?"

Mr. Give's voice rang in Elijah's ears like thunder, making it hard for him to think. He was flooded with emotions, fear and sadness, confusion and anger. Mr. Give stepped over and stood straddle of him, then bent down and got eye to eye with Elijah. His breath smelled of death and decay, and Elijah could see the fires of Hell in his eyes.

"Behold, all souls are mine. As the soul of the father, so also the soul of the son is mine."

A blinding flash of light filled Elijah's eyes, and then Mr. Give and Happy were gone and Seraphina was back. This time she wore a black dress of mourning with a hood that covered her head and surrounded her face with tendrils of black lace. Long sleeves fell far past her hands, and she was barefoot. She circled Elijah, never looking at him, but instead, she lifted her face to heaven and raised her arms to the sky.

"He was a murderer from the beginning and has nothing to do with the truth, because there is no truth in him. When he lies, he speaks out of his own character, for he is a liar and the father of lies."

The ground underneath Elijah began to boil and turn black. Flames leapt out of the earth, surrounding him, and he began to fall down a fiery shaft. As he fell, he saw Seraphina continue to circle with her hands, and her head turned to the heavens. He tried to scream her name, but instead, he woke up drenched in sweat and his pillow soaked with tears.

* * *

Elijah sat at the table reading Seraphina's Bible while Happy played on the floor next to him. Elijah was so confused from what he had seen in his dream the night before. Was Mr. Give Satan, the real devil? Elijah always had pictured the devil as a little imp with red skin and a pointed tail. To be honest, he had never believed all those stories about the devil. He figured they were just nonsense that parents told their kids to get them to behave.

But Seraphina believed, and so did the minister and Mrs. Jones. He had been reading the Bible all morning, and he still didn't know how much of it he understood. One thing seemed certain, and that was that he and happy needed to get away. He closed the book and looked over at little Happy playing with his toes in the baby basket.

"I think we're in trouble, Happy."

A few minutes later, Elijah had packed all their important belongings in the old carpetbag and had placed Seraphina's Bible on top before securing it closed. Carrying the bag in one hand and Happy in the other, Elijah hurried from the house. He tossed the bag into the back of the old truck and placed Happy on the passenger's seat before running around and getting in behind the wheel. The old truck roared to life on the first try, and Elijah threw it into gear and pushed the pedal to the floor.

"I think this is for the best," he said as the little cottage they had called home grew smaller in the rearview mirror. "We gotta get some miles between us and Mr. Give. I've been readin' that book, and it says to turn away from evil and that is just what Mr. Give is. *Evil*."

The truck bounced off the dirt road onto the highway, leaving skid marks in its path.

"The book says the devil tempted Jesus three times, and every time Jesus turned him away. I don't think we can turn him away 'cause I signed that paper. But one thing we can do is run like hell."

Suddenly, Happy began to cry. He made horrible wheezing sounds with each breath.

"You okay there, buddy?" Elijah reached over and tried to comfort the baby, first stroking his head, then rocking the basket. But the more he tried, Happy cried harder, his cries interrupted with ragged gasps for breath.

Elijah pulled the truck over. He picked Happy up out of the basket, put him on his shoulder, and patted his back. He started to sing to Happy the first song that came to mind, *Amazing Grace*.

From out of the cloudless sky, a lightning bolt struck an old oak tree on the side of the road, splitting it in half and setting its leaves on fire.

Happy went limp in Elijah's arms.

"God help me he knows."

Still holding Happy in one arm, Elijah put the truck back in gear. The tires squealed in protest as he did a U-turn, whipping the truck back onto the dirt road.

"Come on baby, breathe! You gotta breathe!"

The truck bounced down the dirt road with Elijah trying to control it one-handed.

Elijah skidded to a stop outside the cottage. Instantly, Happy sucked in a deep breath and began to cry.

"Oh, thank God, thank God!" Elijah held the crying baby to him and kissed his head in relief. Happy took a shuddering breath and began to calm down as Elijah opened the door and slid out of the truck.

As he started toward the house, Mr. Give came out on the porch from inside. "Well, if it's not good old Elijah, or shall I just call you Pappy? Where you been boy?"

Elijah stopped in his tracks. *He knows.*

Panicking, Elijah said the first thing that came to mind. "Nowhere, sir. I just took Happy here for a ride." Elijah hoped Mr. Give didn't notice the quiver in his voice. "He sure does like to go ridin' in this truck you so kindly give us."

"Is that so?" Mr. Give stepped off the porch and casually walked up to Elijah and Happy. A big smile spread across his face as he looked down at the baby. That smile went away when he turned his attention to Elijah.

"You wouldn't be lying to me now would you, Elijah? You know the rule, you never lie to me."

Mr. Give reached out toward Happy and touched his forehead. The baby immediately turned ashen and went limp in Elijah's arms.

"I'm sorry, Mr. Give, I'm sorry!" Elijah, no longer caring if Mr. Give heard weakness in his voice, began to beg. "I'll never lie to you again, I *swear*! Please bring him back, please!"

"Why should I?" Mr. Give pivoted around and strolled back toward the porch. "Maybe letting little Happy die would finally teach you a lesson." Mr. Give took down the dipper that hung above the rain barrel and got a drink of water. Happy's cold body lay limp in Elijah's arms as he sank to his knees in front of the old truck. Mr. Give smacked his lips and took his time hanging the dipper back in place before turning back to Elijah.

"I thought sure you would get the message when I took your woman away, but you didn't, did you?" Mr. Give stooped in front of Elijah, reached down and grabbed him by the ear like an angry mother would a disobedient child. "I own you, and I don't PLAY!"

Mr. Give released Elijah's ear, and he dropped forward, sheltering the unmoving baby with his body, his forehead landing on Mr. Give's boot.

"Yes, sir, yes, sir," Elijah sobbed.

Mr. Give jerked his foot out from under Elijah, causing him to fall face first in the dirt which immediately turned to mud when mixed with his tears.

"I'm sorry! Just bring him back. Kill me if you want to, but let my baby live!"

Mr. Give lowered himself to one knee in front of Elijah. Feeling his eyes on him, Elijah raised his dirty face to look up at him.

"I'm not gonna kill you, there's so many other things I could do to you that's worse than dying. But the truth is, I need you to play guitar till someone else comes along."

Mr. Give touched Happy's forehead, and the baby's still body began to move as life poured back into it. A strangled cry sounded as air filled Happy's lungs.

Elijah snatched the baby up in his arms. His tears mixed with Happy's as he pulled him to his chest and rocked him.

Mr. Give smiled and walked past Elijah into the hazy afternoon.

CHAPTER 9

Elijah needed answers, and since that day in the front yard when Mr. Give had shown his true self, Elijah had been searching. He knew that the answers he needed were somewhere in Seraphina's Bible, and today as he had done every day for the last six years, Elijah sat at the table reading. He only stopped his search long enough to play his weekly set at Mr. Give's club and to sleep a few precious hours each night. He had stopped carrying the Bible with him on his weekly trip into town, deciding it best to let Apollyon, the Asian woman, and Mr. Give himself believe that he had learned his lesson.

Today, as with many days in the past six years, he was frustrated by what he read. At times it seemed to him that the book contradicted itself, seeming to talk in circles. Other times, he got encouragement from its words, and they gave him strength to continue searching its pages. He wished that the minister was nearby so he could ask him questions, sure that someone more educated could help him understand it better.

He ran his hand over his once-dark black hair now turned mostly gray from worry. He held the Bible close to him in order to read the small print. Without Marie to keep up the house it had fallen into disarray. Pots and pans were stacked on the stove, clothes were piled on the couch, and dust and dirt covered the floor. It had been months since it was last swept. Everything inside the house was dull and covered in a layer of filth. Cobwebs, turned black from the lamp soot, hung in every corner.

Happy, now an active six-year-old, came in from playing outside, but Elijah didn't notice as he was engrossed in reading the Bible.

"What'cha doing, Pappy?"

"What does it look like I'm doing?" Elijah snapped at him not wanting to be interrupted. "I'm trying to figure out how to get us out of this mess we're in and I'm sure the answer is somewhere here in the Good Book."

"Praise Jesus!" Happy put one hand on his heart and raised the other toward the ceiling.

Elijah looked over at the boy, and a warm smile erased some of the age from his face. Happy stepped over to him and Elijah lifted him into his lap.

"Just look at you." He brushed some dirt off the boy's knees. "You're an absolute mess."

Happy reached for the Bible and roughly shuffled through its pages, pretending to read. Elijah placed his hand over the boy's and stopped him before he could cause any damage.

"What's so special about this old book, anyway?" Happy asked, as Elijah pushed it farther away from him across the table.

"You remember how I told you about your momma passin' when you was born? Well one of the last things she did was to hold tight to this very Bible. I think it comforted her. When I put her in the ground and shoveled the dirt over her, I made her a promise to keep you safe, and I'm afraid that I have done just the opposite of that."

Happy turned and looked at him, his eyes big with concern, then snuggled against his chest. Elijah placed an arm around him and began to rock him gently as he had done when the boy was an infant.

"We ain't safe here and I guess we never have been. I keep readin' this one part of this book from a section called Exodus, and it says that you are not to allow a witch to live. I been thinkin' on that, and I would say that the boss is about as close to a witch as I have ever seen, but for the life of me, it don't say nowhere in there how to kill one."

Happy started to squirm, so Elijah sat him down on the floor to play and went back to his reading. He continued to read, obsessed with finding an answer to his questions.

The day passed, and Elijah never stopped reading. He read while making dinner for Happy and while putting him to bed. He took the book out to the front porch and sat in his rocking chair, reading until the setting sun became too dim for him to see the print. Back at the table, he read by lamplight, pouring over the words and trying to get them all to make sense.

A knock on the door caused Elijah to jump in surprise. With his heart racing from the unexpected interruption and with the Bible in hand, he went to the door and opened it.

Apollyon stood there, his massive frame filling the doorway. Before Elijah could say a word, he snatched the Bible out of his hands and threw it across the room. Elijah turned, following the path of the book, until he saw it in Mr. Give's hands.

Apollyon pushed Elijah back into the room. The sheer force of Apollyon's shove carried him across the floor until he landed face down in front of Mr. Give. Elijah looked up into his face and again saw the fires of hell burning in his eyes. Apollyon grabbed him by the back of the shirt, hauled him to his feet, and held him there with his toes barely touching the dirty floor of the cottage.

"What's the matter, Elijah?" Mr. Give asked, as he began slowly walking the perimeter of the room. Apollyon turned Elijah in time with Mr. Give and kept him facing him. "A home, money, a nice truck, and all the food you could eat not good enough for you?"

Mr. Give ruffled the pages of the Bible then slammed it shut and held it out, pointing it at Elijah like an old-time preacher making a point.

"Do you think *God* is gonna save you? What has he done for you so far except to kill your wife and leave you stuck with a baby? Do you think *God* is just going to swoop in here and carry you off to a better place? Well, I for one would love to see that."

Mr. Give raised the Bible to the sky, then lifted his face to the ceiling. "God, oh God!" he called out. "You have a man here needs your help."

His eyes grew big and he turned one ear upwards, listening, waiting as if expecting something to happen. "Maybe he's asleep," he whispered to Elijah.

Mr. Give stepped back and this time he raised both hands in the air, arched his back and shouted at the top of his voice. "Hello God! Are you up there?"

He paused again, listening with his arms outstretched, then when nothing happened, he let his arms drop and his hands slap against his thighs as if disappointed. He stood there silently for a few seconds, then to Elijah's surprise, he performed a perfect pirouette that left him standing with his legs crossed at the ankles and his head bowed.

Slowly, he lifted his head and looked straight at Elijah. A knowing smile took over his face exposing his teeth and lifting the corners of his eyes. The pure evil pouring from this man, this *devil*, made Elijah try to look away, but Apollyon placed his huge hand on top of Elijah's head and guided it back to face Mr. Give.

"Looks like you are shit out of luck," Mr. Give said. He clapped his hands in excitement and let out a laugh like an insane circus clown.

Apollyon spun Elijah around and tossed him into a chair, then stepped behind him and placed a hand on each side of his head. The demon's grip was like a vice, and Elijah felt like his eyes were being forced out of their sockets.

Mr. Give tossed the Bible on the table in front of Elijah before stepping over to where Happy was still asleep on the couch. He looked down and reached his hand in the direction of the sleeping child's head. Elijah screamed and tried to get up but was held in place by Apollyon's strong grip.

Just as Mr. Give's finger was about to touch Happy's forehead, he stopped and looked back at Elijah. "Nope, not this time, I have plans for this little one."

Mr. Give pivoted on his heal and scanned the room until he saw the guitar leaning against the bedpost. He picked it up and looked lovingly at it before placing it back where it was.

Chuckling, he walked over to the stove and lit the burner. He danced his hand through the open flame, then reached down and pulled a piece of kindling out of the wood box. He held up the stick and examined it closely like a jeweler would examine a diamond bracelet or an expensive watch. With a nod of approval, he placed the smaller end of the wood into the fire. Immediately, the room filled with the smell of burning wood, a smell that at any other time Elijah would have enjoyed. But today, with Apollyon's hands putting constant pressure on the sides of his face, Elijah could only think of the pounding in his head and the fear coursing through him.

Mr. Give walked back to the table, picked up the Bible, and ruffled through the pages. "You're not going to have much use for this from now on. Apollyon told you to burn it, but you just wouldn't listen, wouldn't do as you were told. Oh no, I gave you a perfectly good woman to take your mind off it, and you ended up getting her killed rather than ridding yourself of this cursed thing."

Mr. Give took the Bible over to the stove and dangled it by one cover over the flame there. "Maybe *I'll* burn it for you."

Elijah tried to get up, tried to break free of Apollyon's grip but managed only to let out a choked cry that was part "no" and part "please."

Just as the pages began to smoke, Mr. Give pulled the Bible away from the flame and blew on the smoldering paper. The embers there turned red then went out.

"But really, what good would that do? If I burn this one, you'll just find a way to get another one."

He tossed the Bible back on the table in front of Elijah. Mr. Give turned back to the stove and lifted the burning stick from the flames. He took the two steps that carried him over to the table slowly, like a bride walking down the aisle. He stopped next to Elijah and let the glowing tip of the stick lightly trace a line across Elijah's forehead. The pain was immense and immediate. Elijah tried again to move his head away, but Apollyon's grip only tightened, causing him to see ripples in his vision.

Just as he thought he was going to pass out, the demon let go of him. Elijah took in a deep breath, filling his lungs with oxygen, then flung himself away from the table. Apollyon was too quick and grabbed him by the collar of his shirt and dragged him back to the chair. This time he put Elijah in a headlock. One of the demon's massive arms encircled his neck, cutting off his air and forcing his mouth closed. Elijah tried to struggle. He hit at the massive figure's arms and legs with his fists, but it made no difference. He was where Apollyon wanted him and that was where he was going to stay.

"Hmmm, let me think," Mr. Give continued. "What can I do to make sure that this is the last time you read that book?"

Mr. Give circled the table while waving the burning stick around like a demonic band leader conducting an orchestra of the dead, humming to himself the whole time. When he returned to the stove, he placed the stick back in the flame, then turned to face Elijah and Apollyon.

"Ah yes, I think I know exactly what is needed to remedy this nasty situation." Mr. Give placed two fingers in his mouth and blew. The whistle that resulted was so loud that Elijah's ears began to ring.

"Really boss?" Apollyon said. His voice sounded weak— almost as if he were afraid. "That seems pretty drastic."

"Oh, I'm sure," Mr. Give answered. "I'm *very* sure."

The unmistakable clop clop clop of a horse's hooves on gravel echoed off the surrounding hills. It came to a stop outside the cabin. A second later, someone or *something* walked across the porch and stopped outside the closed front door.

Mr. Give and Apollyon stood in silence, watching as if they expected the door to be blown off its hinges at any second. Elijah's already racing heart began to beat even faster. If there had been any sound in the room, he wouldn't have been able to hear it over the blood rushing through his ears. Apollyon's body tensed, and his grip on Elijah tightened. A low grumbling noise began deep in the demon's chest and vibrated against the back of Elijah's head.

With the slightest little click, the door latch disengaged and the door slowly swung open. Apollyon jumped at the sound as Mr. Give nodded in anticipation.

The doorknob struck the wall behind it with a soft thud, and again the room fell silent. Outside, the full moon was bright, and its pale blue light cast a shadow on the open door.

A cowboy stepped into the room. Each heavy step was accompanied by the jingle of spurs. He had to bend over to fit through the door. Once inside, he straightened up to his full height and Elijah could see the horror that he truly was.

His chaps, hat, and canvas shirt were stained brown from blood, and a scar ran down his forehead across to his right eye. There, the eyelid was split and curled back like a curtain revealing a white glob of dead tissue. The scar continued down his face till it came to his upper lip which had also been split open exposing the rotten black gums and decay-ridden teeth that lay beneath.

The cowboy walked across the room until he was face to face with Mr. Give.

"So nice of you to join us," Mr. Give said politely and moved to the side.

The cowboy stepped over to the stove. As he passed Elijah and Apollyon, his stench flooded over them. Despite the grip Apollyon had on him, Elijah gagged and felt the contents of his stomach start to come up.

"Oh no you don't," Apollyon whispered in his ear. "If I can't puke, I sure as hell ain't gonna let you." With that, his grip tightened closing off Elijah's esophagus and his windpipe at the same time.

Elijah's head started to swim from lack of oxygen and he prayed that he would pass out, but just before that happened, Apollyon's grip lessened and Elijah was able to draw a breath.

The cowboy picked up the burning stick from the stove and stepped over to the table. He bent down low and looked into Elijah's eyes. When Elijah tried to close them, Apollyon's other massive hand landed on the top of his head and two meaty fingers pulled back the delicate skin of his eyelids. The cowboy's breath stank of rot and disease as he stood there, eye to eye with Elijah.

"What are you waiting for?" Mr. Give said, more a state-ment than a question.

The cowboy looked at Mr. Give, then turned back to Eli-jah. Moving so fast that his hand and the glowing stick it held appeared to blur, the cowboy plunged the burning stick into Elijah's right eye.

Pain engulfed Elijah, it passed through him like a bullet through the barrel of a gun, causing his stomach to empty its contents and his muscles to convulse. Elijah's scream echoed through the cabin as the cowboy removed the stick and placed it again in the flame leaping out of the stove's fire box.

Elijah writhed in Apollyon's grasp, twisting and turning. His body only wanting to be away from the source of the pain. Throughout it all, Apollyon's grip never faltered, even as the blood and other liquids that trickled out of Elijah's mouth and ruined eye socket flowed down over the demon's arm.

"You know, Elijah," Mr. Give said, leaning in and taking the cowboy's place. "I told you before that I own you. When you signed that piece of paper years ago, you sold your immortal soul to me. But I guess you figured that part out. How's that working out for you?"

Elijah weakly shook his head, as much as he could shake it in Apollyon's grip.

"Don't beg, it's not very becoming. Believe it or not Elijah, I like you, and it pains me to have to treat you like this. But just like any spoiled child, you must be taught a lesson. Spare the rod and spoil the child, right? But because I like you, I'm going to do you a favor. Once we are done with you tonight, I'll see to it that Happy doesn't remember a thing about our life together. You two will just live in this little house, and you'll raise Happy to be a big strong boy. And, you will teach him to play that guitar."

Mr. Give stepped back over to Elijah's side.

"Now you make sure you teach him good, cause one day I might just need another black boy to play a little guitar for me."

The cowboy stepped back in front of Elijah and brought the flaming stick up to his remaining eye and held it there.

"And always remember," Mr. Give continued. "If you say one thing to that little boy about what occurred here tonight, I will know. Then I'll just have to come back and see to it that he suffers a fate worse than yours. Do you understand what I'm saying?"

A tear ran from Elijah's remaining eye, and he nodded.

"That's good, that's real good."

Mr. Give winked at the cowboy who then finished the job he had been called to do, fully blinding Elijah. This time Apollyon let go of him as his screams filled the night air.

PART 2

HAPPY

CHAPTER 10

1950

As the morning sun was just peeking over the horizon, turning the gray night landscape into a vibrant green, Happy Parker drove his father's old truck down a narrow two-lane road toward the little town of Plainesville, Mississippi.

Happy was tired. Tired of this beat up old truck, tired of his job hauling garbage, tired of taking care of his old man, and tired of living like the dirt-poor black man that he was. He wanted more, and he wanted out.

He turned the truck off the highway and onto the deserted main street of Plainesville. Like most small southern towns, Plainesville's main street was lined with little shops all painted in bright colors, except for the important buildings like the bank and mayor's office which had stone walls and brass plaques by their doors.

Mr. Macon, the tailor, was watering the plants that grew in a box below his display window. Across the street, Mrs. Mc-Clure was putting clothes on a mannequin in the window of her dress shop. Happy paid them no mind. Long ago, he had lost interest in the little town and what went on there. He would be glad for the day to come when he could leave Plainesville in a cloud of dust and watch it disappear in his rearview mirror.

At the town's only intersection, Happy turned right then right again into an alley that ran behind the main street stores. He pulled to a stop outside of a red wooden door with the word *Kitchen* painted on it in peeling white paint. The City Café had served the fine people of Plainesville for over twenty-five years, but Happy had never eaten there. He was not the kind of people they served. But he *was* the kind of people they allowed to pick up and haul off their garbage every Tuesday, Thursday, and Saturday morning.

Three large metal barrels sat beside the café's back door, and Happy went about the business of transferring their contents into one of the large, fifty-gallon drums strapped into the bed of the pick-up. As he emptied the second barrel, the kitchen door opened and Mr. Sample, the café's owner and only cook, came strolling out and watched as Happy placed the barrel back where he had found it. The fat man lit a match off the sole of his shoe and touched it to the tip of a cigarette he had pulled from behind his ear.

"Morning, Hap. Looks like it's gon' be another hot one."

"Yes, sir, it sure does."

Happy never stopped emptying the garbage cans and never made eye contact with the cook. Just as Mr. Sample never took his eyes off Happy and never made a move to help. Happy emptied the last can and started to get back into the truck. He knew the game and he played it, or else he wouldn't get paid.

Mr. Sample stepped up to the passenger's side window. It was down as it had been for the last four years. It wasn't so bad in the summer months, but when the weather turned cold, Happy had to carry an old blanket with him on his rounds to try and stay warm.

"You tell your pappy hello for me, ya hear."

"Yes, sir, I'll do that," Happy said as he started the truck and put it in gear.

"Hold on there a minute." The cook slapped a meaty hand on the door for emphasis, then turned and went back inside.

Happy did as he was told even though it was making him late to his other stops.

Mr. Sample returned with something wrapped in a greasy piece of butcher's paper and handed it through the window to Happy. "Had a ham bone left over from yesterday's dinner. Take it home with you and make your daddy some soup."

Happy took the bundle and placed it on the seat.

"You know I used to watch your daddy play guitar at an old shack out on the highway when I was younger." The man leaned his elbow on the open window as he talked. "He could really tear that thing up. Shame that all had to come to an end, seeing how he is and everything. What happened to your daddy anyway?"

"I don't know. I mean, Pappy's all right, something just happened to him back before I can remember, really messed him up. He still plays a little but it's mostly Jesus music nowadays." Happy left it at that, then motioned to the bundle on the seat. "Thank you for the ham bone, and I'm sure Pappy will say thank you, too."

The cook stepped back from the truck and watched as Happy pulled away.

* * *

Happy pulled to a stop outside Elijah's cottage. The once quaint house was no longer quaint, now it appeared more of a relic of the past that had been forgotten and ignored. It's once white paint and blue shutters had faded and peeled away, leaving it looking shabby and uncared for. Hot summer sun and wet winters had caused the wooden shingles to curl and break away only to be replaced with old pieces of tin and sheet metal. The front porch where Happy had spent so many warm summer evenings listening to his father play guitar now drooped to one side.

Elijah sat on the porch in an ancient rocking chair humming to himself. As the truck pulled off the road and came to a stop, he turned to face it, then sat still as a statue. His old, wrinkled hands grasped the arms of the rocker ready, to push him up into a standing position at the slightest sound of trouble.

Happy looked out the truck window at his father, at the gray hair and the hunched back that made him resemble an eighty-year-old man not a man of fifty. Then there were the scars, the long white burn marks that stretched out from each eye and wrapped around to his temples. The scars, combined with the ashy grey puckered skin of his eyelids, made it look like his father was wearing a mask. Happy always thought of it as a mask of pain. Growing up, he had asked his father about the scars and his blind eyes, but all the man would do was just shake his head. Now, with him in the condition he was in, Happy guessed that the secret would go with him to his grave.

Happy opened the truck door causing it to squeak, and Elijah immediately let his guard down, having recognized the sound.

An old rain barrel sat against the corner of the porch with a dipper hanging on a nail above it. Happy filled the dipper with water and poured it over his head before taking another dipperful and drinking it. The water was warm and tasted like old wood, but with no running water in the house, he had become used to it.

His father was humming and rocking again. Happy used to love the sound of his voice, but now it only served to remind him how little of his father remained in that body. At times he wished that he would just die and get it over with, but when those thoughts came, so did the feeling of emptiness and pain that he knew would only be intensified when he had to put the old man in a grave. As far gone as his father was, Happy still loved him, he only wondered if he was still able to feel the same for him.

"You all right old man?" Happy spoke gently. His father didn't answer, he seldom did anymore. He just rocked and hummed, his blind eyes looking up to heaven.

"Pappy, it's Hap. I'm home."

The old man's lips started moving, and a whisper of a voice reached Happy's ears. The longer he talked, the stronger his voice became, and Happy could start to make out what he was saying.

"See ye not all these things? Verily I say unto you, there shall not be left here one stone upon another, that shall not be thrown down."

Happy stepped up on the porch and crossed over to his father. He knelt and looked at his weathered face, looking for any indication of sanity, any sign that would tell him that the father he loved was still in there.

"And as he sat upon the Mount of Olives, the disciples came unto him privately, saying, tell us, when shall these things be? And what shall be the sign of thy coming, and of the end of the world?"

Happy gently touched his father's knee, he could feel the bones there hiding beneath the thin covering of skin and cotton. His father had grown thin—he hardly ever ate. His days and nights were spent just sitting and staring out into his dark world.

He turned his face toward Happy as if in conversation. "And Jesus answered and said unto them, take heed that no man deceives you. For many shall come in my name, saying, I am Christ and shall deceive many."

Happy walked back to the truck leaving the man with his nonsense. He started the truck, drowning out the verses, put it into gear, and drove around the back of house.

Two years before, Happy had found a pregnant sow wandering down the side of the road and had brought it home. He parked the truck beside a pig pen that he had made for her there. His drove had grown to seven pigs now. The original that he called Momma, three males, and three females. He had traded a boar from Momma's first litter for one from the farm across town, ensuring that future litters would be healthy. Since then, he had brought in two females from another farm, and they were both expecting their first litter later in the season.

Happy Parker, Pig Farmer, he thought to himself.

He rolled the full barrel of cafe garbage to the end of the truck bed then lifted it off. It was heavy and smelled horrible, but his pigs liked it, and it was free feed for them. He kept an old metal bucket beside the pen's fence and used it to move the garbage from the barrel into a wooden trough he had buried in the ground, just inside the fence. At the sound of slop hitting the trough, the pigs came running, bumping into each other and squealing. This little pork parade always made

Happy laugh, and as the pigs put their heads snout deep into their dinner, he reached down and scratched Momma behind the ears.

"Fatten up, boys," he told them. "Enjoy it while you can 'cause before you know it, you're gonna be lunch."

He reached down and scratched another pig behind its ears then returned the barrel to the truck. He had been talking to the town butcher about selling him some of his pigs, but so far, the money the butcher was offering would barely cover the cost of driving the pigs into town. The butcher seemed to think that black equaled stupid.

Happy was well aware that he would never be paid the same as a white farmer for his pigs, but he refused to be robbed blind. If he had to, he would slaughter the pigs himself and peddle the meat out of the back of the truck. Folks wouldn't welcome him at their front doors, but a good deal on pork that came to the back of the house was hard to turn down.

He picked up the cook's package from the seat of the truck and walked around to the front porch where his father was still rocking and humming.

"Come on Pappy, let's go make some dinner."

He took the old man by the arm and helped him get up from the rocking chair.

The inside of the cottage had not fared any better than the outside. The furnishings were sparce; when something would break Happy would use it for firewood and it never got replaced. Another rocking chair, a table with a book under one leg, and two wooden chairs were about all that was left. The old bed remained in one corner, its mattress sagging from years of wear. Happy had replaced the couch with an army cot that he used for a bed. His father's guitar leaned against the wall, its once reflective finish now dull and scratched. Happy led him to a chair at the table, then lit a fire in the old stove.

"The cook at the cafe gave us a ham bone. Ain't much on it, but if I boil it long enough, we might get a little soup out of it."

"Therefore, I say unto you, take no thought for your life, what ye shall eat, or what ye shall drink, nor yet for your body, what ye shall put on." His father spoke to the room as if addressing a congregation. "Is not the life more than meat, and the body than raiment? Behold the fowls of the air, for they sow not, neither do they reap, nor gather into barns, yet your heavenly Father feedeth them. Are ye not much better than they?"

Happy placed a pot of water on the stove to boil, then handed his father the old guitar. The old man immediately stopped speaking and started to play. As he played, he began to rock his body in the chair to the rhythm of the song.

Happy had seen this before, a trance-like state that would only end when Happy took the guitar away and placed his father's hands on the soup bowl and spoon. Happy watched him for a few seconds, wondering just what was going through the old man's head. Did he even know that he was playing, or was it all just muscle memory? Was his father aware of the passage of time, that his son was a man now and needed to feel like he had a purpose beyond this shack? He wanted so bad to leave but the longer he watched his father the more he understood that as long as the man was living that would never happen.

* * *

Happy and the old man sat at the table with the remnants of their small meal in front of them.

His father's pouch of fixins was sitting next to his plate, so Happy opened it up and rolled him a cigarette. The old man struck a match off the tabletop, lit the cigarette and exhaled a thick cloud of smoke.

Happy picked up the guitar and began to pick out a song. He stretched his hand to make a C chord then an F and a G. His father's playing was in a whole other league and that knowledge frustrated him. Happy leaned the guitar against the table and started to clear away the dirty plates. After a bit his father picked up the guitar and began to play again, his hands traveling gracefully across the strings. A slow melodic tune filled the cottage.

Happy stopped washing dishes to listen. "That's real pretty, Pappy."

"Make a joyful noise unto the Lord, all ye lands. Serve the Lord with gladness. Come before his presence with singing."

"That's all real good when you can play like you do, but I just ain't got it."

Happy turned to face the old man, amazed at how effort-less his playing was.

"If I had half of what you got old man, I'd take that old guitar and get out of here. I'm sick of hauling trash and eating scraps from them white folks. I'd have me a nice car, a pretty girl, and a real bed to sleep in. I'd strike a match to this old pile of sticks and say good-bye!"

His father stopped playing and set the guitar aside. He started to stand, reaching out to Happy for help. Happy stepped up to him and helped him get to his feet. He reached up and touched Happy's face, his fingers replacing his blind eyes as he felt for Happy's expression, then he took his hands away. They stood there facing each other for a moment then his father reached out and took both of Happy's hands in his.

"Know ye that the Lord he is God. It is he that hath made us, and not we ourselves. We are his people, and the sheep of his pasture."

Happy let his father's hands go and turned back to the dirty dishes.

"Yeah, then why do I feel more like one of his pigs than one of his sheep?"

His father just stood there, not moving. Even with his back to him, Happy could tell what was going on. These spells were becoming more common, especially at night.

"I wish I knew what's going on inside your head," he said as he turned and tossed the dish towel on the table. "It'd be nice to have a real talk with you sometime. Come on, it's time for bed."

Happy took him by the arm and lead him over to the bed. He unbuttoned his father's shirt, hating how threadbare it had become, then helped him out of his trousers. His father laid down on the sagging mattress and immediately fell asleep.

Happy stood over him watching the rhythmic rise and fall of his chest. He missed his father; he missed their long talks and how he showed him how to make chords on the guitar. He longed for his father's wisdom and guidance. He would have given anything to her him say, I love you, then for him to reach out and run his hand over Happy's hair like he had done so many times when he was growing up.

Happy picked up the old oil lamp, carried it out on the porch and set it on the flimsy box that served as a table. He stepped out in the yard and looked up at the stars. He thought again of going away, of leaving all this rubble behind him, and a tear ran down his cheek. He brushed it away, then picked up the lamp and went back inside.

* * *

Every Tuesday, Thursday and Saturday Happy was up before the sun to haul garbage, and every Tuesday, Thursday and Saturday he hated every minute of it. Each day, hauling garbage was the same, starting with Mr. Sample's café. Then it was off to the town butcher to pick up his meat scraps and finally, the Fancy Fork Diner outside of town.

"Ain't this the life?" he asked the empty cab of the truck as he turned off Main Street. He pulled to a stop outside the café's kitchen door, and before he could empty the first bucket, Mr. Sample came outside for his morning smoke break.

"How many stops you make now, Hap?" he asked as Happy dumped the first bucket of garbage into one of his barrels.

"Just you, the butcher, and the diner out on 74," Happy replied. He wiped his hands on the leg of his pants, trying to get the some of the slick slop water off them before picking up the next bucket. "Things is getting slow around here."

"Tell me about it. Somedays I don't think anybody would care if I didn't open up."

"Yes, sir, I understand."

Happy dumped the second bucket, then went back for the third. To his surprise the third bucket was empty. Maybe Mr. Sample was telling the truth after all about things being slow.

"There's a new supper club opened up out on Golden Road," he told Happy. "I went out there last night after I closed up, and they're doing big business. I hear tell the parking lot's full every night. Might be worth checking out to see if they could use you."

"Thank you, sir." Happy took off his hat and held it in front of him when he spoke to Mr. Sample. It was an expected sign of respect, whether it was honestly felt or not. "I'll go by there on the way home."

"You do that..."

Happy cast his biggest fake smile and dipped his head to the cook again before turning back to the truck.

"Oh, and Hap, bring your Pappy around one night at closing, and I'll feed y'all dinner. Just come around here to the back door."

Happy started to say something about what he could do with his back door then decided better of it.

"Yes, sir," he said, instead. "I'm sure he'd like that."

* * *

Golden Road intersected with the main highway about ten miles outside of the Plainesville city limits. Happy had never had a reason to come out this way, so he watched for a sign, finally seeing one that read State Route 13/Golden Road.

The old truck's transmission made a grinding noise as Happy wrestled it into a lower gear and made the turn. The gravel was loose and he had to watch his speed to keep from fishtailing. The last thing he needed was to slide into one of the drainage ditches that separated the road from the fields of corn and tobacco that were passing by him on either side.

Dark clouds started to form on the horizon, and a wind from the south stirred up dust, giving birth to little tornados of dirt that danced in front of the truck before spinning out and breaking apart.

The road took a hairpin curve, and Happy had to slow the truck to a crawl to safely make it around. In the distance he saw a large structure silhouetted on top of a nearby hill. As he drew closer, he saw it was a low wooden building with a tall front facade designed to look like an old-west dance hall. Above the front doors was a large hand painted sign that read, *Mammon's Mountain*. The once bright red lettering had faded to a dark rust color outlined in gray. Happy assumed that it must have been black many years before.

He stopped in the parking lot and gave the building the once over. It seemed odd that he had never heard of it before; from the look of the place it had been here longer than he had been alive. The parking lot was empty and a heavy chain with a padlock was strung between the thick wooden handles of the front doors. The place looked deserted, but it was still early.

He had about decided to go home and come back later, but he thought he should check around the back for a kitchen entrance first. Could be the cook was there getting ready for the dinner crowd, so Happy dropped the truck in gear and pulled around to the rear of the building. The back wall was empty except for one unmarked door. Happy drove the truck up close to the building and stopped. From where he sat, it appeared that the door was not only unlocked but it was standing slightly open.

When he stepped out of the truck, the sun was directly overhead, but the storm clouds he had seen earlier were still slowly rolling in. As Happy took out his handkerchief to wipe the sweat off his forehead, a bolt of lightning flashed off to the west, followed a few seconds later by a deep rumble of thunder. That was when he first heard the music.

The sound of a guitar filled the air as if it had been created by the lightning and had ridden in on the thunder. It came from far away, traveling from somewhere deep inside the club.

He stepped up, put his ear to the crack in the door and listened. The music was haunting and beautiful.

Happy knocked on the door, not sure what to expect. The music continued, but no one answered. So, he knocked again louder. No response. He tried a third time. Still no answer, but the door swung open enough for him to look inside.

All he could see through the crack in the door was a narrow hallway stretching the entire distance of the building to his left and right. With what little light seeped in, he could make out an old mop and bucket across the hall from him, but that was about it. The music seemed to be coming from somewhere off to his left.

What are you waiting for? he thought to himself. *The door's open, just go on in and ask the question you came to ask.*

Still, he hesitated. A cold sweat ran down his back despite the hot midday sun.

The haunting melody continued and got in his head. He was finding it hard to think, to concentrate. He moved back a few steps. Creating some distance between himself and the door seemed to clear his head a bit.

The first few drops of rain struck the dry ground around him with a quiet patter almost like the sound of a drum. He wasn't sure, but he thought the tempo of music from inside changed to match that of the falling rain. But that was ridiculous. No one was capable of that, and besides, the person inside had no way of knowing that it was raining much less how fast the drops were falling. Thunder rumbled directly over his head, and the rain started to fall more steadily.

Happy turned to get back in the truck, then stopped.

"This is stupid," he said to the empty parking lot. "I'm a grown man, what have I got to be scared of?"

He turned back toward the door and took a step in that direction, then stopped, again listening to the music. It seemed very familiar like he had heard it in a dream or some-time back in his childhood. It captivated him, and even though he was standing in the rain getting soaked, all he wanted to do was listen.

Lightning streaked across the sky and a crack of thunder followed so loud that Happy ducked and covered his head with his hands. He looked up at the angry sky in time to see another lightning bolt form. This one struck a tree on the edge of the parking lot, engulfing it in flame. The accompany-ing thunder was so intense that it physically moved Happy toward the building. Without any further thought, he opened the door and stepped inside.

It was dark in the hallway, and before he could do any-thing about it, the outside door closed. He fumbled around in the darkness looking for the knob so he could reopen the door and let a little light in, but there wasn't one. He ran his hands along the wall both high and low, not only could he not find the doorknob, he couldn't find the door. All he felt was a cold block wall.

I must have come farther in than I thought I did. Doors don't just disappear, he thought to himself.

Inside the hall, the music was louder. It seemed to be com-ing from everywhere and nowhere at the same time. Happy turned his head one way then the other, straining his ears and trying to figure out what direction it was coming from. He reached out and felt for the wall. When he touched it, it was damp, cold, and slimy under his fingertips.

Happy inched his way along using the wall as a guide, go-ing in what he hoped was the direction from which the music was coming. As he walked, the music became more rhythmic, matching the speed of his steps. When he slowed down, the music would slow down, and when he stopped, the music stopped. He tested it by taking two quick steps, then stopping, then doing it again. the music followed suit producing staccato notes. When he resumed walking, the music became very melodic.

The hallway seemed to go on forever. The building wasn't that big and Happy felt like he should have come to a corner before now. He stopped to try and gather his thoughts. The music stopped as well. In the newfound silence he heard water dripping from somewhere behind him. Each drip echoing through the darkness, followed by another drip, then another. After a moment, those stopped as well. The silence was deafening, and he could feel the emptiness beginning to surround him.

It was then that he noticed a word painted on the wall. He leaned in close, thinking that his mind must have been playing tricks on him, but no, he could just barely make out the letters S...T...A... If he could see them, then there had to be a little light coming from somewhere. He took another couple of steps, causing the music to begin again, and there it was. A crack of dim light coming under what appeared to be a curtain.

Happy reached out for the curtain, and when he touched it, the music stopped. He dropped his hand and stood perfectly still, listening.

"You're in here now, boy," came a voice from the other side of the curtain. "There's no turning back, so step on in here and let me take a look at you."

Happy hesitated, then turned and took a step back in the way he came. From the next room, an angry discordant blast of sound blared out, and Happy jumped.

"You don't want to go that way, boy. No telling what's waiting for you back there in the dark."

A scraping noise began from somewhere in the darkness, a sound like something large with sharp claws was scurrying across the floor. It got louder the closer it came to Happy. He panicked and did the only thing he could. He turned back to the curtain and opened it enough to step through.

The room he entered was large and dimly lit. Shadows hung across it, thrown from a few dirty windows near the ceiling. As his eyes slowly adjusted, he could see that the room was filled with tables. Their chairs were stacked upside down on them as if someone had recently been cleaning the floors. At the opposite end of the room was a dark stage where the shadows all seemed to end.

With a loud pop and crack, stage lights came on and revealed a man sitting there in a straight-back chair, holding a guitar. He was tall and stocky, his dark suit appeared to be made from the same material as the shadows. He had on a white shirt and a string tie, its clasp caught the light and reflected it into Happy's face. He raised his hand to keep it out of his eyes.

The man on the stage reached up and pushed his flat-brimmed hat back on his head as he turned to face Happy. "What's the matter, boy, don't you speak?"

Happy just stared at him, unable to fully take in all he was seeing.

"I tell you what, if you don't come up here and introduce yourself, I guess I'll just have to call the police."

Happy opened his mouth to speak, but nothing came out. His thoughts were swirling around inside his head so fast that he couldn't manage to pull them together enough to form a sentence.

"What do you think they'd say when I tell them that I was just sitting here strumming this old guitar and minding my own business when a sweaty nigger boy stinking of garbage broke in my back door and tried to rob me?" The man paused, and a knowing smile appeared on his face. "Hell, boy, the chief had dinner here last night, and I set him up with a pretty little thing for dessert. Now I don't know about you, but I doubt he would appreciate you being here uninvited."

Happy forced himself to take a step in the direction of the stage.

"Yes, sir." His voice cracked, so he cleared his throat and tried again. "I'm sorry I... I... I just... I just wanted..."

"Suck it up and talk to me straight, boy. I ain't got time for foolishness."

Happy stepped up to the foot of the stage, removed his hat, and held it in front of him. Old habits died hard.

"Yes, sir," he said, trying to sound confident. "My name is Hap Parker and I haul garbage for folks. I was just wondering if you had need of my services."

The man didn't speak, he just sat there holding the guitar and looking down at Happy like a weasel looks at a chicken that's gotten out of the coop. His stare made Happy very uncomfortable; he could feel sweat dampening his shirt under his arms. Happy clutched his hat harder, squeezing and releasing, trying to get control of all the tension that was churning inside of him.

"What kind of name is Hap?" the man asked, finally breaking the silence. "Your momma must not have liked you too much to hang that on you."

"No, sir. I mean, I don't know nothing about that," Happy explained. "My momma died right after she had me. My pappy named me *Happy* 'cause he said momma took one look at me and smiled real big before she passed. Folks just call me Hap for short."

The man stood and leaned the guitar against the chair before moving to the edge of the stage. He lowered himself down on one knee, then leaned forward to get eye to eye with Happy. The man's cologne was strong, but underneath it Happy thought there was a musky, dirty smell like old cigars or decay. The man never blinked.

"Must be hard knowing that the first thing you did on this earth was kill your momma."

His words stung and Happy, not wanting to hear anything else the man had to say, turned to leave.

"You don't ever want to turn your back on me, boy," the man said very matter of fact and the tone of his words caused Happy to stop. He turned back to the man, planning to tell him where he could shove his business, but he never got a chance.

"I tell you what Hap," the man said, getting back to his feet. "I love a good sob story, so I'll let you haul my garbage, on one condition."

"I'm sorry, what?" Happy replied. Was this man actually offering to hire him after what he had just said about his mother?

"What's the matter, boy, you got garbage in your ears? I said, I'll let you haul my garbage on one condition, and that condition is that I want you to come up here on this stage and play me a song on that guitar."

"I don't think so," Happy said, growing tired of the man's games. "I mean, I can't. That is, I don't know how, I—"

"Don't lie to me, boy. Don't ever lie to me." The man went back over to the chair where he had left the guitar. He looked at it lovingly then picked it up and showed it to Happy. "I know full well you know what to do with this."

He placed the guitar back on the chair and moved away. "Now get up on this stage and play." It wasn't a suggestion; it was a direct order.

Happy thought it best to do as he was told. He was starting to get the feeling that this was not a man he wanted to mess with. He would play one song, then get out and never come back.

He walked slowly around to a short set of steps that led up to the stage. The lights were blindingly bright, and for a moment, he couldn't see anything. He took a couple of tentative steps toward the center of the stage and realized that the man was no longer there.

Happy picked the guitar up and gently touched the strings.

"Hurry up, boy, I ain't got all day."

Happy turned toward the sound of the man's voice. He was now seated at a table, holding a glass of whiskey over ice. The whiskey bottle and an ice bucket were sitting on the table beside him.

Something was very wrong, Happy felt it to his core. He sat in the chair and strummed a couple of chords. He purposely took a few seconds to move from one chord to the other, trying to seem like he really didn't know what he was doing. If he could get the man to believe that, then hopefully, this whole thing would end soon.

"What's the matter, boy, didn't you learn nothing from your pappy?"

Happy stopped playing and looked back out at the man.

"That's right, I know your pappy. I know your pappy well, and I know he taught you better than that. Now quit with the bullshit and play."

Happy began to pick out a rhythm using the finger-picking style he learned from his father. As he continued to play, the man began to smile, and eventually, he laughed and clapped his hands in time to the music.

"Now you're doing something!" The man stood up and danced a little jig in a circle around the table. "Yeah, you got something there, boy!" He danced his way to the edge of the stage. "With picking like that you could really go places, with your talent and my know-how, you could be famous. Rich and famous!"

Happy continued to play as he let the man's words sink in. Could he be telling him the truth? Could he really be good enough to make something out of this? Would people really like the way he played?

"Here's to my newest discovery!" The man was back at his table, holding the glass of whiskey up toward Happy in a type of salute. "You're good boy, real good, and you know what happens to good pickers, don't ya?"

He set the glass back on the table and clapped his hands twice. A spotlight came on, its light falling on a doorway off to the side of the stage. The door opened and two women came out and started dancing their way toward Happy. He watched as they moved to the music he was making. They never stopped their liquid movements even as they climbed the steps up to the stage.

One woman was black, the other white, and the gowns they wore were the opposite of their skin color. The thin white gown that the black woman wore became practically transparent in the harsh stage lights, and Happy couldn't take his eyes off her. The swivel of her hips hypnotized him, and he started playing harder and faster just to see if she could keep up.

The white woman stepped between him and the other dancer, the stark contrast between her milk-white skin and the black low-cut gown made him forget the other woman's swaying hips. He had never been this close to a white woman before, much less one wearing so little. His mouth was suddenly dry. He licked his lips, and the girl giggled. She playfully pushed one of the gown's straps off her shoulder, then leaned in over him and placed one hand on each of the chair's arms. She began to sway side to side, giving him an uninterrupted view down the top of her gown.

Happy's thoughts disappeared into a haze of light, music and flesh. He began to feel the music he was playing run through him.

When the black woman stepped up behind him and pulled his head back to rest on her breasts, he went with it, enjoying the feel of her fingers as they worked their way through his hair. The other woman's hands came off the chair and settled on his thighs. A low moan, perfectly in tune to the music, escaped him. It continued when her hands trailed down his legs as she knelt in front of him.

"Keep playing like that boy and you can have it all!" the man shouted from the front of the stage. Happy heard him, but paid no attention. He was lost.

"It can all be yours! A nice car, a soft bed to sleep in, and all the stuff you ever wanted! Black stuff, white stuff, maybe even a little slant-eyed stuff."

The man clapped his hands again, and an Asian woman walked through the tables, carrying a rolled piece of paper and a quill pen. As she passed the man, their eyes met. He raised his eyebrows, then gave a quick nod toward the stage.

Happy saw her appear before him, silhouetted by the stage lights. In his haze she appeared to be floating. As she drew closer, the harsh stage lights dimmed and were replaced by a soft light from behind him that revealed her features. She floated closer and settled beside him next to the woman whose head was now in his lap. She unrolled the paper on the woman's back and the other dancer stepped around to hold it in place. The Asian woman then took Happy's hand from the guitar and placed the quill pen in it before guiding it to the paper.

"Just sign your name, baby, and it's all yours."

She looked down at herself, and the gown she was wearing turned to smoke and floated away.

Happy signed his name.

* * *

Happy jolted awake inside the cab of his truck. The storm had passed, and the hot afternoon sun was shining in through the front windshield. He looked around, not understanding how he got there.

He smelled perfume and lifted his shirt to his nose. The sweet aroma was there, faint under the scent of sweat and garbage. Then it all started coming back to him, the strange man in the black suit, the guitar, the girls. Had he signed something? Seemed like he did, but that part was still a little hazy.

He felt his pockets for his key, and when he didn't find it there, he ran his hands across the dash. The key was there, along with an envelope. His name had been written on the face of it in a very feminine handwriting. He lifted it to his nose, took a deep breath, and let his lungs fill with the sweet fragrance. Inside, he found a fifty-dollar bill, along with a note written in block letters.

BE BACK HERE TONIGHT AT MIDNIGHT. BUY A
NEW BLACK SUIT AND BE READY TO PLAY.

Happy read the note again and rubbed the fifty between his fingers. He had never seen a fifty-dollar bill before, much less held one in his hand. Maybe picking a little guitar in the club might not be such a bad thing after all, it appeared to pay pretty good. He let the idea settle in, take up residence. Yeah, he could do that. It beat the hell out of hauling other folks' garbage.

He started the truck, then tucked the bill back in the envelope. He was going to return the note as well when he noticed something written on the back.

DON'T CROSS ME.

It was signed, *Mr. Give.*

Happy sat there for a minute looking at the three little words written in block letters with the name scribbled below them.

What have I gotten myself into? he thought, then put the truck in gear and drove away into the hot afternoon sun on his way to buy a suit.

* * *

After a hot day, the cool of night settled in as Happy busied himself around the cottage trying to make sure everything was ready before he left for the club. After some discussion outside the front door of the Plainesville Tailor Shop, he had made a backdoor deal for a black suit and matching Fedora hat. He had rushed home and found his father's old dress shoes and polished them till he could see his face reflected in them. All the while, his father had sat silently at the table, turning his head to follow Happy by the sound of his footfalls on the old wooden floor.

Happy started cooking dinner for the two of them. He mashed potatoes from their little garden patch and cooked two thin porkchops he had purchased with the remains of the money Mr. Give had given him. He turned to get his father's plate off the table and was surprised to find the man standing in front of him.

"Labour not for the meat which perisheth, but for that meat which endureth unto everlasting life which the Son of man shall give unto you. For him hath God the Father sealed."

His father stood so close to Happy that their noses nearly touched, and Happy could smell his breath when he spoke. Happy didn't say anything, they had played this game before. Instead, he took his father's arm, guided him back to the table, and helped him to his seat there.

"Whatever work you do, do it with all your heart. Do it for the Lord and not for men," his father said with a nod and turned to the table.

Happy took the man's plate off the table and returned to the stove. He cut one of the pork chops into bite-sized pieces and placed those on the plate, along with a healthy helping of potatoes. Then he filled a cup half full of coffee and placed it and the plate on the table in front of his father.

"Dinner's on the table, Pappy, and your coffee is to the right of your plate."

Happy watched as the man slowly reached out with his right hand until he felt the cup. He brought it to his mouth and deeply inhaled through his nose, then smiled. His father had always loved the smell of coffee. He gently blew on it before taking a sip.

"Lo, children are a heritage of the Lord, and the fruit of the womb is his reward."

Happy returned to the stove with his back to the room and smiled at his father's words. It had been almost eight years since his father had begun speaking only in scripture, but somehow the old man still managed to make his feelings known. Still, Happy missed the days when they actually *talked*.

For as long as he could remember, his father had been blind from some farming accident, but he always told Happy of better days, days when he and Happy's mother traveled together from farm to farm. He had talked about the people they met and how they felt that even if the whole world was against them, that they would still manage to survive.

Happy remembered his father teaching him to read, using the only book they owned. That Bible that had his mother's name carefully printed on the first page was his textbook, and as his reading improved, Pappy had asked him to read it to him more and more. As he read, his father would mouth the words along with him, always ready to correct him if he got one wrong. One day he had stopped reading to get a drink of water, and Pappy had just taken up where he left off, speaking the scriptures from memory. From that afternoon on, Pappy had never spoken another word that didn't originate in the book.

For a long time, Happy hated that book with a passion, that book that had taken his father away from him. That book that replaced stories of his mother with stories of arks and crosses, giant whales, and mustard seeds. He wanted so much to tell his father how much he hated Plainesville, how much he hated hauling garbage, and how much he hated this nasty little cottage. But he couldn't. What good would it do?

As far as Happy knew, his father's mind was gone and all his understanding with it. Happy loved him. He loved him with a passion that only existed between fathers and sons, but sometimes he caught himself longing for the day when the man would die, and he could turn his back on the place and get away. Right now, *away* sounded really good, but away would have to wait. His father had always taught him that family came first; nothing was more valuable than family.

Happy forked the remaining pork chop onto his plate and put a heaping spoonful of potatoes beside it. He sat down at the table next to his father and started cutting up his chop. He dipped his fork into the potatoes, then stabbed a piece of meat and stuffed them in his mouth. The first bite was always the best, and he savored the salty taste of the pork and the smooth creamy potatoes as he chewed.

"I got us a new stop today, Pappy." He wiped his mouth on his sleeve and took a sip of water. "New fella out on Golden Road."

His father had just put his own forkful of potatoes and pork in his mouth, and he turned to face Happy, chewing slowly as he listened.

"Strange kind of fella, made me play the guitar for him before he would give me the job."

His father swallowed hard, and obviously forced the food down too soon. He coughed to clear his throat, then reached for his coffee and took a drink.

"He wants me to come back out there tonight. Even give me money for a suit, too."

His father's hands began to tremble, and he dropped the cup of coffee. It struck his plate, sending both the plate and cup tumbling to the ground. He stood quickly, facing Happy as food and coffee ran down the front of his clothes.

Happy grabbed a rag off the stove and started trying to clean up the mess the man had made.

"But he turned, and said unto Peter, Get thee behind me, Satan." His father's words were frantic, and he slapped at Happy's hands as he tried to wipe a glob of potatoes off his shirt. "Thou art an offense unto me, for thou savourest not the things that be of God, but those that be of men."

"Now look what you gone and done! Ain't I got enough on my mind without you making a mess?" Happy, having done what he could do to clean up his father, picked up the plate and cup from the floor and placed them back on the table.

As he stood to start wiping up the mess, his father grabbed him by his shirt and pulled him close. "Watch and pray, that ye enter not into temptation." His voice was just above a whisper, his words intense. "The spirit indeed is willing, but the flesh is weak."

Happy pulled his father hands loose and took a step back.

"What's gotten into you Pappy? This is a good thing. I'll be making more money, and we can maybe get this place fixed up a little bit."

The man took a step toward Happy, and this time his words were pointed and aggressive. "Lay not up for yourselves treasures upon earth, where moth and rust doth corrupt, and where thieves break through and steal. For where your treasure is, there will your heart be also." He reached out and pushed Happy as if trying to make his words stick. For an old man he was still strong from all the years of farm work and the blow caught Happy off guard, causing him to stumble.

He landed against his new suit, knocking it to the ground. Happy braced himself against the wall, then stepped back to his father. Taking him by the arm, Happy roughly guided him back to his chair and made him sit down. He turned and picked up the suit and began to brush off the dust it had picked up from the floor. With every wipe at the dust on the suit, Happy grew angrier. He hung it back on the nail and turned on his father.

"Have you lost your mind? I'm trying to better myself!" He knew his words might not be reaching the old man sitting hunched over in the chair, but at this point, he didn't care. He was angry and the words were going to come out regardless. "Just because you ain't never had nothing don't mean I can't!"

Happy looked back at the suit and noticed a small spot on one leg. He snatched the rag he had been using off the table, dipped a corner in his glass of water, and returned to the suit to try and remove the spot.

"Mr. Give says I've got something special. I want to see if he's right." Happy continued to scrub the stain. "I'm going to that club tonight and I'm gonna play for them folks."

His father straightened up and slammed both of his fists on the table, sending plates and cups tumbling to the floor. "Honor thy father and thy mother!" he screamed at the top of his lungs. "That thy days may be long upon the land which the Lord thy God giveth thee!"

Happy had heard enough. He threw the rag at the man and hit him in the face. "Not this time Pappy. For once, I'm going to do what I want to do, and you ain't gonna stop me!"

His father reached up with a trembling hand. He pulled the wet rag from his face and let it drop to the ground. His chin fell to his chest, and he gathered his hands in his lap, running one shaking thumb over the gnarled knuckles of the other hand.

Happy saw what his words and actions had done to his father. He had never seen him look so defeated. He stepped over and knelt in front of him. Happy placed his hands over his father's and the man lifted his face.

"I've got to do this for me, Pappy, can't you see that?" Happy asked. "Do you even understand what I'm telling you? Mr. Give says I got something special, and I believe him. So, I'm going out to that club tonight, and I'm gonna give it all I got. I want to go with your blessing, but blessing or not, I'm still going."

"For by grace you have been saved through faith," his father said in a desperate pleading tone. "And this is not your own doing. It is the gift of God, not a result of works, so that no one may boast."

Happy released his hands and walked over to the suit hanging on the wall. "I'm sorry Pappy, I gotta do this. We'll talk some more later tonight when I get home."

Happy saw the guitar leaning against the wall and took it over to his father. He accepted it and began to play a slow melancholy tune. Happy brushed away a tear as he stood and watched his father's gnarled old hands caress the neck of the guitar and his fingers gently pluck the strings.

"I love you, Pappy. I'll be home soon. You'll see, everything's gonna be just fine." He leaned in and kissed the old man on the top of his head. If he noticed, he didn't make any movement that let Happy know. Happy started to say something else, then thought better of it. He took the suit from the wall and left the house, closing the door behind him.

Outside, Happy put the truck in gear and pulled away from the house, throwing a spray of gravel from beneath the truck's tires. As he moved onto the road, he couldn't shake the feeling that something was different this time from all the other times he had started into town. Then it dawned on him. For the first time, he was leaving to do something for himself. This was going to be the beginning of a bright new future. No more hauling garbage and slopping hogs. From here on out, everything was going to change. Tomorrow was going to be a better day.

* * *

At the sound of the truck's engine starting, Elijah stopped playing and looked up. His lips trembled as he tried to say Happy's name but was unable to form the words.

Elijah ran his fingers down the neck of the guitar, his trembling hands unable to make a chord. He lifted his face to heaven and a moan started deep inside of him, growing ever louder until it burst from his mouth as a scream of rage and fear.

He grasped the neck of the guitar with both hands, then stood and slammed the guitar's body against the tabletop. Again and again, the guitar met the table and began to splinter and break apart. Years of pent-up anger, of heartbreak and fear, drove him to destroy the instrument. Pieces of wood flew about the cottage. A large splinter lodged in the side of Elijah's hand, and the blood that flowed from the wound made the neck slick.

Elijah raised the remains of the guitar over his head, planning to bring it down again on the table, but this time it slipped and flew from his grasp. The battered and busted instrument flew across the cottage and landed on the stove, causing the skillet of hot pork grease to turn over and immediately burst into flame.

The flames jumped from the stove to the curtain on the window that overlooked the pig pen and Happy's little garden. From there, it only took a few seconds for the entire cottage to be engulfed, its old, weathered boards providing the perfect fuel for the growing fire. Elijah felt the heat surround him. He stretched out his hands, attempting to feel for a cooler area through which he could escape, but there was none.

Confused by the heat and choking on smoke, he took a step toward what he hoped was the front door. A flame from the wall leapt out and scorched his palms. Before he could step back, the roof of the little cottage that had been his and Happy's home collapsed on top of him.

Outside the house, a black sedan was parked on the edge of the road. Its driver and passenger watched as the cottage walls fell in on themselves.

* * *

Happy pulled into the parking lot at Mammon's Mountain at five minutes to midnight. In stark contrast to earlier in the day, the parking lot was packed. Cars of every make and color stood in lines outside the club, whose sign was now lit by bright lamps that managed to bring new life to the faded façade.

Inside, the air was thick with smoke, and the sounds of people drinking and gambling made conversation nearly impossible. Waitresses dressed in short skirts and low-cut tops made their way through the crowd with trays of whiskey and beer. The occasional pat on the rump or whispered proposition was just part of the job, but the tips were good.

Mr. Give stood at the end of the bar, looking over his domain. He held a shot of whiskey over ice that he swirled around, watching as the ice slid along the sides of the glass. It was important that he look the part of the well-to-do bar owner, but he never took a drink. Whiskey was for the weak. He looked at the clock behind the bar, 11:58.

Mr. Give smiled and turned to greet Happy who had just stepped inside. "Well, if it ain't the garbage man," he said almost jovially. He circled Happy, making a show of checking him out. "And he's wearing a mighty fancy suit to boot!"

Mr. Give laughed at his own joke, then with a wave of his hand, the bartender handed him a guitar from behind the bar.

He placed the guitar in Happy's hands. At exactly midnight, the house lights winked out, and with an electrical snap, a spotlight came on, its light encircling Happy and Mr. Give.

"This is your night garbage man, don't screw it up," Mr. Give whispered in Happy's ear. Then, placing his arm around Happy's shoulders, Mr. Give led him to the stage.

CHAPTER 11

1952

Happy opened the curtains to let the morning sun into his room on the top floor of the hotel where he had spent the night. The sunlight immediately warmed his skin, and he was tempted to let the towel he was wearing around his waist drop to the floor so he could feel it all over.

A sleepy groan came from behind him where a white woman was lying naked on the bed. Her name was Beverly and he had met her two nights earlier. He was in town for a two-week engagement at the Troubadour Theater. Usually, he didn't find a companion on the first night in a new town, but when she came backstage to interview him for the local newspaper, they had hit it off, and she hadn't been back to work or home since.

"Wake on up, I ordered room service," he said to her.

Beverly didn't move. She just let loose with another sleepy moan.

He turned back to the window and looked out at the town below him. For the life of him, he couldn't remember what town he was in, but it really didn't matter. All these towns were the same, all the theaters were the same, and to be honest, so were all the Beverlys.

He had done all right for himself over the last two years. Mr. Give kept the show on the road, and in every town the theaters got bigger and the crowds louder. Happy played his guitar for his adoring fans, and they paid handsomely for the privilege of being in his presence. It beat the hell out of Plainesville and the garbage business. Too bad Pappy couldn't be there to be a part of it.

There was a knock on the door, and as Happy passed the bed to answer it, he slapped Beverly on her perfect backside.

"Food's here. Cover up."

Beverly did as she was told, wiggling around until she could find the sheet and pull it over herself. Before he opened the door, Happy took a quick look over his shoulder to make sure she wasn't going to give the waiter a thrill. The room service waiter wheeled in a cart overloaded with food.

"Just put it at the end of the bed," Happy directed him, then walked over to the dresser to get the young man a tip from his wallet.

"Anything else I can get for you, sir?" the waiter asked.

"No." Happy pressed a twenty-dollar bill into his outstretched hand.

"Thank you, sir!" the waiter grinned and made a quick exit.

Happy looked down at his wallet where he kept the only photo he had ever had of his father. He missed the old man. There were times he wished he could hear his voice again even if it was just rambling Bible verses. He had always found comfort in his father's voice, and he could use a little of that comfort now.

"Are you going to eat or what?" Beverly asked from behind him.

He turned to see her sitting on the edge of the bed eating a piece of toast with jelly. A drop of jelly fell on her chest. She giggled and wiped it off with one finger that she then licked clean in a gesture that was far from innocent.

"Oh yeah, sorry. I got distracted."

Happy crossed over to the bed and sat down beside her. She kissed him and her lips tasted like grape jelly mixed with alcohol and cigarette smoke from the night before.

"So, what had your attention so much that you forgot about breakfast?"

"I was looking at a picture of my father," he answered. He wasn't sure how far he wanted to let her into his world. "I called him Pappy. He died a few years ago."

"Oh, I'm sorry. What happened?" She sounded like she actually cared, and when she looked up at him with her baby blue eyes and he saw caring there also, he decided to open up a little and let her in.

"He burned to death in a house fire, but to be honest he was gone a while before that."

"What do you mean?" Beverly munched on her toast.

"Well, it's kind of a strange story. You see, for the last seven or eight years of Pappy's life, he only spoke in Bible verses."

"Bible verses? I don't get it."

Neither do I, Happy thought to himself and that made him laugh. "Yep, that's what I said. Bible verses, and he was blind."

"Okay, now you have my attention. Go on."

Happy took a piece of bacon and bit the end off. The salted pork and the smell of coffee took him back to so many breakfasts he had spent with his father around the little table in the cottage.

"Pappy was blind for as long as can I remember, but we used to have the best talks. He was the one who taught me to play the guitar." He took a sip of coffee and let it wash down the lump that was forming in his throat. "But there always seemed to be something under the surface bothering him." He turned on the end of the bed so that he was facing her. She reached out and stroked his thigh with a touch that was too loving to be coming from someone he had only known for a few days.

"I remember one time I asked him what was wrong," he went on, "and he just waved me off. Any time after that when I would try to talk about it, he would just get up and leave the room."

"That's awful." The girl reached for another piece of bacon.

"When I got older and started learning to read, Pappy had me practice using my mom's old Bible. The better I got at reading the book, the more he asked me to read to him. It started out being at night, after dinner, then as time went on, he would want to hear some before breakfast. Before long, it seemed like if I was home, I was reading that book to him. That's when he started repeating back to me what I had just read. Somewhere along the way I stopped reading, and he just kept on going without me. I guess whatever it was eating at him finally just took him over."

"So let me get this straight. You're telling me that you are the son of a blind, blues playing, religious fanatic who died in a house fire, but not before he was able to teach you to play guitar enough for you to become a rich and famous musician?"

"Yeah, I guess so." Happy couldn't help but laugh when his life was laid out in front of him like that.

"I call bullshit," she said frankly, then broke into a smile.

"You do, do you?"

"Yeah, I do." The sarcasm in her voice made her laugh as well. "What you gonna do about it?"

Happy looked around at the breakfast tray and picked up a pitcher of syrup.

"This."

"Oh, no you don't!" She held up her hands in mock protest as Happy covered her naked body in the warm sticky syrup.

* * *

Rehearsal at the Troubadour was scheduled for three o'clock, but after Beverly left to find an outfit to wear to the show that night, Happy began to feel restless. He called for a car and decided to see what the town had to offer. A limousine picked him up outside of the hotel, its portly white driver held the rear door open for him as he stepped out of the building and made his way to the car.

"Where to, sir?"

"I honestly have no idea. Can we just drive around and see where we end up?"

"Yes, sir."

As the man walked around to the driver's door, Happy saw him remove his hat and wave it in the direction of the hotel.

What's that all about? he wondered.

The driver settled in behind the wheel and pulled the car from the hotel parking lot and out into traffic.

Happy watched out the window as a generic middle-American city passed by with its shops and restaurants, parking lots, and business parks.

I've come a long way, Pappy, he thought. *This sure beats the way we used to live.*

The limousine turned onto a back street into an area with strips of older shops, many of which looked closed and abandoned. A few homeless people with all their belongings in sacks wandered the street. He wondered if Plainesville looked this way now. Were its pretty little flower boxes filled with weeds? Were the butcher shop windows now soaped over with a *For Sale* sign taped to the front door? He hoped so. He hoped that when he left, the town had just dried up.

As he was enjoying his moment of self-importance, a storefront caught his eye. The hand-painted lettering in the shop window read, *Gloryland Way Café and Soul Food Kitchen.* He was immediately transported back to his days picking up garbage outside the restaurant with the red door and the fat cook that promised to sneak him and Pappy in the back after hours for a meal. They had never eaten that meal, but that didn't mean that Happy couldn't stop and eat here, and he would go in through the *front* door to do it.

Happy leaned forward and tapped on the window to get the driver's attention. The man lowered the window that separated the haves from the have-nots.

"Yes, sir?"

"Pull over. I want to grab a bite to eat."

"Yes, sir, but I should remind you that you have rehearsal in less than an hour."

"I realize that, but I'm hungry, and I would like to eat first," Happy said firmly.

"Yes, sir."

The driver pulled the car over and parked it against the curb outside the café. As quickly as his rotund form would allow, he rushed to Happy's door and opened it for him. Happy stepped out of the car and took another look at the deserted street.

"Stay here until I get back," he instructed the driver, who answered him with a nod of the head.

"Yes, sir."

Gloryland Way was a small place that appeared to have been in business for many years. When Happy opened the door, a little bell rang. He looked around at the worn seats and peeling linoleum on the floor and started to second guess his decision to stop. The room was bathed in a yellow light coming from the filthy plastic covers on the two florescent lights attached to the ceiling. A large fan hung below them distributing warm air to every corner of room.

There were two booths along the front wall next to the large plate-glass window. The plastic seats were discolored and cracked from years of exposure to the sun. Two metal, four-top tables sat in the center of the room, surrounded with mismatched chairs. A small counter with four stools ran along the back wall at the end of which sat an old cash register. Mounted to the wall above the counter was a letter board containing the day's specials. It was Tuesday, so the special was pot roast and asparagus. They must have run short on letters, so the person that had put up the sign had made the regrettable decision to abbreviate. The sign read:

POT ROAST AND ASS

Happy laughed.

He took another look around the dingy café and was just turning to leave when someone called out to him from the back room.

"Well, hello there, young fella." The voice was thick and rich with age and experience. Happy was not surprised when a large black woman wearing red stretchy pants, a blue shirt with a yellow daisy pattern, and black soft-soled shoes appeared through a door marked *kitchen staff only*. A stained apron covered her ample chest and belly. An order pad was sticking out of the front pocket. Her long gray hair had been pulled into a knot at the back of her head and the ends hung down past her shoulders. A chipped and dirty name tag was pinned to her shirt, it read, *Esther*.

"Woo-wee aint you a fine-looking young man," Esther said as she drew close to Happy. "You come right over here to this booth by the window and take a seat."

Esther passed him on the way to the booth and motioned for him to follow. He took a seat in the booth, sliding in carefully so the ripped plastic cover wouldn't tear his pants.

Esther took her place at the end of the table. "Some of these girls around here see you sitting there in my window, and I'm liable to have to start taking reservations!" She belly laughed as she removed the order pad from her apron and started fishing around for something to write with.

"Now what in the world have I done with that pencil? I'm always losing that blasted—"

Happy pointed to her ear.

Esther smiled and reached up to get the stub of a pencil that was resting there. That lead to another belly laugh that Happy found contagious.

"All right handsome, what can I get for you?"

"It's Happy," he told her. For some reason he just felt like she needed to know his name, and that if she called him by it, he would feel loved.

"Honey, we don't serve that here, but if we did, we would be a heck of a lot busier!" Again, the big laugh. Her joy spread out through the room and Happy couldn't remember why he had started to leave.

"No, my *name* is Happy," he corrected her with a smile.

"Good to meet you, Happy. I'm Esther, but you can call me Essey. Everybody does."

"Okay, Essey, what's good today?"

"Now that's a loaded question." She put the stub back behind her ear and motioned with her thumb toward the door. "The old man is back in the kitchen, and so if I was you, I would go with the special."

"Okay, what is the special?"

"I call it Ham Bone Soup. The old man calls it *Garbure*." The last word came out in a horrible French accent that brought that big lovable laugh with it. "He don't do nothin' but boil an old ham bone and dump a bunch of veggies in there. Then he throws yesterday's leftover bread in it to thicken it up. It don't sound like much, but I gotta admit it tastes pretty good."

This time it was Happy's turn to laugh as she stood there and looked down at him with a smile that would lift the spirits of even the most-sullen man.

"Okay, you convinced me. I'll try it."

"All right, sugar. I'll go get that for you. And how about a piece of buttermilk pie for dessert? It's good, I make that myself."

"Sounds perfect."

"All right, sugar. I'll be right back." Esther smiled and headed toward the kitchen.

"Hey old man, I need a bowl of *Garbure*!" she yelled out, emphasizing the fake French pronunciation.

Happy laughed, then turned to look out the window. Through fingerprints and street dirt that had collected there, he watched a squirrel wrestle to get a crumb off a piece of wax paper someone dropped. Prize in hand, the squirrel disappeared into a downspout.

A movement from the front of the limo got Happy's attention, and he watched as the driver sat behind the wheel. His lips were moving like he was talking to someone, but he was the only person in the car.

Happy didn't have time to consider this weird situation because just then a bowl of soup and a piece of pie was set down on the table in front of him. "Thanks, Essey, that was quick"

"You're welcome." The voice was ragged and hoarse, and Happy looked up to see an old man standing there. His hair was long and gray, bound up inside of a hair net, and he had a salt-and-pepper beard. A dirty white apron hung down over his khaki pants but had done nothing to protect his scuffed black boots from getting stained by spilled food.

"Oh, sorry," Happy apologized. "I was expecting Ess—"

"Is that your stretch sitting out there by the curb?" The old man interrupted his apology.

Happy turned to look again at his limo, then back to the old man.

"Well, it is today," he said, a little embarrassed.

"What are you, some kind of superstar or something?"

"I'm doing okay, I guess." Happy was starting to feel a little uncomfortable with the attention his transportation was getting.

"I say better than okay," the man continued, not taking his eyes of the limo. "By the looks of your ride anyway."

Happy picked up his spoon and dipped it into the soup. He raised it to his mouth and tasted it. The thick hot soup coated his throat and warmed him. It tasted like *home*.

"Wow, that's really good."

Not taking his eyes off the car, the old man stepped over and slid into the booth across from Happy. "You know, a long time ago, *I* left home to be a star." The man finally tore his eyes from the car and turned to face Happy. "Before I left, my momma, who was a big fan of the Good Book, told me that somewhere in there it says to watch and pray, that ye enter not into temptation. The spirit indeed is willing, but the flesh is weak. She said that meant that if something seemed too easy, then it probably was, and I should avoid it."

The sound of his words echoed through Happy's memory. Hadn't that been the same thing his father had said that first night he had left to play at the club, the night his father had died? He shook off the thought and took another spoonful of the soup.

"So, let me guess," Happy said slowly. "You took those words to heart and became the next Frank Sinatra, and you're just cooking here so you can be close to your adoring fans." He didn't like the sarcasm he heard in his own words, but it didn't seem to faze the old man.

"No, it didn't work out so good for me, but it did get me here where every once in a while, I get to meet and talk to a superstar like you."

Happy didn't know what to say to that, so he just finished eating his soup. Just as he took the last bite, Esther arrived at the table with a to-go container.

"Get up out of that booth and leave this boy alone," Esther said to the old man. "He come in here for a warm meal, not to be bothered by an old cuss like you."

The old man slid out of the booth and stood behind Esther as she handed Happy the container.

"I brought you some pie to go." She motioned with her head in the direction of the waiting car. "From the way that man is pacing out there, I'm betting you need to hit the road."

Happy turned and looked out the window. His driver was pacing nervously back and forth by the side of the car.

"Thanks, I don't know what's gotten into him. What do I owe you?"

"Nothing, son," the old man said. "Sometimes the best things in life don't cost us a thing."

Esther smiled and nodded in agreement.

Happy stood and shook hands with the old man, then turned to Esther and extended his hand to her.

"Oh no, you ain't getting away that easy." Esther pulled him into a bear hug, her big arms wrapped around him squeezing him tight against her. "Just be careful out there. ol' Essey will be praying for you," she whispered in his ear.

Esther released him, then stepped over and opened the door, causing the little bell to ring. Happy stepped outside, then turned back to the odd couple standing in the doorway.

"Thanks again, for everything."

The driver rushed over and took him by the arm, leading him away from the café. "Holy shit, where have you been?" He sounded panicked and practically pushed Happy into the back of the car. "They're looking for you. Apollyon said if I didn't get you to the theater soon, he would kick my ass. He can do it, too."

The driver slammed the door before practically jumping into the driver's seat and starting the car. As the car pulled away from the curb, Happy looked back at Gloryland Way, expecting to see Essey and the old man waving goodbye. But instead of the restaurant with the faded floors and cracked seats, he saw only an abandoned storefront. In the dirt on the window in big letters someone had written *Stevenson Blows*, and below that in the lower corner of the window was written, *matt2641*.

As the car moved away, Happy could only stare as the strip of abandoned businesses were lost in the distance.

* * *

Later that night, Happy stepped into his penthouse room at the hotel, and for the first time in a long while, he was alone. He had told Beverly that he had a headache and he just wanted to get some sleep. She had protested that she needed to come with him, to take care of him. In the end he had gotten angry and short with her, and she had fled the theater in tears. He would call in the morning and have some flowers sent to her home. Flowers always worked.

He walked over to the window and pulled the chain to open the curtains. He was surprised by his reflection in the glass. Tall and lean, wearing a black suit and a black hat, he looked like a man totally in control of his destiny. But since leaving Gloryland Way, or wherever he had been that afternoon, he was feeling anything but in control.

He made it through rehearsal and the show that night, but something Esther had said to him was bothering him. She had whispered, "I'll be praying for you," in his ear just before he had left. Why so secretive? Surely, she wasn't embarrassed to say something like that in front of the old man, so why whisper? And what about the old man and that story about how his mother had told him the same thing that Happy's crazy blind father had said to him the last time they ever spoke? That couldn't be coincidence, could it?

He sat on the edge of the bed and kicked off his shoes, then tossed his hat toward the dresser. He missed, and the hat fell on the floor. The afternoon seemed so much like a dream that Happy was afraid if he thought about it too much it would fade completely, and he would never understand it. What had been written in the window as they pulled away? Not *Stevenson Blows*, he had seen that written in a lot of windows on his travels, but it was the small print down in the lower corner, *matt2641*. Was that someone's name or some kind of code? It gnawed at him, and he couldn't let it go.

He ran his hands through his hair, frustrated. Maybe a shower would help clear his mind, help him to think straight. He stood and took off the rest of clothes, leaving them in a pile at the foot of the bed.

The bright bathroom light hurt his eyes. He switched it off and turned the knob that started the heat lamp in the bathroom's ceiling. The room was filled with a soft red glow, and its heat came down in waves on his shoulders.

Happy turned on the shower and trailed his hand through the falling water until it got warm. He stepped in and let the warm water flow over his head and down his body. He tried to clear his mind by concentrating on how the water felt running down him, over his chest and back, then down his legs.

His mind started to drift back to when he was a child in the old cottage, to how his father would heat water on the stove and use a rag to wash him off after a long day playing outside. Even though he was blind, the man never missed a spot of dirt. It was often during those baths that he would tell Happy about his mother and how he knew she would be amazed at how big and strong he was getting. He liked to talk about how they had spent many nights, while Happy was still in her belly, talking about how they were going to raise him to be responsible and hardworking.

It seemed like every story involved his mother taking out her Bible, the very Bible he was using to learn to read. His father had told him that her favorite part had come from the book of Proverbs, and it said: "Train up a child in the way he should go, even when he is old he will not depart from it." Happy had tried to find that verse the next time they sat down to read and couldn't.

"That's 'cause they don't write out the words full like at the top of each page," his father had told him. "They shorten them so instead of looking for P R O V E R B S you just look for P R O V."

Happy snapped to attention in the shower. That was it. *matt2641* wasn't a name or a code. It was an abbreviation. Matt stood for Matthew, and 2641 must be the chapter and verse.

He got out of the shower and wrapped himself in a towel, then picked up the phone and dialed, *0*. The front desk answered after four rings.

"Front desk, how may I help you?" the sleepy voice said on the other end of the line.

"Hello, I have an odd question."

"No question is too odd or any request too strange when it comes from one of our guests," the voice answered.

"Okay, great. Do you have a copy of the New Testament down there that you could send up to my room?"

"Yes, sir, we do. I'll send it right up."

"Thanks."

Happy hung up the phone and immediately there was a knock at the door.

"Wow, that was fast!" he said as he walked over and opened the door, expecting to see a bellboy standing there holding the book. Instead, Apollyon put his hand against Happy's chest and pushed him back into the room.

The big man stepped inside, closing the door behind him. "Exactly what in the hell do you think you're doing?" Apollyon asked before Happy could say anything.

"Apollyon," Happy stuttered, trying to pull himself together. "What are you doing here? I haven't seen you in over a year."

"Yeah, well I've seen you." Apollyon moved closer to Happy, forcing him to sit on the bed to keep from being stepped on. "I've seen you with a different piece of ass after every show. I've seen you drinking champagne. I've seen you smiling like the cat that ate the freaking canary when your fans ask you for an autograph. Pretty sweet life you got here, so you need to remember who put you here and don't screw it up."

Happy pivoted to the end of the bed and pulled on a pair of under shorts before standing up and facing Apollyon.

"I haven't forgotten anything. I know I have Mr. Give to thank for all this."

"Then shut off the light, go to bed, and forget all this Bible nonsense."

Apollyon clapped his hands. The room was thrown into darkness.

Happy sat quietly and listened. When he didn't hear the big man moving around, he got up and switched on the dresser lamp. When he was sure that he was alone, he let his guard down and began to shake. He made his way to the bed, sat down, and pulled the comforter tight around himself.

* * *

Happy woke with a start. He had been dreaming. In his dream his father had come to him at the Troubadour dressed in a suit that was half black and half white. Even the hat and sunglasses that he wore were split down the center into the two different colors. Happy had been onstage playing when the audience had parted, letting the old man through to the foot of the stage. There, a beautiful angel descended from above, unfurled her wings and wrapped them around Elijah like a protective shield. It was Seraphina. Happy didn't know how he knew that the angel was his mother, but he was sure of it. At the sight of her and his father together again, he had begun to cry in his dream.

The tips of Seraphina's wings touched Elijah's chest. Their razor-sharp points cut through the old man's suit coat and shirt and entered his chest. The angel shrieked, making a sound like a wounded eagle, as a blood-red stain started spreading across her wings. When the stain reached her torso, the angel's face—his *mother's* face—began to swell and redden like a tick gorging itself on a dog's back. Her beautiful skin stretched and bubbled as if being boiled from the inside. Trapped in the angel's grasp, Elijah began to call out, "Eloi, Eloi, lama sabachthani?"

Happy tried to go to them, but he could not get up from the stool he was seated on. His hands would not stop playing the guitar so he just watched in horror as the tips of the angel's wings went further into Elijah's chest and began to pull apart his ribcage.

"Pappy!" Happy screamed, but he could not be heard over the noise of the crowd that had suddenly come to life, clapping their hands and chanting his name.

"Happy, Happy, Happy!"

A gaping hole was now visible in Elijah's chest, and inside it was Seraphina's Bible. Arteries and veins ran into and out of the book, and it swelled and receded as it pumped. Elijah punched one hand through the angel's wing, sending red feathers floating to the floor, then plunged it into the open cavity in his chest and grabbed the Bible. With great effort, he tore the book loose and threw it on the stage. It landed at Happy's feet and he saw that it was open to the book of Matthew, the twenty-sixth chapter, and that a red line circled verse 41.

Seeing the book lying there on the stage in a growing puddle of blood, the angel released Elijah and disappeared. Elijah stood there for a moment, and the crowd grew silent. He reached out to Happy with a blood-covered hand.

"My son," he whispered. Then he fell to the floor and was covered by the crowd as it rushed to the stage again chanting Happy's name.

"Happy, Happy, Happy!" they cried out, clapping and stomping to the rhythm of their chant.

Happy realized that he had stopped playing and was trying to stand. He dropped the guitar and knelt beside the Bible, then with a trembling hand, he reached out for it. The Bible vibrated, and the pool of blood surrounding it began to rise in the air. Suddenly, a blinding flash of light shot from the book and struck Happy in the chest.

That was when he woke up.

It was still dark outside. and Happy reached for the clock that sat on the bedside table, its glowing phosphorescent dial a soothing green. *Four-thirty.* He had only been back in the hotel for a little over two hours.

He got to his feet, went to the dresser, and picked up a note that was lying there. He switched on the light and looked at the note before carrying it back to the bed and setting it beside the telephone. Holding the handset between his ear and shoulder, he dialed the number written on the note, making sure that the rotary went around all the way before removing his finger from the hole. If he misdialed, he wasn't sure he would have the guts to try again.

"Hello," a sleepy and confused female voice answered on the sixth ring.

"Beverly, it's Happy. I'm sorry to wake you, but I need to ask a big favor."

* * *

Thirty minutes later, there was a soft knock on the hotel room door. Happy, who had been pacing around the room, rushed to it.

"Who's there?" he asked through the crack between the door and the jamb.

"It's me," came the soft reply.

Happy opened the door for Beverly, who had not bothered to change out of her pajamas before rushing across town. She stepped inside and wrapped her arms around Happy's neck and kissed him deeply.

He broke off the embrace and pushed her away. "Did you bring it? The Bible? Did you bring it with you?"

Beverly swung her purse off her shoulder and reached inside it. She pulled out a small New Testament that she had gotten at Bible camp when she was nine, the year before her parents had divorced. She had prayed for them to be happy and to stay together, but when that didn't happen, she had stuck the Bible in a drawer, and that is where it had stayed until she got Happy's call.

"I don't get it," she said. "What's so important that you needed me to bring you a Bible now, instead of just going in the morning and buying one for yourself?"

Happy didn't answer her. Instead, he sat on the bed and ruffled through the pages until he found what he was looking for.

Matthew the twenty-sixth chapter and verse forty-one.

"Watch and pray, that ye enter not into temptation. The spirit indeed is willing, but the flesh is weak."

* * *

The next few weeks were a blur of concert dates and travel. After Beverly brought him the Bible, Happy told her about his dream and the odd happenings at The Gloryland Way Café. He confessed to her that he was scared and that he thought he had made a big mistake signing on with Mr. Give. He asked her to go on the road with him because he needed her companionship. That was true, but he also needed her as a cover to keep Apollyon and Mr. Give off him while he tried to figure out exactly what he had gotten himself into.

During the day, Happy and Beverly carried on the lifestyle of a couple that had everything and weren't afraid to abuse it. They would proudly walk arm and arm into stores, laughing at the shocked stares they would get there. A tall skinny black man with a buxom blonde on his arm was quite a sight. Then those same people would gasp out loud when he would pull out a wad of cash to buy Beverly a coat or a purse.

At night, they would attend whatever party they were invited to. After a few hours, Happy would slip away and return to the hotel to study the Bible while Beverly partied till sunrise. Day after day and night after night, from one town to the next, it was the perfect plan. Mr. Give was nowhere to be seen, and Apollyon on his occasional visits would see what Happy wanted him to see and move on. That was until the night Beverly didn't come home.

* * *

Happy had fallen asleep reading at the desk in his suite and was startled when the telephone began to ring. He stood and stretched trying to loosen up his stiff back then walked over to the bedside table. He picked up the ringing phone then had to stifle a yawn before he answered.

"What...? It is...? What time is it? Yeah, yeah, okay, we'll be right down."

Happy stood up and stretched again, wincing at the pain that shot up his back and into his shoulders.

"Hey you, we overslept. The limo is waiting for us downstairs, get up and get dressed."

When he didn't get an answer, his shoulders slumped in exasperation. Beverly had begun to enjoy this lifestyle way too much, and he was going to have to put a stop to it before she got in too deep and couldn't get out.

"Beverly," he said a little too harshly as he turned to the bed. "I said you gotta get up. You can't run with the big dogs during the day if you—" He stopped short.

The bed was empty.

Happy stepped over to the closet where Beverly kept her clothes and opened it. Everything was there and the alligator suitcase that he had bought for her in New York was still sitting in the floor.

He checked the bathroom; her make-up and toothbrush were on the counter, and there was a pair of panties kicked into the corner. Beverly had become a little too accustomed to housekeeping as well and had started leaving her clothes wherever she took them off for the maid service to pick up.

He walked back over to the telephone and dialed *0* for the front desk.

"Yes, Mr. Parker, how may I assist you?" the front desk clerk answered, far too enthusiastic for this early in the morning.

"Did Miss Rachels leave a message for me?"

"No, sir," the clerk replied. "I haven't seen Miss Rachels since she left with you for your performance last evening."

"Okay, thanks."

"My pleasure, and just a reminder, your limousine is waiting for you at the front entrance."

"Yes, I know, thank you. Oh, can you ask for housekeeping to pack my things and send them along to my next stop please? I'm running late and don't have time to pack."

"Certainly, sir, and where is your next stop?"

Happy had to think about that for a moment.

"I have no idea," he admitted.

"No problem, Mr. Parker. I'll inquire and gladly forward on your belongings."

Happy hung up and looked around at the empty room. He went to the desk that had served as his bed the night before and took out a piece of paper and a pencil and wrote a note for Beverly.

> *Limo's here and I have to go. Hope everything is all right. Here's some money for bus fare. Hopefully you know where we are going. If not call the office and find out.*
>
> *Happy*

He stuck a hundred-dollar bill and the note in an envelope that had the hotel's logo in the upper left corner. He would drop it off at the front desk on his way out.

Fifteen minutes later, he was showered, dressed, and on his way. He grabbed Beverly's Bible from the desk and tucked it into his guitar case. Usually, it was her job to carry it, but today that wasn't an option. He hurried out the door, closing it behind him. The envelope, completely forgotten, was still sitting on the desk.

* * *

Happy stepped out of the elevator and into the hotel lobby where his driver was leaning against a doorframe and chatting up a waitress from the hotel restaurant. When he spotted Happy, he snapped to attention and rushed ahead to open the limousine door for him.

Happy tossed the guitar case in the back seat, then climbed in himself. The driver smiled and closed Happy's door before getting in behind the wheel and lowering the partition that separated the back seat from the front.

"Good morning, sir. Just settle in and get comfortable. We have about a nine-hour drive ahead of us."

"Thanks."

"I've placed the morning paper in the pocket on the seat back for you in case you want to read while we are on the road. Is there anything else you need before we get started?"

"No, I'm good, thanks."

"Very well then," the driver started to close the partition and Happy stopped him.

"Driver?"

"Yes, Mr. Parker?"

"Where are we going?"

"Mobile, sir. Southern Alabama."

"Oh yeah, great."

The driver turned around and raised the tinted glass partition.

Nine hours to get to Mobile, Alabama. Happy thought with that information he might could figure out where he had just left.

He didn't have to think too hard about it. When he opened the newspaper, the logo for the Charleston Post and Gazette was the first thing he saw.

A local shop owner had reportedly been robbed by two black men. He had a shotgun hidden behind the counter and killed one of them before they made it out of the building. A police officer had taken care of the other one on the street a block away. The police report said that they had not found any of the shop's merchandise on either of the men, so the police were searching the route the one had taken before being killed, in hopes of finding the stolen merchandise.

There was a sale on shotguns at Sears. The ad contained a sketch of a father and son holding their matching shotguns on their shoulders while dear old Dad held a fist full of ducks up in the air.

The summer Olympics were being held in Helsinki, Finland. William Harrison "Bones" Dillard, a black track-and-field athlete had won gold medals in both the 100-meter sprint and the 110-meter hurdles. They were calling him "The World's Fastest Man."

Happy thought that it didn't matter how fast he was if he'd been in the wrong place at the wrong time in Charleston on a Friday night.

He closed the newspaper and laid his head back against the seat cushion, closed his eyes, and tried to sleep. What made him so different from those two boys in Charleston? Nothing, except that he had signed Mr. Give's paper.

He thought again about how that verse in Matthew kept coming back up in his life. First Pappy saying those words to him the night he died, then seeing it written in the dirt on the window at The Gloryland Café, and again in that awful dream.

Pappy had always told him how his mother had lived her life by that book. Even blind, Pappy had found a way to hear the book's words, and they had become so much a part of him that when he lost his mind, those words had become his every word and thought.

Maybe *he* was losing his mind like Pappy had. That would explain a lot. He had been reading Beverly's Bible as much as he could in hopes of finding an answer, but there didn't seem to be one there.

Before he realized it, he had begun to pray.

"God, if you're there I need an answer. I need to know what's going on. Why are you, if it is you—if there is a *you*—doing this to me? If it's not you then who is it, or am I just as batshit crazy as my old man?"

He opened his eyes, sat up, and looked out his window at the countryside passing him by. A forest of evergreen trees stretched out as far as he could see, all in perfectly straight rows. As they approached a dirt road that cut through them, he saw an old faded sign:

Pappy's Christmas Tree Farm
Open December 1st - 24th
Cut your own tree just like Pappy used to do!

Happy laughed when he read it. They had never celebrated Christmas when he was growing up. Pappy said there was no Santa Claus and nothing that you got for free was worth having. One time, Happy had tried to sneak in a little tree just to try and brighten up the place, he was maybe twelve years old at the time. He had made an ornament out of an old coffee can lid and hung it on the tree.

The next morning, the tree was gone, and Pappy was visibly upset. He sat in his chair by the table, rocking forward and back with his hands clasped in his lap and his head bowed. He was mumbling something. A string of spit hung out of his mouth and was soaking into his shirt.

Seeing his father like that had scared Happy. He walked quietly up to him and touched his shoulder. His father jumped, cried out, and grabbed at Happy, managing to take hold of his shirt sleeve.

"It's me Pappy, it's Happy! What's the matter Pappy?" Happy had cried out. Realizing who he was holding, his father had loosened his grip, allowing Happy to step out of his reach. He remembered his father's next words clearly even all those years later.

"Then another sign appeared in heaven. An enormous red dragon with seven heads and ten horns and seven crowns on its heads. Its tail swept a third of the stars out of the sky and flung them to the earth."

Pappy had begun to cough and Happy went out on the porch to get him some water from the rain barrel. As he reached for the dipper, a glint of light in the yard had caught his eye. He set the dipper down and stepped off the porch.

The gravel was rutted there like something heavy had been dragged across it or like a big snake had traveled through the front yard. He followed the rut till he came upon the object that had gotten his attention. It was the ornament he had made. It was lying there in the dirt, the morning sun reflecting off it.

Happy bent over to pick it up, and that was when he noticed the footprints. Instead of picking up the can lid, he stepped to one side and looked back the way he had come. That disturbed area, the rut, led from the porch steps right up to the lid, then stopped. He looked past the lid toward the road. A single set of footprints began at the lid, then faded as they moved away. Pappy's words about a dragon came rushing back to Happy. He kicked dirt over the lid, then ran back into the house, closing the door securely behind him.

The Christmas tree lot ended and was replaced by rolling hills of corn and cotton. He watched them slide past his window and tried to imagine his parents out there with their picks and hoes working in the dirt, or bent over picking cotton and stuffing it into burlap bags that hung heavy on their shoulders. It was a life that he knew only from the stories his father told him as a child. Fairy tales from the past that only Pappy remembered.

Happy turned back and looked through the partition, out the front window of the limousine. The smoked glass of the partition made the road ahead look like something out of a nightmare. A world in constant eclipse. The dark road ahead was empty for as far as he could see, and he couldn't remember the last time he had seen another car on the road.

He reached for his guitar case to get the Bible he had hidden there. They had hours to go on the drive, so what better time to continue his search for answers. Normally Beverly would have been the one carrying the book, it was one of the ways he had managed to keep it out of sight. How would they know if he had it out here in the middle of nowhere? It was just him and the driver, and he was watching the road, not the back seat.

Happy eased the guitar case up into his lap and soundlessly undid the latches. Opening the case effectively blocked the driver's view of what he was doing if he happened to look back through the glass. He picked up the newspaper and eased the Bible from the case into it and placed it beside him before closing the case and returning it to the seat next to him.

He sat still and watched the driver to see if he had noticed anything. The man was sitting dead still with both hands on the wheel staring straight ahead at the road.

Happy opened the Bible, camouflaged by the newspaper, and began to read where he had left off in the eighth chapter of the book of John:

> And ye shall know the truth, and the truth shall make you free.
> 33 They answered him, We be Abraham's seed, and were never in bondage to any man: how sayest thou, Ye shall be made free?
> 34 Jesus answered them, Verily, verily, I say unto you, Whosoever committeth sin is the servant of sin.
> 35 And the servant abideth not in the house for ever: but the Son abideth ever.

36 If the Son therefore shall make you free,
ye shall be free indeed.

"If the Son shall make you free, you will be free indeed," he whispered those words over and over to himself.

Was this what he had been looking for? Was this the key to getting out of Mr. Give's grasp? If so, then he had to admit one thing to himself, and that was that Mr. Give was not some crazy, rich, white man, which is how Happy had always thought of him, but he was the devil. THE DEVIL.

The limousine began to slow, then pulled to a stop on the side of the road. Caught up in his thoughts, Happy paid little attention, thinking that the driver may have decided to stretch his legs or needed to relieve himself.

When the glass partition began to lower, it caught Happy by surprise. He quickly dropped the book to his lap and folded the newspaper around it. All he needed was to get caught with it by a driver who was just telling him that he needed to water a bush.

"Is there a problem driver?" Happy asked, glancing up from the mess of paper in his lap.

Instead of the round face of his driver, he looked up to see Apollyon staring back at him through the small opening.

"Damn straight there is."

From beside him Mr. Give reached over and removed the wad of newspaper hiding the Bible. Happy jumped at his touch and pushed himself against the limousine's door.

"Mr. Give...how did, where did...?" Happy stammered.

"I never quite understood the fascination that some people have with this book," Mr. Give said, paying no attention to Happy. He flipped the book from hand to hand, seeming to enjoy how the pages fluttered with each movement.

"The Other One's followers have used this as a reason to start wars, they have used it to crown themselves judge, jury, and executioner over their peers. They use it to rationalize their every single sordid thought."

Mr. Give faced him for the first time. Happy saw that his eyes were red, his pupils, dark islands in a sea of blood. "Your own father sacrificed his eyes for this mumbo jumbo, then went crazy trying to remember everything that was in it."

He stopped and set the Bible down in his lap and folded his hand over it.

"That is until your greed burned him alive," he stated, looking directly at Happy.

"That was an accident."

"Sure, it was." Mr. Give's voice was full of sarcastic understanding. "Happy, Happy, Happy. What am I going to do with you?" He shook his head slowly from side to side in a gesture usually reserved for parents disappointed by a child's bad behavior.

Mr. Give picked the Bible back up and made a show of rolling down the window and tossing the book out.

"As I was so quick to remind your father, I own you. You are my property, my cattle, my... "

Mr. Give paused to consider his words.

"My *bitch*. You've had it pretty good so far, and I must admit you have opened a door with your music that many a sad and pathetic soul has walked through. For that I am grateful, but not grateful enough to put up with any of this Bible foolishness. I was too lenient with your Pappy when it came to that little foible, and it cost me a good guitar player and a lot of wasted years waiting for you to get old enough to take his place."

Happy's heart pounded as he stared at Mr. Give and tried to take in everything the man said.

"Oh yes, I've had my eye on you for a very long time, and I plan to keep on using you. But now that you have forced me to show my hand, I guess I do need to teach you a little lesson."

He paused again and looked around at the inside of the car. "First off, let's lose the limo."

Happy nearly stumbled when his feet hit the ground. The afternoon sun began to heat the top of his head and wrap him in a humid oven. The limousine had disappeared, and he was standing at the side of the road holding his guitar case. He looked over at Mr. Give and Apollyon who were standing on the center stripe of the empty highway.

Mr. Give pulled a handkerchief out of his coat pocket and used it to fan himself. "It *is* a scorcher today. Way too hot for that fancy suit you're wearing."

The snug fit of Happy's custom-tailored suit loosened and hung loose on his body. The cuffs slid an inch down over his wrists as his high-dollar suit was exchanged for a cheap thrift store one that was a few sizes too large. The nice new guitar case Happy carried now looked beat up and old, the handle attached by a piece of twine.

"That's better. Now you're really starting to look the part of a traveling blues man, and that is exactly what you are. So, go on Mr. Blues Man and ride your thumb into the next town."

A sporty black car pulled up beside them, and Apollyon got in behind the wheel. Mr. Give looked Happy up and down, smiling, then gave him a wink before getting in the passenger seat and closing the door.

Apollyon stomped the gas and the tires peeled out on the hot pavement, leaving Happy in a cloud of smoke. The car abruptly stopped, then the backup lights came on like two cat's eyes through the fog. It backed up and came to rest with the passenger window beside Happy. For a brief moment, he saw himself reflected in the glass. His face had become drawn, wrinkles had formed at the sides of his eyes and mouth, and his hair had turned gray at the temples.

The window slid down and Mr. Give looked out at him. "Oh, and Happy, no one knows who you are anymore. You've never made a record, never got any awards, *nothing*. Now you are just a down-on-your-luck blues man. One more thing . . ." He reached down beside his seat and handed Happy a bottle of brown liquid. "Take this in case you get thirsty hitching out here in the hot sun. Next time you want to take a peek in-side that book, you just remember how it worked out for you this time."

Mr. Give rolled up the window, and they sped off, leaving Happy in a cloud of dust.

He looked down at the bottle in his hand. In big scrolling letters it read, *OLD CROW*. Happy's mouth began to water and a need to open that bottle and savor its contents came over him in a way he had never know before.

Suddenly, he was very thirsty.

CHAPTER 12

1954

Happy walked with his eyes closed, not caring where he was, where he'd been, or where he was going. All the roads he traveled were dirt, and he had become accustomed to feeling every pebble as they pressed up against the thread-bare soles of his shoes. He was hungry and needed a drink.

He stubbed his toe on a clump of dried mud, stumbled, and fell. The guitar case he was carrying slid into a ditch. He still hadn't opened his eyes. Happy just sat there on the side of the road, listening and hoping for the sound of a truck that he could roll out in front of and put an end to all this.

"Oh no!" he yelled at the top of his lungs when nothing came his way. "No, you won't let that happen will you, you son of a bi. . ." His words trailed off till he was just mumbling nonsense.

He scraped up two handfuls of dirt and threw them in the air, then turned his face up and let the debris fall on him. He laughed at that, then started feeling around for his guitar. He couldn't find it by feel, so he relented, opened his eyes, and laughed again.

Before him stretched an old dirt road for as far as his eyes could see. A road that looked just like the last one he was on, and the one before that. For two years he had been walking on dirt roads that took him to small towns with little bars where he would play for tips, or if he got lucky, maybe a meal and a drink.

The night before, he had played at a little hole-in-the-wall with a bare bulb on a wire over the stage. They had given him a choice of chicken fried steak or whiskey. He had chosen the bottle, and now his stomach was letting him know that he made the wrong decision. But if he had it to do again, he knew he would make the same choice.

A signpost stood on the side of the road. He looked up at the sign and squinted to try and make the words come into focus.

Warm Springs 10

The white letters stamped into the old metal sign had all but faded into the chipped green paint that had once shined like a spring tomato still on the vine. Happy licked at the dirt that had stuck in the sweat around his mouth, then spit at the base of the sign.

He struggled to get to his feet, only to slide down again while trying to get his guitar out of the ditch. When he finally managed to crawl out, he closed his eyes and began walk.

"Ride your thumb into the next town." That was what that damned devil had told him the last time Happy had laid eyes on him. He had tried hitching rides for a while, but who was he kidding? He was an old black drunk. No self-respect-ing white man would be caught with him in their car, and anyone of his kind who would pick him up was as likely to beat him for his bottle and leave him to die as he was to get him where he needed to be.

So, he walked.

After a few miles he started to hear music—a jangly guitar playing a rhythm he knew all too well. His Pappy had called it "playing the train." It was a choppy rhythm that sounded like the chug, chug, chug of a train going down the tracks. If he played that rhythm one time a night, he played it twenty. It was a sound that made the ladies shake their hips and the men smack their lips. It was a sound that put tips in the jar and a bottle in his pocket.

As he drew closer to the music, he began to make out a high tenor voice singing along.

"Singing, hey there Momma, is you gonna take me home?
Hey there Momma, is you gonna take me home?
Well, I'm going away, Momma, cause I gotta roam,
Won't be back, Momma, feets just wanna roam.
Going away, Momma to find myself a home.
You're a triflin' woman and you're goin' home alone."

Happy knew the tune, but the words were new to him. White folks up north called it the blues, but down here it was just colored music. In his other life, he had made records of songs that sounded just like that and folks from New York to Chicago had paid good money to buy those records and to see him play the songs live. Chicken fried steak or whiskey . . . oh how the mighty had fallen.

The sound of the guitar and the high squeaky voice led him to an old clapboard shack that sat just off the side of the road. A wire fence that had seen many better days ran along the front of the house, with a broken-down gate at its center. Big rocks had been placed at the base of each rotten fencepost in an attempt to keep them standing. The walls of the shack had turned black with age, and the front porch drooped noticeably at one end. An old black man sat in a rocking chair on the porch. As he rocked and played, a loose board squeaked and popped in time to the song.

"You're a triflin' woman and you're goin' home alone.
You're a triflin' woman, mmm . . .
Won't take me home, so you goin' home alone.
Won't take me home, now you all alone."

The man was thin as a rail and wore black slacks and a black suit coat over his naked chest. A bowler hat with a chicken feather in the band perched at an angle on top of his head. His mustache was pencil thin, and when he opened his mouth to sing Happy could see that his gums were black and many of his teeth were missing.

He saw Happy and stopped playing.

"Hiya, brother," he called out and raised his hand. "Been a mite since one of our own done come a-callin'." His voice was high-pitched and reedy like nails on a chalkboard.

"I heard you're playing as I was walking along and followed it to you," Happy said, standing outside the fence. "That's some mean picking you were doing."

"Twern't' nothin', just a little something I picked up along the way, but thanks for the kind words all the same." The man stood, reached behind his chair, and picked up a bottle that was sitting on a table there. "You look like a man what needs a little something to grease his gears. Don't be a stranger. Step on up here and share with me."

"You ain't got to ask me twice." Happy pushed down on the wires that separated them and stepped over. At the sight of the bottle, his hands started to shake and as he stepped up to the porch, he reached out for it.

"Uh, uh. Not so fast, brother. The house gets to drink first 'round here."

Happy licked his dry lips and watched intently as the man used his few remaining teeth to pull the cork from the bottle, then spit it on the ground at Happy's feet. The man smacked his lips, then turned up the bottle, letting the amber liquor pour into his mouth. Happy watched as half the bottle's contents emptied before the man finally lowered it. He finished with a loud belch and handed the bottle over to Happy.

"Careful, it's got a kick." The man belched again, then crowed and strutted around the porch in a circle like a banty rooster.

Happy brought the bottle to his lips, then hesitated, thinking about the man's black gums and rotted teeth. When the smell of the alcohol reached his nose, any hesitation he was feeling left him. He pressed the bottle to his lips and drank deeply. The whiskey burned his mouth and throat. He gagged and had to stop drinking to get his breath.

"Haw!" the man crowed. "Told you it had a kick!"

"Kick nothing, that stuff's dynamite."

"Yeah, it is. I brew it out back. Toss in a little kerosene for color."

Happy inhaled deeply, then took another pull off the bottle. This time his throat welcomed the burn, and he started feeling its effects soften reality's edges. A third pull emptied the bottle, and he handed it back to his host, who tossed it in the weeds at the side of the house.

"So, tell me brother, you play that thing or just carry it around for looks, hmm?" The man indicated the guitar case that was sitting next to Happy.

"I play," Happy answered him. "I play for my supper, I play for my whiskey, and I play for my ladies, but not always in that order." The liquor was doing its job, and Happy couldn't help but laugh at his own joke.

"Well how about you whip that thing out and give me a little something? You done heard me pick, now you return the favor."

The back-yard hooch had hit Happy's system hard, and he struggled with the latches on the case. He finally managed to retrieve the guitar and dropped down on a large rock that served as the porch step.

Happy started strumming, and before long he was *playing the train*. The man picked up his guitar and joined in. The sound of the two instruments, Happy's rhythm, and his new friend's lead lines, blended perfectly, and he was carried away on waves of whiskey and sound. He let his body move to the music, swaying back and forth on the hard stone.

"Oh, help me Momma," the old man sang,
"the man done stole my soul,
done stole my soul, it's a hot day down below, mmm.
Well, I'm goin' away, Momma, won't be back no mo'
Won't be back no mo', mmm.
Goin' away, Momma, won't be back no mo'.
Misser Gib dun come an' stole my livin' soul."

Happy stopped playing and looked up at the man.

"Whatchu' looking at, brother? I'm just doing what it is I do."

"What you was just singing..."

"Yeah, brother, you know all about that, no?" He tilted his head when he spoke, looking at Happy like he was trying to get him to admit to some deep dark secret. "Come on now, dis is me you talking to. You know Misser Gib and his big bad buddy what smokes them fat cigars."

"Maybe I do, but what do you know about him?"

"What do I know? What do I know?" The man stood and turned in a circle with his hands outstretched. "I know he give me this beautiful house and this here 'spensive guitar. He set me up but good, and all's I gotta do is pick a little here and there!" The man grabbed the guitar and started again *playing the train*.

> "Oh, that ol' Misser Gib, done gib me this very home,
> this very home, mmm.
> Old Misser Gib, done gib me this very home.
> Misser Gib dun come an' stole my livin' soul,"

Happy picked up his guitar and case and started backing away from the house. Was this what his father had been destined to become? And what about himself when Mr. Give was finally done with him? Would he leave him sitting in a dump like this believing it was a castle, while he drank himself into oblivion?

"Where you goin' brother?" the man yelled from the porch while still strumming the guitar. "I got another bottle back here, come on back. Me and you a lot alike, we brothers, we got the same daddy and him name is Misser Gib!" The man laughed and crowed, *playing the train* faster and faster.

Happy knew he needed to get as far away as he could, he felt like his life depended on it, like his *sanity* depended on it.

He turned to run but forgot about the wire fence. Before he realized what had happened, the wires pulled loose from the rotted poles they were attached to and became tangled around his legs. He dropped the guitar and the case to try and keep his balance, but it was no use. He fell and struck his head on a rock that had been holding one of the poles in place.

* * *

Pure white light encased Happy. A cool breeze blew over his face and he felt like he was floating. A shadowy figure came upon him, blocking some of the light from his face, but still hovering just out of sight. He heard whispers—they seemed to surround him—everywhere and nowhere at the same time. Whispered words and songs, and the sound comforted him. He felt at peace.

"It's okay." A soothing voice cut through the whispers and a hand reached out to touch his face. "It's just a little cut, you're gonna be okay." The shadowed figure above him started to solidify, to come together. It came in closer and became the face of his mother. Her smile warmed him. Tears filled his eyes, and he couldn't understand how he could feel so much love for someone he had never met, but he did.

"You just hang in there," she said, "were almost home."

Almost *home*? Had his mother come to take him home? Was she taking him away from all this suffering at the hands of Mr. Give? Had she intervened for him? Had she...?

The ground underneath him rose up and hit him hard on the side of head. He opened his eyes and bright sunlight blinded him. Happy raised his arm to shield his eyes, and a glance at his surroundings told him that he was riding in a car and laying with his head in an open window.

"Hey, there you are. You had me worried!"

Happy reached out and used the back of the seat to pull himself up fully. His head spun wildly, and he had to shut his eyes and force himself not to cry out. He touched his fingers to the side of his head, and they came back sticky with partially dried blood.

"Sorry about that, I didn't have anything in the car to clean you up with, but we'll be at my place in just a minute."

His head was spinning and with every bump of the car he felt like he would either pass out or vomit his guts up. He managed to slowly turn his head in the direction the voice was coming from. At first, all he saw was a frenzy of yellow hair blowing all around the head of the person behind the wheel, then she reached up and gathered her hair with the hand not on the wheel. He couldn't believe his eyes.

Beverly was driving the car.

She suddenly jerked the wheel to one side to try and miss a pothole in the road but only managed to make the situation worse. The car hit the deep hole at an angle instead of straight on, and the jolt lifted Happy out of his seat, slamming his head against the car's low roof and knocking him unconscious.

* * *

Happy came to again just as the car pulled to a stop outside a small white farmhouse surrounded by cornfields.

"We're here," she said looking around the empty front yard. "I need you to stay here and lay down in the seat until I let momma know that you're with me."

"I don't understand, how did—"

Beverly shushed him by putting a finger to his lips. It smelled of old cigarettes and cheap perfume, but he got the message.

"Now do as I say and lay over here in the seat, and I'll be right back," she whispered. She opened the door and slid out silently, closing the door behind her.

Happy did as he was told and laid over on the seat and listened. His heart was pounding, he could feel it in his temples. Each beat sent a shockwave of pain across his face that settled into his teeth.

He noticed that the radio dial was broken and that there was a fist-sized dent in the glove compartment door. The floorboards were caked with mud, and the dash had split and grown brittle from years of exposure to the sun.

A screen door slammed somewhere outside the car. He heard harried voices drawing closer.

"Well, what was I supposed to do? I couldn't just leave him there in the road to die, could I?" Beverly was saying.

"You didn't have to bring him here. If your pa lays eyes on him, he's gonna' wish you had left him out there," a woman's voice answered.

Two faces appeared in the window, looking down at Happy. One was Beverly, and the other he assumed was her mother. The woman's fat face was ruddy from overexertion, and her breathing came in short bursts. Happy thought that if they had walked another ten yards, she would have been lying out there dead from a heart attack instead of looking down at him.

"Jesus H., Beverly! You've done it this time! Bringing home stray cats and dogs is one thing, but bringing this rode-hard nigger into our home is too much!"

"Who are you calling a rode—"

"Shut up, boy," she shouted at Happy, cutting him off. Her face got redder by the second. "Let me make one thing perfectly clear, you have exactly one shot at living to see tomorrow, and that one shot is me. So don't piss me off, understood?"

Happy didn't answer her. He just kept his mouth shut and tried to hold his anger at bay.

"That's better." She turned to Beverly. "Your daddy—"

"He's not *my daddy*!"

"Fine, your *step*daddy is at his den meeting, so we've probably got about half an hour to get this boy out of sight. Now, go around and haul his ass out of the car, then take him into the corn. Mind you don't break no stalks doing it or Daddy'll know. Once it's dark, I'll tell you that I need you to run to old Miss Baker's to take her some meal that she had asked to borrow to make bread for tomorrow's church social."

She turned her attention back to Happy. "When you hear the car start up you hightail it out to the road, and she'll pick you up and drop you across the county line."

"Yes, Momma," Beverly said, and Happy nodded in agreement.

Beverly came around to the passenger's side of the car and helped Happy to his feet. As soon as he tried to stand, big black circles appeared before his eyes, and the strength started to leave his legs. He slumped against Beverly, and his head rolled back on his shoulders.

"Jesus H. we ain't got time for this." Beverly's mother rounded the car and took Happy's arm to take some of the dead weight off Beverly.

"He's passed out again, Momma."

"I can see that, and he stinks of rotgut whiskey. My Lord, girl, your kind heart is gonna be the death of me, you mark my words."

"I'm sorry, Momma, what do we do with him now? No way the three of us can sneak into the corn without leaving a trail."

"Let's dump him in a stall in the barn. When Daddy gets home, I'll keep him occupied while you sneak out and try to wake this boy up and get him out in the field."

"You think you can do that?" Beverly asked.

"Daddy's always feeling his oats after a den meeting. I think I can find a way."

A loud backfire came from across the field followed by the sound of an engine in dire need of a muffler.

"That's your cousin, Bobby Joe's truck, you can hear it a mile away. Daddy rode with him to the meeting. Haul ass girl, or we're all gonna be in it."

They carried Happy across the yard to a barn that sat on the edge of the closest cornfield. The old barn door screeked in protest as they pulled it open. Inside were four stalls that once held the mules that were used to work the fields. Those mules had been replaced by a tractor last year, and the big machine sat in the center of the barn leaving very little room on either side to pass by it. They managed to open the first stall door and dump Happy inside.

Beverly's mother turned to leave the barn, but Beverly hesitated, looking down at Happy. A shrill whistle got her attention.

"Move girl, git!" her mother commanded.

Beverly followed her out of the barn and latched the door behind them. They ran across the yard and into the house just as a beat up 1935 Ford F1 flatbed pick up pulled into the yard. The old truck backfired and rolled to a stop outside the barn.

The sound of the backfire brought Happy around, and he had no idea where he was. He was about to call out when the old woman's words came back to him. He was supposed to be in the corn but something must have gone wrong, and they had put him in the barn instead.

A truck door slammed, and he chanced a peek outside. Looking through one of the openings between the planks, he could see a short man with a big belly, wearing overalls and a floppy hat, standing next to the truck. The man placed his hands flat against the small of his back and stretched. The exertion caused him to pass gas with a thunderous report.

A big man in khaki pants and a baby-blue cotton shirt buttoned up tight under his chin appeared around the front of the truck. He stopped suddenly, put his hands on his knees, and let out with a bray that any mule would have been proud of.

"Wee haw Willie, did that come out of you?" The man's teeth were yellow from chewing tobacco. He spit a stream of brown juice at his feet then wiped a dribble off his chin with the cuff of his shirt. "Carol Ann's gonna have to wash your drawers out in the back yard after that 'un!"

"Shut up, Bobby Joe," Willie said. His low voice rumbled like thunder. He spoke in a slow manner that could have been taken as sign of a feeble mind if not for the meanness that it carried in its tone.

Willie reached inside the truck and pulled out a hickory walking stick. The solid piece of wood had been worn smooth from years of use. He wrapped his meaty hand around the top and started making his way to the house.

He passed gas again, and Bobby Joe snickered.

"One more sound out of you, and it it'll be your last." Willie stopped and held the walking stick out in Bobby Joe's direction and Bobby Joe stepped back. Willie took that as a sign of contrition, so he lowered the stick and continued on.

Happy watched as the two men crossed the yard and went inside. A few minutes later Bobby Joe came back out holding a basket of eggs. Beverly's mother was close behind him.

"Mind you don't break any of them eggs, Bobby Joe. Your granny's gonna need every one of them to make them butter-milk pies of hers for the church social."

"Yes Ma'am, Carol Ann. I'll be extra careful and I'm gonna tell Granny to set aside one of the pies special for you and Willie."

"No need for that. If you make it home with all them eggs, there'll be pies enough for everybody."

Bobby Joe opened the passenger's side door of the truck and gently placed the basket of eggs in the seat. He then climbed in behind the wheel and started it up.

The old truck backfired, frightening Happy so badly that he stumbled and fell against the wall, rattling some metal tools hanging there. He quickly quieted them, then stood perfectly still, hoping that Bobby Joe had not heard anything. A moment later, the old truck's gears grinded into place, and the truck pulled away.

Happy eased back to his spot beside the wall and looked out again. Beverly's mother was standing on the porch, staring directly at him. Another backfire came from Bobby Joe's truck as he pulled out of the driveway onto the main road. Carol Ann looked in that direction, then went back inside.

* * *

As the sun set, its light shone full against the front wall of the barn, sending shafts of dusty beams to brighten the stall where Happy was sitting. For the first time since he had been dumped there by Beverly and her mother, he was able to fully see his surroundings. A polished wooden cabinet sat against one wall, looking out of place with all the tools, twine and leather tack that covered the other surfaces in the room. Happy peered through his crack toward the house to make sure that no one was coming, then went over to the cabinet.

He noticed that the straw and dust that covered the floor had all been pushed aside by the cabinet door as if it had been opened recently. He figured that it was full of parts for the tractor that stood outside the stall door. Probably some cans of oil and a rusty funnel. But he hoped that somewhere in the cabinet, maybe tucked away in a dark back corner, ol' Willie might have stashed a little something to take away the chill of a cold winter morning. Didn't all those hayseed farmers have a still somewhere hidden back in the hills?

Happy was hurting for a drink. He just needed a little taste to settle his nerves and to help him think.

He reached a trembling hand out and grasped the wooden handle of the first door. He made a silent wish and opened it. He was right, it was full of tools, oil cans, and funnels. A slightly larger lower section contained a pair of rubber mud boots. He blew out his breath and closed the door. Feeling let down and expecting to find more of the same, he stepped over in front of the second cabinet door and this time didn't hesitate. He grabbed the handle and pulled the door wide open.

A tall white figure reached out for Happy, and it was all he could do to jump back out of the way of the outstretched arms. He threw himself on the ground and curled into a ball, covering his head with his arms. He prepared himself for the blows to come, but none did.

He listened, but there was no sound inside the stall, except for his heavy breathing and pounding heart. Cautiously, he lowered his arms and glanced up at the cabinet where his attacker had been hiding, then started to laugh silently.

Hanging inside the cabinet was a bleached white robe with a pointed mask attached. He stood, stepped back over to the cabinet, and closed the door. Then as he had done just a moment before, he snatched the door open. The suction created by opening the door caused the robe's long arms to rise, then slowly settle down again.

Trying to contain his laughter, he closed the door, then couldn't help himself. For the third time, he snatched it open with the same results.

"You won't be laughing if Daddy catches you out here messing with his den uniform."

"Shit!" Happy jumped back at the sound of Beverly's voice. He tripped over his own feet and fell against the wall, hitting his head on a stud and threatening to reopen the earlier wound there.

"Shhh," Beverly whispered. She came into the stall and closed the door behind her. "Momma took Daddy into the bedroom so I could get you out of here, but if he hears you making a bunch of racket, ain't nothing Momma's got'll keep him in that bed."

"Sorry," Happy whispered. "It's been a hell of a day and I was hoping there might be something in there to calm my nerves."

Beverly looked down at him sitting in the dirt and straw and took pity on him. She turned to the robe hanging in the cabinet and pushed it to one side. Leaning in, she came out with a gallon jug full of clear liquid with a corncob stopper.

"Bobby Joe's got a still up yonder in the hills. I think this stuff is the only reason Daddy lets him hang around. That and he's got a big enough truck to carry the cross on burning nights."

Happy let that sink in for a minute, then stood and took the jug from Beverly. He pulled the cork out with a satisfying *pop* and put the jug to his lips. Having learned his lesson earlier in the day, he just took a small sip. The clear alcohol swirled around inside his mouth. It came alive with the first touch and created a tingle on his tongue, then a second later the fire that he craved traveled down his throat. His second taste was deep and satisfying, and as he raised the bottle for a third, Beverly put a hand on his arm to stop him.

"You've had enough to steady your nerves. Now we need to get you out of here before Daddy starts wondering where I got off to."

Happy nodded and shoved the corncob back in the mouth of the bottle. Beverly took him by the arm and led him over to the stall door.

"I'm gonna stand watch while you sneak past the Farmall and out the back. Open that door back there real easy 'cause them hinges are rusted and they squeal if you move 'em too fast. Once out the back, you'll be about four good steps from the edge of the corn, just slip in there and follow the rows all the way to the other side. That'll take you to the main road. Hunker down there out of sight, and I'll come get you as soon as I can."

Happy nodded, then slipped out the door and down past the red Farmall tractor. When he got to the rear of the barn, he looked back at Beverly. She was peering out through a crack she had opened in the front door. After a few seconds, she turned back and motioned for him to go on. Happy put his shoulder against the barn door and applied a small amount of pressure. The door didn't move. He looked back at Beverly just in time to see her open the barn door, step out into the fading afternoon light, and close the door behind her.

He panicked. He was stuck in the barn of a low-talking, short, fat, angry Klansman and the only chance he had of surviving this had just left him stranded. His heart raced as thoughts of what that farmer might do to him ran through his mind.

Then he realized that he still had the jug of moonshine in his hand. This was not the time for another drink, or was it? He was probably about to die; wouldn't that go a bit easier if he were drunk?

He leaned his back against the barn door and tried to resist the urge to take a drink. He closed his eyes and softly banged his head against the door. That sent a wave of pain through him that broke what little reserve he had left. He reached down and wrapped his hand around the piece of corncob that served as a cork. He pulled, hoping for that satisfying *pop* that signaled that the bar was open. The cork didn't budge. He pulled harder, but still nothing. Then he remembered how the man he had met earlier, how his *brother*, had opened that bottle, and he lifted the jug to his mouth and sunk his teeth into the cork.

The door behind him opened, and he fell out into the grass, landing flat on his back. The jug he had been trying to open slammed into his mouth, opening a cut in his lip.

"Get up! Get up!" Beverly whispered and made shooing motions with her hands toward the cornfield. Happy half rolled and half crawled to the edge of the field, then stood and slipped into one of the rows.

Beverly followed him in.

"Where did you go?" he whispered. "I thought your father had come out."

"I remembered that Daddy put a latch on the back door to keep anybody from sneaking in through the field to steal the tractor. That's why you couldn't open it. Now go do like I told you and get to the other side of the field." With that, Beverly stepped out into the barnyard and disappeared.

Happy turned his back to the barn and headed off through the corn toward the highway.

* * *

The corn was thick with ripe ears that Happy had to duck and dodge as he made his way through. Their husks hung down and felt like spiderwebs when they touched his face. He did as Beverly instructed and followed the row he was in.

After about fifteen minutes, he started hearing traffic noises. He eased up to the outer edge of the field and peeked out. A two-lane, black-topped road ran along the edge of the field just as Beverly had told him.

Happy went back about ten feet and settled down, figuring he was far enough from the road to keep from being seen. Now he just had to wait till Beverly came to get him. It could be hours, hours of sitting in the corn. Hours alone with his thoughts. Hours with nothing to do. Just him and the full bottle of white lightning.

He reached out and ran his hand down the side of the clear glass jug. It was cool and a little condensation had formed on the surface of the glass. He wanted nothing more than to turn up that bottle and let the cool liquor drain from it down his throat. He longed for the numbness that it would provide his tired mind. He needed to feel the burn in his stomach spread out through him.

It was a bad idea, and Happy knew it. He needed to stay sharp and focused. He needed to be prepared to jump in the car and make his getaway when Beverly arrived. He needed to stay sharp and listen for her old man in case he came for him through the corn.

He needed a drink.

Happy pulled the cork out and brought the bottle to his lips. He lifted the bottom just enough for a splash to escape the neck and wet his mouth. It was as amazing as he knew it would be, and he savored it. He licked a stray drop from his lips, then brought the bottle up again and drank deep. A wave of heat passed through him, and his nervous tension started to fade.

Happy set the bottle down and closed his eyes. A part of him hated the need, hated the dependency. Another part of him, a larger, stronger part loved it, embraced it, and called it home.

"You don't need none of that, boy."

Happy started when he heard the voice and tried to stand, but the alcohol made itself known and he drifted to one side, then sat back down hard. He looked around at the thick stalks that surrounded him, trying to see who had spoken. There was no one there. He stared at the bottle in his hand, forcing his eyes to focus and stay still. It must have just been his con-science talking, reminding him that if he was too drunk to get in the car when Beverly arrived, then he was as good as dead.

Happy shut his eyes and leaned his head back against a cornstalk. His head swam under the effects of the drink, and he loved and hated the feeling at the same time.

"You better pull yourself together and fly right."

This time the voice came from behind him. He threw himself on the ground and looked in the direction from which he was sure it had come. Nothing, just corn rising above him like the bars of a cell. He closed his eyes and rested his head on his arm. Lying there on his stomach in the middle of a cornfield, Happy fell asleep.

* * *

Footsteps.

Happy awoke but didn't move. He lay perfectly still and listened. The footsteps came again, this time accompanied by the sound of corn leaves being pushed aside. A breeze floated past him and carried on it the scent of soap and vanilla.

Happy opened his eyes and was surprised to see that the sun had set. It was dark in the cornfield. The breeze came again, and this time it brought an acrid animal smell with it. He wrinkled his nose at the offensive order, like a wet dog that had been rolling in garbage.

A low growl came from deep in the corn somewhere to his left, the angry wet growl of an animal on the hunt. Happy slowly pushed himself into a seated position, trying to not make any sounds or sudden moves that would lead whatever it was out there to him. He wrapped his hand around the neck of the jug, prepared to use it as a weapon, even if it meant losing the joy it contained.

The vanilla smell came again, this time stronger. A dim glow appeared off to his right. As he watched, it floated to one side, then back in the other direction. It passed behind a thick clump of stalks that blocked it from his view, only to reappear a few feet farther away.

From behind him, the growl came again, this time closer. Happy turned his head, and red eyes stared back at him from two rows over. Whatever it was had found him. His eyes locked with the animal's in what felt like a life-or-death staring contest. *First one to blink loses.*

Fear rose inside of him, and he fought to control his breathing. Animals could sense fear, and if this animal sensed weakness in him he might never leave this field. Given a choice between death at the hands of a short, fat Klansman or in the jaws of a wild animal, Happy thought he might prefer the Klansman.

Never breaking eye contact, Happy pulled his legs under him and managed to get on his feet. The animal chuffed and its growl turned high pitched and threating.

Happy gulped. A large dog with fangs bared pushed forward through the corn. The animal was massive, easily standing four feet tall. Its broad shoulders parted the cornstalks with ease as it stepped into a pool of moonlight. It was missing an eye and the empty socket had scarred over. A deep gash ran down its muzzle and split its nose. The dog lowered itself into a crouch and extended it neck in Happy's direction. It growled again and a white foam dripped from between its clenched teeth.

Happy took a deep breath, preparing to run for his life. The dog woofed again and took another step in his direction, daring Happy to run. Happy was about to do just that when a bright white light and the smell of vanilla engulfed him.

"GO! GO NOW!" the voice from earlier screamed inside his head. Happy dropped the bottle, sprang to his feet and ran in the direction of the road. The dog yelped, followed by the sound of a struggle, then the light went out and Happy was plunged into darkness.

An angry howl came from behind him. He heard the dog running through the rows. It was on his scent, and it wouldn't take long for it to make up what little lead Happy had managed to gain.

A light appeared a few yards ahead of him through the corn, and thinking it was headlights on the highway, Happy started in that direction. If he could manage to get to the highway, then he might be able to wave down a car and make his escape. The dog's heavy breathing got closer behind him. He imagined that he could feel it nipping at his heels.

As Happy approached the light, it moved to his left. He made a course correction to continue following it. The light disappeared, then reappeared again farther along, leading Happy in a zig-zag pattern.

Happy didn't know how much longer he was going to be able to keep running like this. His lungs burned and his left calf threatened to cramp.

The light moved again, and this time when Happy turned to follow, his foot struck something lying on the ground. He fell face first in the dirt. He landed with his hand touching something hard, smooth, and wooden. He instinctively grabbed it and pointed it in the direction of the dog, hoping to hold it off.

The dog burst air-bound through the corn and struck the front of Happy's weapon at full speed. There was a wet sound followed by a howl of pain. The impact was enough that it knocked Happy over and wrenched the wood from his hand. The piece of wood he had been holding began bouncing around on the ground and slapping at his legs and the corn-stalks around it. After a moment, it stopped thrashing and lay still.

Cautiously, Happy got to his feet, and with the little bit of moonlight that filtered through the corn lighting his way, he followed the length of the wood to its other end.

The wood turned out to be the handle of a pitchfork that someone had abandoned in the field. The light had led him to it. He had managed to raise it up just in time, and the dog hit it hard enough to bury the rusty tongs in its skull. The once-fierce creature now lay still at Happy's feet. Even with a pitchfork in its head, the dog still felt like a threat. Happy nudged it with the toe of his shoe, then jumped away in case the dog sprang back to life. But it didn't move.

Happy breathed a sigh of relief.

When he turned to try and orient himself, the blinding light that had given him the head start from the dog surrounded him again. An angel hovered above him with its arms outstretched. A golden halo encircled its head, and its wings were tipped in the same gold. The angel's light began to dim, and it settled to the ground in front of Happy. Its wings disappeared into its back, and its halo morphed into white streaks in its hair. It stepped down onto the earth as if stepping off a low step and walked up to Happy.

Mother . . .

Seraphina reached up and started to place her hand on Happy's face but stopped and took a step back. A tear ran down her cheek and dropped to the ground. Where it landed a lily burst from the dirt in full bloom.

"Mother?" He reached out for her, but she stepped back farther to avoid his touch.

"There is evil inside you. You have accepted the embrace of the devil. You must repent and turn your back on the father of lies before it's too late."

"It *is* too late. I signed his paper, I took his deal, I..." Happy broke down and fell to his knees in front of Seraphina. He buried his face in his hands, unable to look at her.

Seraphina knelt in front of her crying son, longing to touch and comfort him, and at the same time repulsed at what he had become. "It's only too late if you've given up. If you have faith and believe it..."

The dog convulsed next to Happy, and a deep growl formed in the animal's midsection. It rolled over and tried to stand up, unable to raise its head because of the pitchfork still buried there.

Happy recoiled and jumped to his feet. The dog shook its head, swinging the pitchfork handle left and right. It slapped at Happy's feet and the surrounding cornstalks.

Happy turned to his mother for help, but she was gone. The dog lunged at him, but the weight of the pitchfork caused it to fall to one side. Seizing the opportunity to get away, Happy jumped back into the corn and ran. He had no idea where he was going, but anywhere was better than where he had just been.

A car horn beeped three times somewhere in front of him. Three short bursts that meant freedom to him. He poured on the speed, ignoring the corn fronds that scratched his face and the ears that reached out to strike his shoulders and arms.

He burst through the last row of corn and spotted Beverly standing by her car less than fifty yards away. He ran toward her waving his hands and motioning for her to get back in.

Beverly stared at him, not understanding why he was acting so strangely.

As he got closer, he started yelling at her. "Get in the car, get in! We have to go now! Get in and start the damn car!"

Beverly did as she was told. When Happy jumped in, she threw the car into gear and roared back out onto the highway with tires squealing and leaving two clear skid marks on the road.

Happy twisted around in the seat so he could see out the back window, expecting at any moment for the dog to come running out of the field. When that didn't happen, he settled into the seat and let his head fall back against the headrest.

"My God, what happened to you?" Beverly had looked away from the road and obviously noticed his dirty clothes and scratched face. She put her attention back to her driving, but glanced his way with another concerned look.

"Please watch the road," Happy said. "After what I've just lived through, I don't need you to kill me in a wreck."

They traveled on in silence for a while.

"What happened to you in that field?" she finally said. "I know it wasn't Daddy 'cause once Momma was through with him, all he wanted to do was eat and go to sleep."

"It was a big dog. I fell asleep and woke up with this big dog after me. Then an Ang... Never mind it was just a big angry dog."

"You poor thing. I've got some of Daddy's clothes in the trunk. I swiped them so you would have something to change into. I'll pull over and get 'em for you."

"*NO!*" Happy sat up in alarm. "No don't, not here. Let's get as far away from here as we can."

Beverly looked over at him with concern.

"I mean in case...you know..." Happy sputtered, realizing that he had overreacted. "You know, in case your father wakes up and comes looking for you."

Beverly nodded and went back to watching the road. They drove on for another hour. Happy spent the time looking out his window as Beverly searched for music on the radio. She finally landed on a country station broadcasting out of Nashville. As the last few bars of a two-step melody played out the announcer came on.

"That was the classic, *Devil and the Dance Hall Girl* made famous by Joe Mann who lost his life outside the Dixie Tabernacle after making his first appearance on the Grand Ole Opry twenty years ago this very night. Next up, it's Tennessee Ernie Ford with *River of No Return*."

The song's opening strings swelled and filled the car with music. When Tennessee Ernie Ford started singing, Beverly hummed along with the melody. She had a beautiful voice, and as it blended with the song, Happy began to feel the tension that had held him in its grip since getting out of the cornfield start to fade.

He looked over at the instrument panel then back up to Beverly as she yawned, covering her mouth with her hand. "Looks like we're gonna be needing some gas soon," she said. "Maybe it's time to pull over for the night and get a fresh start in the morning."

About a mile farther on, Beverly spotted a dirt road coming out of a line of trees. She turned onto it and found a field hidden from the main road. She pulled the car into the field and stopped. "I brought some food for us, so why don't you go scout some firewood while I get things ready."

Happy slid out of the seat and walked over to the trees they had just driven through. The moonlight shone brightly in the open field, and in a short amount of time, he had gathered an armful of dry twigs and small branches.

They sat by the small fire and ate leftover chicken and biscuits and washed it down with water from a nearby stream. After he had eaten his fill, Happy laid over on his back and lit a cigarette. He blew the smoke up toward the full moon that hung high above him, watching as it dissipated and thinking about the angel in the corn. About what she had said about faith and belief. Was it that simple? It couldn't be, could it?

Beverly stretched out beside him and took the cigarette from his hand. She wrapped her lips around it, inhaled, and blew out an impressive plume of smoke.

"You seem very familiar to me," she said, giving him back his smoke. "It's like I knew you before. That's why I stopped and picked you up outside that old shack. You looked so pitiful just lying there."

Happy took another draw off the cigarette and flicked it into the fire before rolling over on his side to face her. The firelight played off her features, and he could see that she had aged since he had last seen her back in Charleston. She didn't remember him, but he was familiar to her all the same. Mr. Give had made him disappear from fame and fortune, had made the world forget his name, but maybe he missed something. Something deeper inside of folks. Maybe he wasn't as all powerful as he wanted folks to believe.

"I brought you a little something else." Beverly smiled and went to the car. She opened the trunk then came back with something hidden behind her back.

"Aww, ain't you sweet," Happy teased. "You didn't need to bring me nothing."

"I think you're gonna like this." She brought a jug of moonshine out from behind her back. "Daddy gets it by the truckload from an old fella up in the hills and sells it to a fella and his brother in the next town over." She handed the bottle to Happy.

He used his teeth to pull out the corncob stopper and started to take a drink then pointed the bottle at Beverly. "Ladies first!"

She took the bottle and used the crook in her arm to turn it up like an old pro and drank deep.

"Woah, woah, woah there little lady. Save a taste for me!" Happy laughed at the sight of little Beverly with the bottle to her lips.

She lowered it, belched, and handed it back to Happy. "Burns!"

"I bet it does, sucking it down like that." Happy took a deep drink for himself before passing it back to her.

Half an hour later, the jug was empty. Happy dozed and enjoyed the buzz running around inside his head with Beverly curled up beside him next to the fire. She stirred, stretched, and pushed herself up tight against him. He was very aware that her breasts and midsection were touching him. She breathed in, causing her chest to rise in a very tempting manner, and when she exhaled, her breath tickled his ear.

"Why did you leave me back in Charleston?" she mumbled, half asleep and half drunk.

Happy turned his face to her and studied her closed eyes. Beverly moved her shoulders, attempting to get more comfortable, but didn't say anything else. Happy shook her gently and her eyes fluttered open.

"What, what's going on?" she asked sleepily.

"Nothing, sorry. I thought you said something. I must have been dreaming."

Beverly gave him an understanding smile and drifted back to sleep. Happy carefully rolled away from her and stood up. He was still a little lightheaded from the moonshine but managed to walk a mostly straight line over to the trees to empty his bladder.

Relieved, he hitched up his britches and turned to go back to the fire. As he came closer to their little camp, he stopped. A dark figure was hunched over Beverly and had her arm in its grasp.

"Hey, you!" Happy yelled as he ran toward them. "Get away from her!"

The figure stood.

He was tall in his cowboy hat and boots, and the fire's light reflected off a long scar that traveled from his forehead to mouth. The cowboy stood there, unmoving. His message came through loud and clear; I could kill you right now, but that's not why I'm here. Moving slowly, the cowboy turned and stepped away from Beverly.

Happy dropped down beside her, but before he could see if she was okay, a loud bang came from the direction of the car. Happy looked over there in time to see the cowboy step away from the now-flat back tire. Angry and not thinking, Happy grabbed a burning log from the fire and hurled it toward the cowboy. Just as the flaming missile was about to strike its target, the cowboy faded from sight and the burning wood landed in the open trunk of the car.

Happy turned back to Beverly and shook her. She groaned and rolled over, exposing a syringe in her arm. Happy pulled the needle free and tossed it into the fire where the glass cylinder broke and the residue inside it caused a tendril of dirty brown smoke to rise. He shook Beverly violently, but her head only rolled from side to side as she mumbled incoherently.

"What a shame." Mr. Give's voice came out of the darkness.

Happy laid Beverly down and got to his feet just as Mr. Give stepped into the flickering circle of the fire's light. He stood with the fire between him and Happy, the flames reflecting in his eyes as it illuminated his face.

"I do hate to see a pretty little thing like her hooked on the smack."

"You, it was you! You did this to her!" Happy's anger welled up and he pointed and shouted at Mr. Give. "Why? She meant nothing to you. She's no threat to you!"

"She's not now," Mr. Give said with a little chuckle. "She might have given you hope, and I can't have that. She might have given you something to live for, to *fight* for, and I can't have any of that either. Oh no." He paced back and forth like a teacher lecturing.

"You see Happy, I need you to know that you have no hope and there is nothing for you to live for. At the same time, I refuse to let you die because I need you traveling from town to town making sure that all the little sheep have a reason to come to my bars and stay there. Come for the show, have a few drinks. Enjoy the show and have a few more. Then come back the next night and do it all over again. Then once I have my hooks in them, well..."

Mr. Give stopped talking and looked up at the moon as if enjoying the thought of whatever came next.

"Anyway, enough about all that." He reached into his coat pocket and pulled out a small pad and pencil. "Let's see where you stand, shall we? "You killed your mother at birth." He used the pencil to make a check mark beside each thing as he spoke. "Twenty-something years later, you got greedy and signed my little paper. After that you caused you dear blind old Pappy to burn to death when you left him alone to follow your dream of being rich and famous."

He turned back to Happy with a big grin and surprised look on his face.

"And look right here," he pretended to show Happy the pad. "You did get rich and famous, but that wasn't good enough for you. Oh no. You had to go and start digging in stuff that was none of your business."

He closed the pad and put it and the pencil back in his pocket

"I don't need notes to remember what happened then. I snatched it all away from you and set you off with nothing but a beat-up old guitar and warm bottle of rotgut. I figured that would have been proof enough that I don't play, but I guess not 'cause here you are messing around with this little white girl all over again."

Mr. Give paused and rubbed his chin between his thumb and forefinger.

"Well, who am I to try and separate two people that fate seems to be insisting stay together?" He made a big show of waving his arms about like some kind of vaudeville magician and ended his act by snapping his fingers. Then in a poof of smoke he disappeared.

Happy was stunned. He just stood there staring at the emptiness where Mr. Give had been a split second before. Beverly moaned behind him and he turned to see if she was okay. She was sitting up cross-legged and to his absolute horror, she had another syringe and was pushing the brown fluid into a vein in her arm.

"No!" He dropped to his knees in front of her, grabbed the syringe, and pulled it from her arm, leaving a long scratch there in the process.

Beverly screamed and that was when the car exploded.

CHAPTER 13

1958

Every dressing room in every bar in every town that Happy played looked alike. The paint may have been a different color, but it was always peeling. One place may have a lighted mirror where another might have one that is small and hard to see yourself in, but they were always cracked. Only two things stayed exactly the same: Beverly was there, and Happy was drunk.

He had no idea what town they were in. Wherever it was, they had a bar that had a stage, and Happy was there to play on it.

He sat in the dressing room in a straight-back chair, smoking and having a drink. He had lost count of how many he had already, but the bar had left him a bottle, and he intended to drink it all before he went on stage.

Happy looked over at the worn black suit that Beverly had laid across the back of the room's only other chair and laughed. He lifted his glass to it in salute, then emptied the amber liquid into his mouth. Some of the whiskey dribbled down his chin and landed on his stained undershirt. He could have wiped it off, but why bother?

A ragged loveseat sat against one wall, and for a second, he considered lying down. Then he remembered the bottle he had in his hand and his plan to empty it before the show. A man had to have his priorities, so he poured another two fingers of whiskey in the glass and drank it down.

The dressing room door flew open, and Beverly came in. She was very thin, almost skeletal. The dress she wore was three sizes too big, and she continually pushed one of the straps back up on her shoulder. She had broken the heel off her shoe but hadn't noticed.

They had been in town all of three hours, plenty enough time for Happy to find a gig and for Beverly to find a fix. She was flying high. Happy could tell from her bloodshot eyes and the way she was stumbling around.

She sauntered up to him and grabbed the cigarette out of his hand. She took a deep draw, then she smiled and blew the smoke out through her black, rotten teeth. When Happy didn't laugh at her little joke, she just shrugged and dropped the butt into his whiskey glass.

He looked at the butt floating there, then picked it out, tossed it on the floor, and finished his drink.

"You know where we are?" she asked, slurring her words. She made her way over to a cracked mirror hanging on the wall above a small shelf. "This is where we started four years ago. We're in Cartersburg, my hometown." Beverly turned and leaned against the shelf. "My cousin, Bobby Joe's, out there in the bar. Bobby Joe was always good for a little something to take the edge off. He says my daddy's dead, burnt up at a rally one night when some of the local niggers decided to fight back. I'm guessin' Bobby Joe don't know you're one, or he wouldn't be here. Bobby Joe loves music but he hates niggers worse than Daddy did." She leaned in and looked at herself in the mirror.

"I still got it." She smiled, then watched as Happy's reflection in the mirror stood up. "*I* still got it, but you look like shit." She laughed.

Her laughter was cut short when Happy flung the glass he had been holding and it shattered against the wall next to the mirror.

"You stupid piece of sh..." she mumbled and turned on him with her hand raised to slap him.

He beat her to it. His closed fist caught her in the jaw, causing spit and blood to fly across the little room. He grabbed her by her hair and shook her, then pushed her onto the loveseat where she crumpled into a ball, crying.

"Stupid bitch," he muttered to himself.

Beverly pushed herself up off the couch and went to the door. She showed Happy her middle finger then left, slamming the door behind her.

Happy just chuckled and shook his head. This wasn't the first time this scene had played out in a dressing room. Beverly would go out in the bar and have a drink or maybe find a fella who would give her a fix for five minutes of fun in a nasty bathroom. It always ended the same way, with Happy on stage and Beverly passed out. After the show, when she woke up, it would all be forgotten, then they would ride their thumbs to the next town.

He walked over and opened his guitar case. Inside, there was a little brown bottle. Happy opened it and shook two white pills out into his hand. He walked back over to the shelf under the mirror where he had left his whiskey and drank half of what remained in the bottle to wash the pills down.

Happy turned to face the mirror but looked down instead. He hesitated, not wanting to see what he had become. He had grown to hate mirrors because they made it impossible to ignore the shambles that his life had become after signing Mr. Give's paper. Mirrors didn't lie, they only held the truth in their reflective surface.

He forced himself to look up.

His father was standing behind him dressed in a black suit, hat, and sunglasses exactly like the one's Happy was about to put on. He turned, hit his hip on the shelf, and knocked it off the wall. His whiskey bottle fell and shattered on the dressing room's concrete floor.

No one was there.

Happy rubbed his eyes and looked again at the cold empty room. At the straight-back chairs, the old loveseat and the broken bottle leaking the last of its contents out on the floor. He kicked at the broken glass with the toe of his shoe. He imagined himself reaching down and picking up one of the shards and pulling its sharp edge against his wrist. It would hurt, but the pills would dull the pain. *The pills*. There were at least twenty more in the bottle. He could swallow the rest of them, then slit his wrist. He nodded, that would do it, that would get him out of this mess of a life. Or would it?

He walked over to the case and pulled out the bottle of pills. He opened the cap and poured the contents out in his hand. At least twenty, maybe twenty-five.

There was a knock at the door.

"Show time!" It was the owner.

Happy looked back down at the pills in his hand, poured them back in the bottle, and got dressed.

* * *

The walk from the dressing room to the stage was about four steps, but to Happy if felt like a mile. He walked with his head down, carrying his guitar by the neck. He didn't care if it touched the ground or knocked against one of the graffiti-ridden concrete block walls. He had learned a long time before that it didn't matter how good or prepared he was, it only mattered that he was there. Any monkey with a guitar could do what he did.

He climbed the three narrow steps that led to the stage and stopped there. The pills he had taken were doing their job, making him not care and not think. He would just walk out on the stage and go to the stool that was sitting there waiting for him. He would play his songs and smile at a room full of people that didn't care, and forty-five minutes later he would be back in the dressing room cracking the seal on another bottle.

Standing there in the dark, he made the decision that this was going to be the last time. The last time he walked on a stage, the last time he played the guitar, the last time he did anything. He was done, and if Mr. Give didn't like it, then he could suck it. Just like Happy was going to suck down those pills.

The bar owner stepped up behind him and placed a hand on Happy's shoulder, bringing him out of his stupor.

"You all set?" he asked.

Happy nodded and turned back to the stage. Beside him, the owner started pulling the thick rope that opened the curtain. The stage lights came on, and Happy squared his shoulders, ready to get it over with. That's when he saw his father standing in the wings on the other side of the stage.

"Pappy!" he shouted. Happy moved forward onto the stage and into the light.

His father turned his back on him and stepped into the darkness.

Happy raced across the stage, knocking the stool over in the process. He reached the other side only to find his father gone.

The noise in the room quieted as the audience became interested in what was unfolding on stage. Happy stepped around some junk that was being stored in the wings, looking for his father, but he was nowhere to be seen. He took a few tentative steps backward, unaware that he was again standing on the stage.

It must have been the pills; they had never made him see things before. Anything could happen when you mixed pills and booze. *Like you could die*, he thought to himself.

Maybe that was it, maybe he was dead, and Pappy had come to drag him to Hell.

"Get on with it already!"

The crowd had been watching him stand there staring into the dark. They started yelling and clapping to the rhythm of their frustration.

Realizing where he was, Happy straightened up and gave the crowd a wave. He righted the stool and sat down to play.

The crowd pushed forward and stood shoulder to shoulder at the foot of the stage as Happy lifted the guitar into position. He happened to glance down at the front row just as two people stepped aside to let his father in.

Happy jumped up and ran to the front of the stage. The audience started to boo, and a beer bottle whistled past Happy's ear. He reached out to his father but instead of him, he extended his hand to a fat man with a long beard who slapped it away. Happy stumbled back to the stool and sat down. Confusion, barbiturates, and booze clouded his thinking, and he just sat there, unmoving.

"What the hell's the matter with you? Play something already before these people tear the place apart!" the club owner yelled from the wings.

Happy looked over at him, at his red face and frantic motions, but felt nothing. Happy's world was a colorless, soundless blur. Another beer bottle flew at him from the audience and connected with his shoulder.

He looked back at the faces there. Some were yelling and others laughing. They had no way of knowing that his long-dead father was haunting him, and that he wanted nothing more than to die right there on the stage so his nightmare of a life could finally be over. Hell couldn't be any worse than his actual life, just a little hotter.

Happy lifted the guitar into position. His hands were shaking badly as he began to play.

* * *

Happy rushed into his dressing room, needing a drink like he had never needed a drink before in his life. Seeing the broken bottle on the floor, he turned and went to the table where his guitar case was. He opened the case and in the accessory compartment next to the bottle of pills was a pint of whiskey. He downed it, then threw the bottle across the room, shattering it against the wall.

His head was pounding, and he beat his fists against his temples trying to make it stop. Tears filled his eyes, then flowed down his cheeks. Happy stumbled over to a chair and sat down with his elbows on his knees and his head in his hands. His heart raced in his chest, and his breath came out in short bursts.

Over the sound of his blood rushing through his veins, he heard the dressing room door open.

"GET OUT!" he screamed. He stood with his arm outstretched and his finger pointing at whoever had dared come in. When he opened his eyes, his father stepped in through the open door.

The man just stood there looking dapper in the black suit. Around the edges of his sunglasses, Happy could see the burn scars.

Behind him in the hallway, people were passing the open dressing room door paying no attention to what was happening inside.

"Pappy?" Happy slurred, his tongue suddenly too big for his mouth. He took a tentative step in his father's direction, then swooned and stepped back to hold onto the chair for stability.

His father raised his badly burned hands and the hallway behind him filled with fire. Happy lifted his arms to shield his face from the inferno but he could still hear the sounds of the people in the hall. He tried again to go to his father but again he stumbled, this time falling face down on the cold concrete floor. When he looked up, his father was gone, and the door was closed again.

"Pappy!" he screamed at the top of his lungs. "Pappy! NO!"

The door reopened. This time, the owner came in and knelt beside him.

"Come on man, its okay, you've just overdone it. Sit here and I'll go see if the Doc has a little something to perk you up." He helped Happy back into the chair, then left to find the doctor, who always spent his evenings drinking at the bar.

Happy rubbed his hands across the top of his head, then made a fist and started hitting himself in the chest and shoulder, just wanting to feel something real. Panic and frustration built up inside of him to a point he thought his brain would explode. He also feared his heart might melt from the friction of beating so hard in his chest.

He stood and screamed till his voice cracked, then he screamed again. He grabbed the chair he had been sitting in and slammed it against the dressing room wall, sending pieces of splintered wood in all directions.

Breathing hard, he ran from the room and down the hall. He pushed anyone against the wall that was unfortunate enough to be in his way. He hit the latch bar of the clubs backdoor so hard that he bent the thin piece of metal. The door flew open and banged against the brick wall behind it.

Happy stopped in the middle of the alley and paced like a caged animal. In the frigid air, he could see his breath coming out in short bursts, but the alcohol in his system kept him from feeling the cold.

A group of people formed in the open door behind him. He could hear their whispers:

"What's the matter with him?"

"I think he's drunk."

"Someone should call the police."

A movement at the end of the ally got his attention. He turned in time to see his father pass the by the opening. Happy knew what he had to do. He had to catch the man and beg him to tell him what was going on. Pappy had always had the answers. Even when he was crazy and speaking in verse, he always knew what to say. His father would make it better. He could make all this madness make sense.

Happy ran to the end of the alley and out into the street. A car horn blasted, and he jumped back onto the sidewalk as a big black sedan barreled past him. He looked to his left then back to his right, but his father was nowhere to be seen.

He ran to the right since that had been the direction his father had been going when he had passed by the alley's entrance just a moment before. When he reached the next corner, he spotted the man standing midway up a flight of concrete steps.

"Pappy, wait!" he called out and stepped off the sidewalk. Car horns blared and tires squealed as drivers swerved to miss the crazy man running across the street. One car barely stopped in time, and Happy slammed his hand down on its hood and shot the driver a dirty look.

He reached the steps and grabbed a stone statue there for support, trying to catch his breath. He looked up to where his father had been, but he was gone. The steps were empty.

A bell began tolling in a belltower far above him. Happy looked up toward the sound of the bell and saw that the statue he was leaning on for support was a depiction of Christ with his arms outstretched, welcoming everyone in. Tears filled Happy's eyes as he sank to the ground. Kneeling there at the foot of the Savior, Happy cried like he had never cried before. All the anger and anguish rushed out of him in wave after wave of sadness.

Happy felt a feather light touch on the top of his head. The air filled with the scent of vanilla and a strange warmth filled him. When he lifted his face, a bright light filled his vision. From inside the light, his mother emerged. She didn't speak or look at him. Instead, she ascended the steps of the church and passed through the closed doors.

Happy stood and started to follow her, but his way was blocked when his father appeared at the top of the stairs between him and the doors. He looked Happy in the eyes and tried to speak but was not able to make a sound. The old man tried again; his lips moved, but no sound came out. A tear fell from his eye, and Happy understood what he had been trying to tell him.

"It's okay Pappy, I understand. You did what you had to do for us."

The man nodded and a smile pulled at the corners of his mouth.

"You did what you did out of your love for me," Happy continued. "But *I* can't say that, can I?"

His father's smile faltered, and it was replaced by a look of concern and sadness.

"I need to go in there, Pappy. I don't know why, but you led me here, and Momma just went inside. I don't know what good it's going to do, but I plan to find out."

His father nodded and stepped aside, allowing Happy to continue up the stairs. At the landing, he turned to say something else to his father, but the landing was again empty. He grasped the handle of the door and pushed, fully expecting the door to be locked, but it opened easily.

Happy stepped into a church for the first time in his adult life.

* * *

The interior of the church was dimly lit. The only light came from a representation of Christ crucified hanging on the wall behind the pulpit. A bright light mounted above it in the high ceiling illuminated the figure. Unlike the welcoming statue outside, this version of Christ was in anguish. Its mouth was pulled back in an expression of pain, and a crown of thorns was on its head. Where the thorns met its scalp, small rivulets of blood ran down toward its eyes. The figure was naked, except for a tattered garment wrapped around its waist. Large square nails protruded from its palms and its crossed feet.

Happy heard crying coming from far away. He looked around the sanctuary, surprised that he wasn't alone at this late hour. A small woman sat on the second row, her head bowed and her shoulders shaking with her sobs. Happy approached slowly, not wanting to startle her. As he drew closer, her crying subsided and she sat silently in the pew.

Happy reached the end of the row where she was sitting and stopped. He blinked hard, trying to understand what he was seeing, or *not* seeing, as it was. The woman was there, but Happy could see through her. He could also see a squirming baby that she held in her lap.

She gently touched the blanket the baby was wrapped in. The child stopped moving, and the covering fell away from its face, except there was no face there. Where Happy expected to see the smiling features of an infant, there was the cloth face of a black ragdoll with white X's where it eyes should have been.

The woman let the doll fall to the floor where it vanished, then she turned toward Happy and rose to her feet. Her drab clothes began to change, first draining of color before turning a bright white. The cloth flowed over her like water as wings formed on her back. Happy watched, transfixed, as the now-angel rose above him. She filled the sanctuary with her light, then faded away, leaving the room dark again, except for the glow around the man on the cross.

Happy stepped up to the altar and fell first on his knees, then all the way over so his forehead touched the floor. Emotions welled up in him, and he cried out the only prayer he remembered from his reading.

"Our Father who art in heaven, hallowed be Thy name! Thy kingdom come, Thy will be done on earth as it is in heaven!"

The doors of the church slammed open.

Mr. Give appeared on the landing. "What do you think you're doing, boy? I don't remember telling you to come to church. That thing you're praying to is just a bunch of plaster and wire. Your salvation is out here with me."

Happy rose to his feet and turned to face him. His heart pounded so hard in his chest that he feared it would burst, but he didn't let that stop him. He gathered his nerve and took a step toward Mr. Give.

"My Pappy had a verse he used to quote all the time, he'd say, *watch and pray, that ye enter not into temptation for the spirit is willing, but the flesh is weak.* I've been weak Mr. Give, but I ain't gonna be weak no more."

"Like you have a choice. You *are* weak, garbage man, just like your Pappy was weak. He could have had it all, just like you. But no, he decided to break the rule. You remember the rule don't you, garbage man?"

"Yes, sir. Don't ever lie to you."

"But you just did lie to me, didn't you, boy? You just lied when you said you weren't gonna be weak no more. You are weak and you are a liar. But I tell you what, Happy, you come on out of this empty shrine and kneel before me like you were kneeling before that ridiculous hunk of clay, and I'll forgive you."

Mr. Give reached into his pocket and brought out a bottle of whiskey. Happy's mouth went dry at the sight of the bottle, and he hated himself for wanting a drink so badly.

Mr. Give removed the top from the bottle and tossed it away, then reached back in his pocket and pulled out a crystal glass full of ice. He held the bottle high, then made a show of filling the glass to the rim with the whiskey. Mr. Give brought the glass to his nose and sniffed the amber liquid like a connoisseur would a fine wine, then tilted the glass toward Happy, spilling some of the contents on the ground.

Two women—one white and one black—wearing negligees, stepped from behind Mr. Give and placed their heads on his shoulders. They smiled and giggled like little schoolgirls with their first crush. One of the girls reached out and caressed Mr. Give's chest, while the other stood on the toes of her bare feet and leaned in to place a kiss on his cheek.

"You are weak Happy, and I know your every weakness. I know what you like."

He gave the glass a little shake, making the ice rattle against the sides.

"How about it Happy? Need a little something to wet your whistle after all the praying you was just doing?"

One of the women slid down Mr. Give and wrapped her arms around his thigh. He handed her the bottle, and she suggestively put it to her lips, tasting the rim with her tongue. Then in one long drink, she finished off its contents.

Happy was sweating, and his hands shook. He tried to resist, but the want, the *need*, for a drink was too strong. He took a few steps in Mr. Give's direction, then heard the woman crying again and looked back over his shoulder.

His mother was standing at the foot of the crucifix, weeping. Beside her was a full-size rag doll dressed exactly like Happy. Its black cloth face bore two white stitched X's where the eyes should have been.

Startled at the sight, Happy stumbled over his own feet and fell.

"Get up boy, get up!" Mr. Give commanded.

Happy, head down, let out a howl of confusion and pain, then started to crawl toward the door and Mr. Give. If he could just have one drink to settle his nerves, just *one*, he could work this all out.

Two worn black shoes appeared in front of Happy, blocking his way. He stopped crawling and a loud sob escaped him. Happy slammed his fist against the hard church floor.

"*NO!*" he screamed. "No more, just let me have a drink!"

He looked up and through his tears he saw his father standing over him. He didn't move, he just stood there looking down at Happy through his black sunglasses. Happy couldn't take it anymore and he cried openly as he lay down flat at his father's feet. Happy's body shook and convulsed from sheer agony.

"Get up boy, pass him by!" Mr. Give yelled through the door. "He can't save you! Hell, he couldn't save himself. Oh, he tried, just like you're trying to, but just like you, it was too late, and he knew it was. He couldn't play no more, couldn't sing no more, couldn't *see* no more, so I left him home to die. And thanks to you, he did just that."

"I'm sorry, Pappy! I'm sorry I didn't listen to you." Happy lifted his head but couldn't bring himself to look up into his father's face. "I'm sorry about the fire, I'm sorry about everything."

His father didn't move. He just continued to stare down at Happy with pity on his face.

"He had his chance, boy, and now you have yours. But this is the last one. So, get up and join me!"

Happy slowly got to his feet and stood face to face with his father. Still unable to look at him, Happy stood there with his eyes down.

"I am weak, he's right. I *am* a liar," Happy whispered. "I'm sorry."

His father dropped his head and faded away, leaving nothing between Happy and Mr. Give.

Happy took another a step toward the devil.

"That's it, boy. Mr. Garbage Man!" Mr. Give spoke like he would to a dog which is exactly what Happy felt like. A dog willing to do anything for a bone, even willing to die for it.

Seraphina, who had watched all this play out from her place at the statue's feet, turned and faced the representation of the Savior. She raised her hands and began to pray. Her lips moved nonstop as tears fell from her eyes and ran down her cheeks, disappearing before they struck the floor. She prayed as so many others had while in the church. She prayed for the son she never got the chance to know. She prayed for her husband who had tried his best to keep their son safe, but ultimately had made the wrong decision for all the right reasons. She prayed for their salvation. She prayed in the name of the Father, the Son, and the Holy Spirit.

Seraphina reached up and her fingers touched the tattered garment that was all that remained after the Roman guards had cast lots for Jesus's clothing.

"Please, God!" she cried. "Save my son."

An electric arc formed in the aisle in front of Happy, followed by a blinding light. He was pushed into the pews by an unseen force. Where Happy had been, now Elijah stood. His black suit had been replaced by a white one and the sunglasses that had hidden his burn-scarred face and blind eyes were gone, along with the scars. His eyes were clear, and he looked at Mr. Give no longer with fear but filled with a confidence that he had never felt before.

"The Lord rebuke you, O Satan!"

Elijah raised his hands and in each was a golden cross. With arms outstretched he walked toward Mr. Give.

"The Lord rebuke you, O Satan! The Lord rebuke you, O Satan! The Lord rebuke you, O Satan!" Elijah's voice grew stronger with each step.

The two women at Mr. Give's side ran down the steps, leaving him standing alone. As Elijah drew nearer to Mr. Give the crosses burst into flame and began to burn in his hands. Elijah raised the burning crosses over his head and threw them at Mr. Give.

Mr. Give stepped back, and the church doors slammed shut. With their target gone, the flaming crosses turned to smoke and faded away. Elijah pivoted around and walked over to Happy. He reached down and helped his son to his feet. With a smile and a wink Elijah faded away, just as a minister stepped out from a room next to the altar.

"Can I help you, my son?"

Happy hadn't noticed the man enter the room and jumped at the sound of his voice.

"It's okay," the minister said in a comforting tone as he approached Happy. "You're in God's house. You're safe now."

Happy smiled, then his knees went weak and he sat down hard. The minister walked up and slid into the pew beside him.

* * *

The church doors swung open. The minister stepped out on the landing with Happy close behind. Happy took in a deep breath of the cool night air, then turned to the minister and shook his hand.

"The Lord has heard your prayer, Happy, and he forgives you, but that's just the beginning." The minister placed his other hand over Happy's and held it there. "Now the hard part happens. Now you must follow through on your promise to stop drinking and devote your life to His service. Now you must atone for your past. Just accepting Christ as your savior doesn't erase what you've done before it opens the door to a brighter future. You can't earn salvation, that's a gift from God, but you can earn happiness, Happy."

"Thank you, Father."

The minister gave him a warm look and released his hand.

"Now go and make today the first day of your new life."

"Thank you. Thank you so much."

They shook hands again, and the minister turned and went back inside, pulling the church doors closed behind him.

Happy looked out over the city with newfound joy. He watched as the few cars still out and about passed by him, then descended the steps and headed back toward the club.

After a block, he stopped. *Why go back there*, he thought to himself. *That's my old life. The father said to make this the first day of the rest of my life and that's just what I'm going to do.* He smiled at the thought, turned around and walked in the opposite direction.

No more night clubs, no more drinking, no more playing guitar, and *especially*, no more Mr. Give.

Happy had his hands in his pockets and walked with a lighter step. For the first time in his adult life, he felt like he was free. He didn't know what was waiting for him around the next corner, but whatever it was, he intended to face it head on. With God's help, he would be able to make the next part of his life better than the first.

He came to the end of the block and the symbolism of the corner he was approaching was not lost on him. He stopped, looked to the heavens, and gave God a wink. Happy smiled, took a deep breath and stepped around the corner.

Beverly was standing there with three big white men. There was a red welt across one side of her face, and her lip was swollen. The front of her dress was smeared with dried blood.

"That's him!" she shouted at the men and pointed at Happy.

The men lunged for him, but he was able to sidestep them. He took his chances and ran across the street. Dodging traffic, he made it safely to the other side. He looked back over his shoulder. The men were still standing there with Beverly.

The largest one is probably her cousin, he thought to himself. *What was his name? Jerry, Jim, no it was Joe,* Bobby Joe, *and Bobby Joe hates niggers.*

As Happy watched to see what they were going to do, Beverly slapped Bobby Joe across the face. "What are you waiting for?" she shouted at him while pointing at Happy. "Get him! Get that bastard!"

The men glanced at each other, then stepped into traffic. A yellow Studebaker couldn't stop in time and hit Bobby Joe. The big man landed on the car's hood, denting it, then rolled off onto his feet as if nothing had happened.

Happy had seen enough. He took off running in the opposite direction. He was faster than the men chasing him and soon had close to a two-block lead on them. Still, years of smoking and drinking were taking their toll, and he needed desperately to find a place to stop and catch his breath.

He jumped into an alley and sank down behind some barrels there. They were full of garbage and they stunk, but he felt safe there knowing that he couldn't be seen from the sidewalk.

Happy leaned his head back against the cold brick wall and struggled to get his breathing under control. He was exhausted, and his head was beginning to swim, so he bent forward and placed his head between his knees. He closed his eyes tight and concentrated on his breathing and trying to stop his head from spinning. Finally, he started feeling better and opened his eyes.

Two scuffed black shoes were the first thing he saw.

"Pappy, thank God," he started, then remembered that the last time he saw his father, he had been dressed entirely in white.

He slowly looked up into the face of Apollyon.

"Did you really think you would get away with this?"

Apollyon reached down, and with a grip like iron, he grabbed Happy by his shirt. The demon flung Happy out of the alley and onto the sidewalk, right into the path of the three men that had been chasing him.

Epilogue

Sunrise was always Elijah's favorite time of the day. He loved to watch as the sun crested the foothills and feel its rays bring the first warmth of morning to his waiting skin. This morning's sunrise was extra special because he was enjoying it with his son.

He looked over at his only child, beaming with pride. Happy had managed to do the one thing that Elijah never had. He had broken his contract with Mr. Give.

Happy turned to his father and smiled. He had missed the old man and was looking forward to catching up with him and learning what had really happened all those years before. But for today, he was just glad to be here feeling the sun on his face.

"Looks like it's going to be a beautiful day, Pappy."

"Yes, Son, I think it is."

Out of the brilliant sunshine, the silhouette of a young woman appeared walking toward them. Elijah raised his hand to shade his eyes and was not surprised to see that it was Seraphina. She stopped and motioned for them to follow her.

They stepped away from the tree they had been standing under. The morning sun reflected off the finish of an old guitar that was leaning there and illuminated the body of an unknown black man hanging from one of the lowest branches.

THE END

Author's Note

"The Devil Plays Six Strings" is a work of fiction in which I have used The Bible, Scripture and Religion in general as a character in the story. Hopefully, I have not taken too many liberties with them. If reading this has piqued your interest and you would like to learn more about the Bible, I highly recommend you go to:

www.StudyJesus.com

Study Jesus is a storehouse for religious study containing hundreds of books, lessons and articles all written without denominational influence. It strives to be a location where anyone of any religious background can come to read and learn.

I hope you enjoyed "The Devil Plays Six Strings." Please watch for the next book in the series, "The Devil and the Dance Hall Girl," coming soon.

Vince Pinkerton
December, 2021